Copyright © 2022 by Melody Tyden

All rights reserved.

The characters and events portrayed in this book are fictitious. Any similarity to real persons, living or dead, is coincidental and not intended by the author.

No part of this book may be reproduced, or stored in a retrieval system, or transmitted in any form or by any means, electronic, mechanical, photocopying, recording, or otherwise, without express written permission of the publisher.

Cover design by: GetCovers

BOOK THREE OF MISMATCHED MATES

MISTAKEN Meanings

MELODY TYDEN

*For the readers who wanted more of Abby and Oliver -
this one is for you!*

Chapter One

~Jerrod~

My mate snarled up at me, her golden-brown eyes narrowed in disgust.

"Is that the best you can do, *Alpha*?"

I hated when she called me Alpha. From anyone else, the word was a mark of respect, even though I wasn't technically an Alpha yet. I would be soon though, it was only a matter of time, and most of the werewolves in our pack treated me accordingly.

Not my mate, though. When she used my title, she did it sarcastically: a reminder that, in her eyes, I wasn't worthy of that title or worthy of her either, for that matter.

I fucking hated it.

I especially hated how much it turned me on.

"If it's so bad, why are you so wet for me?" I growled back at her, thrusting into her harder, our bodies slamming together without an ounce of tenderness. "There isn't a wolf on our territory who can't smell how aroused you are right now. The pups are probably asking their parents what that smell is."

I was exaggerating, of course, but only a little. She was definitely turned on. Her nipples were stiff peaks and her pupils were dilated, though she tried to hide it as she narrowed her eyes at me further. The condom I was wearing was dripping wet with the proof of her excitement.

"If I'm wet, it's only because it's been so long since I've been truly satisfied," she lied, refusing to give me an inch even as she drew closer to her release.

"You're such a fucking liar. No one makes you come like I do, Marissa. No one ever has."

I pressed down on her clit as I pounded her even harder, and her legs began to shake.

"I hate you so much," she muttered just before her orgasm claimed her, and as she tightened around me, her pussy gripping my hard cock rhythmically, I lost control too.

"Not as much as I hate you," I managed to gasp as I emptied myself into the condom.

Before I'd even stopped pulsing, I pulled out, not wanting to stay inside her a second longer than I had to. Wordlessly, I pulled the condom off, wincing as it came loose, and threw it into the trash can next to the bed. She insisted that I wore a condom every time we had sex, saying she was far too young and beautiful to get pregnant yet; her words, not mine. When I pointed out that she could just go on the pill or something, she point-blank refused, saying I was the one who wanted to fuck her so I could take the responsibility.

She was always crude, never subtle, constantly over-the-top instead of understated. She was nothing at all like the woman I used to dream about ending up with.

That familiar pang of loss hit me again as I pulled my pants back on. After many months and countless sessions with our pack therapist, I finally understood what I had done wrong with Abby, more or less, but I still didn't think it fair that I couldn't have another chance. Instead, I was saddled with a mate who hated me, while the girl of my dreams was mated to another Alpha-to-be from a different pack. The whole thing wasn't right. *He* wasn't right for her; I was. She had just never been able to see that.

Marissa's phone buzzed as she finished putting her own clothes back on. We'd be expected at dinner shortly, but I had caught sight of Marissa in one of her ridiculously short skirts, flirting with one of the men who worked security in the house, and I had to remind her whose mate she was. I could swear she only did it to make me jealous, though why either of us should care, I really didn't know.

"Who's texting you?" I asked with that same unwelcome sting of jealousy, watching as she scrolled through the message. It looked to be a long one.

"One of my friends from the Jade Moon pack. They just had a pack meeting and there was big news."

The Jade Moon pack was Abby's mate's pack, but I refused to think of it as Abby's pack, even though that was where she was right now. Her place was still here, whether she recognized it or not.

"What's the news?" I asked, trying to pretend like I really didn't care. The thought that Abby might be pregnant crossed my mind, and for a moment, I thought I was going to be sick.

Thankfully, that wasn't it. "The Alpha's found a new mate. They're saying it's his third-chance mate?"

Marissa looked up at me in surprise, and I had to admit that was unexpected. Third-chance mates were pretty rare. Usually, once a wolf had exhausted a first and second chance, their only options were to take a chosen mate or remain mate-less.

I knew which I'd prefer.

Marissa was my chosen mate, though not chosen by me. We had been fated mates until I rejected her, but then my father and that fucking arrogant Alpha Patrick of the Jade Moon pack had insisted that I take her back. We reforged our bond through marking each other, but that kind of chosen bond couldn't compare to the strength of the fated mate bond, which had been severed forever when I made the rejection and she accepted it.

I still didn't regret doing it. I would do it again if I could. My actions towards Abby were the only things I would change if I had the chance to do it all over again.

The only reason I didn't reject her again now was because it would cast doubt on my 'rehabilitation', which was necessary if the Alpha position was ever going to be mine.

And now that asshole Alpha was getting his own fated mate, for the third time? Life couldn't be any more unfair.

"There's more," Marissa said, her excitement growing as she read on. She always loved a bit of gossip, like the shallow bimbo that she was. "Oliver has a twin brother! He's going to be staying in the pack too, with his new mate."

Oliver. I hated that name. I hated everything about that guy. Usually, I did my best never to think about him unless I absolutely had to, like when my insensitive mate brought him up. She didn't understand the depth of my feelings for Abby. She'd never even tried to.

Marissa was frowning at the phone now before she looked up at me. "Don't twins usually share a mate? Shouldn't Abby be mated to them both?"

The idea of another man having a claim on Abby when I had none made my anger flare once again. "You don't know anything about it. Why do you care?"

Her brief good humour evaporated as her eyes narrowed at me once again. "I care because it's my old pack. Why do *you* care?"

"I don't care. You're the one who brought it up. Hurry up and get ready for dinner."

Leaving her there, I made my way downstairs on my own and found my father just coming out of his office. I took the opportunity to fill him in on what I'd just learned. "I've just heard that Alpha Patrick has a new mate, and possibly a new son too."

That piqued his interest, as I thought it would, and he invited me into his office to share the details I had, which admittedly weren't many. It had taken a long time for my father to begin to trust me again after the fight I caused between our pack and the Jade Moon pack, but we were slowly getting there. He was starting to give me a few responsibilities again, small ones that I couldn't mess up.

I couldn't let him know I still had feelings for Abby. The full restoration of my standing in the pack depended on it.

He had never understood why Abby was so special. If he had, he would have helped me win her over, rather than standing between us every chance he got. I didn't think I could ever truly forgive him for that.

After I passed on what Marissa told me, my dad called over to the Jade Moon pack, putting the phone on speaker so I could hear it too.

"Alpha Patrick?" My dad smiled when the other Alpha answered, almost looking as though the man didn't make his skin crawl the same way he did for me. Had he really forgotten the defeat we'd suffered at Patrick's hands? "This is Alpha Easton from Forest Ridge. I hear congratulations are in order."

"Good news travels fast," the Alpha replied, sounding far more laid-back than he did the last time I'd spoken with him, here in this very room on the day of the battle I instigated. "Thank you, Alpha Easton. It's still very new, but she's an incredible woman. I'm very lucky."

I rolled my eyes and my father shot me a warning look. The message was clear: I was to be on my best behaviour. "My son is here too, he also wanted to congratulate you."

With real effort, I put on a conciliatory tone. "Congratulations, Alpha Patrick. I hope this is a blessing to you and your pack."

The Alpha's response to me was much shorter and cooler than it had been to my father. "Thank you, Jerrod."

"Forgive me for indulging in gossip," my dad continued, "but the rumour is you've also got another new addition to your pack?"

Alpha Patrick chuckled. "Let me guess: is this rumour's name Marissa?"

He wasn't stupid, I had to give him that much. When my dad confirmed it, Alpha Patrick laughed again.

"Well, in this case, she's right. Oliver's twin brother, Elijah, has joined us temporarily. I'm not sure how long he'll be staying, he was previously Alpha of his own pack on the west coast. I'm looking forward to having his input for as long as he's with us."

Wasn't that cozy? They were all one big, happy family, apparently.

My dad and Alpha Patrick exchanged a few more pleasantries before Alpha Patrick's phone rang again in the background. "Please forgive me," he apologized. "Word of my good fortune seems to be spreading."

"Of course," my father agreed. "Congratulations again. I'll see you at the Alpha council conference next week, I hope?"

"Certainly," Alpha Patrick confirmed. "I'll be there, along with Oliver and Elijah."

My ears perked up at that. If Oliver was going somewhere, there was a good chance that Abby would go too. The conference was somewhere I might be able to bump into her without being too obvious, if only I could find a way to be there too. My heart leapt at the thought.

They hung up and my father looked over at me thoughtfully, as if he were thinking along the same lines I was. Well, not exactly the same lines, of course, but about the conference at least. "Maybe I should take you along too, Jerrod. You've worked hard over these past few months and I'm proud of you. Do you think you could handle it? Being in the same room with Oliver West without losing your temper?"

I gave him the serene smile I'd been practicing in the mirror for months. "Of course, Dad. That's all in the past. Representing the Forest Ridge pack would be my honour."

He smiled too, accepting my reply at face value. "Good. We'll make plans to attend then, both of us. And our mates, of course."

Our mates? *Shit.* I didn't want Marissa there, but I couldn't think of a good reason why she shouldn't go. It didn't seem I was going to have much choice.

Although, maybe the idea wasn't a terrible one, all things considered. She'd always had a thing for Oliver. They'd even dated for a while before he met Abby. Maybe this was one time we really could work together since we both wanted the same thing: Oliver and Abby broken up.

How hard could it be?

~Abby~

Though keeping a straight face wasn't easy, I did my best as Storm came out of the dressing room wearing a floor-length pink dress and a deep scowl.

"I look like I've been dipped in cotton candy," she growled as I pressed my lips together even more tightly. She wasn't wrong, and I knew if I made eye contact with Liz, I would lose my self-control entirely.

Liz, Whitney and I were all sitting on the small couch outside the dressing rooms at the boutique Whitney had chosen. We were here to find the perfect dress for Storm's mating ceremony with Alpha Patrick later this weekend.

Storm came to me for help first, since her new mate was my mate's father, but I was hardly an authority on fashion. Liz wasn't much better, so we enlisted the help of our very trendy and fashionable cheerleader friend, Whitney, to lead the way.

Luckily, Whitney was undeterred by Storm's grumpiness as she leapt to her feet and circled around her, examining the look carefully. "The colour isn't quite you," she agreed, much to Storm's relief. "But I think we can work with the style, maybe just with longer sleeves so we don't see quite so many of the tattoos."Storm raised her eyebrows at Whitney, who quickly backtracked.

"They're amazing, of course, they just don't really go with the dress. So, pink is out, but what colour would you prefer?"

"Black," Storm immediately answered, to no one's surprise, but Whitney shook her head.

"This isn't a funeral. It's a... wait, what's it called again?"

That question was for me. As a human who had only found out about werewolves a couple of weeks ago, Whitney was still learning all the lingo.

"Mating ceremony," I supplied. "And Whitney's right, Storm. Alpha Patrick is very traditional, and although he said you could choose any colour, I don't think he meant black."

The mention of her mate softened Storm's expression considerably, making me smile. The way these two tough and guarded people turned to mush around each other was incredible. They were willing to do anything to make each other happy. That was the power of the mate bond: it made you reevaluate what was important and what was worth fighting for.

I should know.

"How about gold, then?" she suggested reluctantly, making an honest effort to cooperate.

Whitney pursed her lips, scanning Storm from head to toe. "I think it might clash with your hair."

Storm's hair was a bright red colour, much too bright to be natural. I had originally thought her hair, her piercings, and her many tattoos would have scared off Oliver's dad, who had once made a point of telling me I didn't look enough like a Luna. He later explained why he said it and apologized for it, but it didn't change the fact that he was a rather old-fashioned man and Alpha. A motorcycle-riding, strong-willed woman who looked like she'd stepped off the pages of a biker magazine hardly seemed like the ideal match for him after the untimely loss of his first mate, Oliver's mother. And yet, they seemed to work anyway. The Moon Goddess knew what she was doing, apparently. Considering my luck with my own mate, I couldn't really argue otherwise.

"Silver?" Whitney suggested, but this time, Storm and I quickly shook our heads.

"Silver is not a good colour for werewolves," I explained. "The metal is so painful for us that we try to stay away from it in general."

"Oh, right." I had told Whitney about that before, she had just forgotten, and I couldn't blame her. Learning about a whole other species and their culture was a lot to take in. "Well, how about red, then? We can find a shade that highlights your hair rather than working against it."

Storm agreed, so she went back into the dressing room to take off the pink gown while Whitney went to look through the other dresses to find something that would work.

That left Liz and me alone, and she leaned back in her seat, looking overwhelmed. "I can't believe they're having their ceremony already. They only met a couple of weeks ago!"

I knew what she was thinking without her having to spell it out more than that. Liz had discovered her own mate, Elijah, the same day Storm and Alpha Patrick met. And despite how much she loved him already, for someone who had grown up thinking she was human, committing to someone so permanently that quickly was hard to imagine.

But for werewolves, relationships worked differently. When the bond kicked in, it was hard to resist and rare for anything to happen to break that connection, apart from death.

Hopefully, that was a long way away for any of us.

"It's fast for humans, but not for werewolves," I told her now. "The bond comes first, and true love develops afterwards. It's a little bit backwards, I know, but in the long run, I actually think it's better. And because Alpha Patrick is an Alpha, the pack is eager to have his mate installed as their Luna too. You and I don't have to worry about all that just yet."

Although Elijah had been Alpha of his pack when he and Liz met, he gave up his position in order to dedicate himself fully to her as she learned how to embrace her werewolf heritage and the powers of her particular bloodline which had been hidden from her for so long. Her learning curve was a big one, and what their future together held was still not entirely clear.

"Okay, I've got a few different options for you," Whitney called out as she returned to the dressing room, passing the dresses in various shades of red to Storm. "One of these will work, I'm sure."

Despite Whitney's confidence, another hour passed before Storm finally emerged in the dress that was the clear winner, and all three of us got to our feet in excitement.

"It's beautiful," I assured her as she looked at herself in the mirror, turning from side to side as though she couldn't quite believe her eyes. The long red dress had a slit up one side and down one shoulder, revealing just a hint of Storm's tattooed arm. The bodice was form-fitting without being clingy, and with a rippled undertone of black that hinted at something unexpected, just like the woman wearing it.

"I actually kind of like it," Storm admitted. "Which can only mean one thing: we've been here so long that I've become delusional."

"Or this dress was meant to be," I countered. "Just like you and the Alpha."

"Thanks, Abby." She gave my shoulder a little shove which I understood was the equivalent of a hug from most people. We were very different people, but it felt like my new stepmother-in-law and I were going to get along pretty well. At least that was one person in the pack I didn't have to worry too much about winning over.

After dropping Whitney off at her house, Liz, Storm and I headed back to the Jade Moon pack land with Storm's new purchases. Whitney hadn't been able to sell her on heels, but at least she got some shoes that weren't full combat boots, so we were counting that as a win.

The pack house was rather quiet when we arrived, and as Storm left to hide her shopping bags somewhere that Alpha Patrick wouldn't find them, Liz and I went in search of our mates. They weren't in the Alpha's office, nor the kitchen, and not at Oliver's workshop either. Finally, I gave in and asked one of the guards if he'd seen them.

He answered us completely straight-faced. "They're both in the hospital."

"What?!" Liz exclaimed, her face paling as I asked the obvious follow-up question.

"Why are they in the hospital?"

The guard simply shrugged. "You'll have to ask them."

Luckily, the pack hospital wasn't too far away, so in a matter of minutes, we were standing in the waiting room with Alpha Patrick. "What happened?" I asked as he turned to greet us.

"They're fine," he assured us. "A few broken bones, nothing that won't heal."

"Broken bones?" Liz was still looking a little nauseated, but on this point, I could reassure her.

"Werewolves heal really quickly, remember? Those bones will be fixed in no time. But how did this happen, Alpha?"

His lips twitched a little in amusement. "They were arguing about who would win in a fight between them. It seems they were both right and wrong, given it ended in a tie."

Seriously? I really didn't understand men sometimes, but Alpha Patrick seemed to think the situation was funny. And I supposed Oliver *had* always wanted a brother, someone he could do stupid things like this with. The fact that they were both adults didn't seem to be stopping them.

We waited with the Alpha until we were told they were ready to see us, and Liz and I walked in to find our identical twin mates in side-by-side beds, both of them shirtless with various body parts bandaged and bruised faces. For a moment, I honestly couldn't tell who was who.

"Sorry, Heels," the one closest to me said with a sheepish grin, and I immediately went to Oliver's side. "We got a little carried away."

"You think?" I shook my head at him as I tried not to laugh. He looked both guilty and pleased with himself at the same time.

"Maybe we can play doctor when we get back to the house," Elijah suggested to Liz, making her blush.

"Eli! Everyone can hear you."

Elijah glanced over at Oliver and me, completely unconcerned. "So what? There's no way Oliver's not thinking the same thing."

I looked down at my mate for confirmation and he simply raised his eyebrows in invitation, making me shake my head once again.

Boys really would be boys, but I still couldn't be happier that this one was mine.

~Elijah~

With Liz supporting me, we made our way back to the room we were sharing in the Jade Moon pack house. The weeks that we'd spent here so far had been a lot more fun than I would have ever anticipated. Being here was kind of like a vacation, not having to deal with all the ins and outs of running a pack as I got to know the family I never knew I had. I spent a lot of my time with Alpha Patrick and Oliver, reviewing the pack's operations and making suggestions, but the final responsibility was no longer my own. I was essentially a consultant, and the role suited me very well. I never had any trouble giving anyone my opinion.

I was also enjoying the chance to get to know my mate and to support her as she grew more comfortable with all her new werewolf abilities. Liz amazed me more every day. Her whole world had been completely turned upside down, even more than mine had, and yet she took it all in stride. I had given up my pack, yes, but she had to accept that she was a completely different species from what she'd always believed. She gave up her job for the summer to stay with me until we could decide what to do next, and although I would support her no matter what she wanted to do, I had my own ideas too.

After all, I had been hunting for the source of power for years. I had a lot of plans for what I was going to do when I found it, and though some of those were immediately quashed when I realized that the source belonged to Liz and not to me, some of them were still valid. I still believed that the Alpha Council could be improved by having someone in charge, and who better than someone of the royal bloodline?

Liz was a queen without a throne, and I intended to build that throne for her, whatever it took.

"I can't believe you and Oliver did this to each other," she exclaimed as we reached our room and she helped me down onto the bed. "Are you sure you should have left the hospital already?"

"I'm fine," I promised her. "A good night's sleep and I'll be good as new."

That seemed to satisfy her. She trusted me when it came to all things werewolf, so she left it at that and moved on to making me more comfortable, taking off my shoes and then adjusting the pillows behind me. As she leaned over, her chest right at my eye level, I couldn't stop myself from bringing up my earlier suggestion once again.

"I wasn't kidding about playing doctor, though. What do you say, Liz?"

Though she rolled her eyes at me, I could see that hint of colour starting to rise in her cheeks. She was starting to get used to how much I wanted her, anytime and anywhere, but there were times like these when it still took her by surprise.

She honestly didn't know how incredible she was, and I didn't understand it. There wasn't a fucking thing about her that didn't turn me on. She usually kept her dark hair pulled back in a ponytail, but I loved the way it looked wrapped around my hands. Her hazel eyes seemed to see straight into my soul, and her body, soft and smooth, was my absolute favourite thing to touch.

"I don't think you'd be a very good patient," she said, trying to give me a disapproving look that held just a little too much desire in it to be truly convincing. "You never do what you're told."

"I promise I'll do exactly what you tell me *if* you help me feel better."

Clearly struggling against her better judgement, she looked me up and down. As her gaze passed over my groin, the blood rushed to that spot, making my already alert cock even harder.

I was always half-hard around her to begin with. It made life a little difficult at times, but I was learning to live with it.

"What kind of help do you need?" she asked, half-reluctant and half-curious, and I grinned up at her from the pillows.

"Well, most of my bones and bruises are healing, but there's this one spot that's getting more and more swollen as we're talking. I think you better take a look at it."

She might still be a little inexperienced, but she caught my drift immediately. "Oh, really? It wouldn't happen to be around here, would it?"

Her hand grazed lightly across the growing bulge in my pants, and even that small amount of contact made me groan. "You see, you're an excellent doctor. You identified the problem immediately."

This time she couldn't help laughing. "Well, you seem to have it all figured out. Maybe you can treat it yourself."

She was teasing me, of course. I didn't believe for a second that she'd leave me hanging. "I think you need to kiss it better."

"Why did I have a feeling you were going to say that?" Again, she tried to look reproachful, but she couldn't quite pull it off, not when her own desire was growing by the second.

She pressed down on me harder, making me groan again.

"Oh, I'm sorry. Does that hurt?" she asked, all faux innocence, and any other time, I would have grabbed her and thrown her down on the bed right there and then. However, at the moment, I honestly was still a little sore from the fight with Oliver. I couldn't do much other than lay here.

"My pants are getting too tight," I told her quite honestly. "It might feel better if you took them off."

Shaking her head at me, she undid my belt and unzipped my pants, pulling everything down to let my cock out, and I breathed a sigh of relief. That really did feel a million times better already.

Liz began to kneel down next to the bed, but I quickly shook my head. As much as I wanted her to touch me, I wanted to make her feel good too, and given my current aches and pains, that was going to be easier in my present position. "Not there."

She looked up at me in surprise. "I thought that's what you wanted?"

"Oh, trust me, I do. I just want you somewhere else."

Her look of confusion was adorable. "Where?"

"On my face."

Her cheeks flushed stronger this time, but she didn't even try to deny that she wanted it too. Standing back up, she quickly shed her own pants, revealing to me the beautiful curve of her hips and that fucking perfect junction between her legs, which was giving off a strong scent of arousal. Hers was the very best smell in the world.

Gingerly, she climbed up onto the bed, facing my feet, and straddled me until her sweet centre was directly above me. I grabbed onto her hips and pulled her the rest of the way down, inhaling her perfect scent until my mouth was watering. If I didn't taste her now, it honestly felt like I might die.

My cock twitched as desire flooded through me, and as my tongue connected with the warm, wet perfection of her, she took me into her mouth too, kissing me just like I'd asked her to.

Saying which was better was almost impossible: the way she tasted and felt as my tongue moved along all the little hidden parts of her, up to her sensitive clit that always made her shudder when I ran my tongue across it, or the way it felt as her own soft tongue stroked my swollen head, exploring each inch of it as she sucked and teased me.

Just when I'd lose myself in one sensation, the other would take over, until I honestly didn't know if I was coming or going – or rather, if I was coming or she was.

Liz's moans of pleasure were muffled by my cock in her mouth, just as the sounds from my own mouth disappeared against her skin while my tongue plunged deeper inside her. My thumb came over to assist, rubbing her clit as I kissed and sucked on her, the sparks of our mate bond adding to the already intense buildup of sensation. She wasn't taking it easy on me either, stroking me with her hand while she took me as deep as she could in her mouth, her other hand reaching around to gently stroke my balls, the twin feelings of need and desire inside me getting stronger and stronger with each movement she made until I couldn't take it anymore.

My whole body tightened in anticipation, feeling the moment of release building, and my mouth moved back to Liz's clit, sucking on it as I plunged my fingers deep into her. Her body shook just as my orgasm hit me, the world exploding around me like a bomb had gone off, like everything had been blown apart.

I came back to my body just in time to lower my lips back to her entrance. Not wanting to miss a single drop of it, I lapped up the sweetness that she dripped down onto my face as little aftershocks of pleasure ran through us both.

When we had both recovered, she gently climbed off me and turned back around so her face was next to mine. Running my fingers through her hair, I pulled her close to me, kissing her mouth just as I'd kissed her pussy a moment ago, tasting myself on her lips and letting her taste her own flavour on me.

I'd never imagined being so in tune with another person was possible, to feel like every emotion and sensation, good or bad, was shared between us.

Liz had given my life a new purpose, and I was determined to do her proud. I wasn't going to rest until everyone else knew what I had already accepted: this woman was made to be worshipped.

Chapter Two

~Oliver~

By the time my father's mating ceremony came around, all my injuries were healed, and Abby gave me an appreciative look as I pulled my suit jacket on.

"You look pretty good all cleaned up," she told me, a smile pulling at her lips. "There's just one problem."

My brow furrowed as I glanced down at what I was wearing. It looked alright to me. "Is my tie crooked?"

"Nope." With a gleam in her pale blue eyes, she walked over and ran her fingers through my hair before curling her hand around the back of my neck possessively. "It's just that you look so good, I want to take it all off again."

I was never going to say no to that. "In that case..."

I started to pull the jacket off again, but Abby immediately stopped me, laughing. "We don't have time right now, but trust me, I'll be thinking about it all night."

Well, now I would be too, and I groaned as I adjusted my dress pants to try to hide the growing bulge there. *Down, boy.*

It didn't help that Abby looked absolutely incredible herself. She was wearing a sweet blue dress that matched her eyes, tight on the top with a skirt that flared out. I didn't have a clue what that kind of dress was called, all I knew was that I couldn't take my eyes off the way it curved around her breasts and hips, or the thought of what lay beneath that skirt.

Months had passed since I first saw her naked, and I still got just as excited about it every time.

But a quick glance at the clock told me she was right, we really did have to get going, and I opened our bedroom door at almost exactly the same time Elijah's door opened down the hall. A second later, he stepped out wearing a suit almost identical to mine, and we both stared at each other in dismay while Liz came out of the room after him and burst out laughing.

"Okay, one of you has to change. You look like your parents dressed you up in matching outfits."

Though Abby tried to hide her smile, she was clearly thinking the same thing.

"I don't have many clothes here," Elijah pointed out, his eyes still fixed on me. "You've probably got a closet full of suits."

I wasn't sure what he thought I spent my time doing, but I certainly wasn't wearing suits most of the time. "Actually, they don't come in very handy in the lab. This is the only one I've got that fits."

We seemed to be at an impasse until Abby stepped in, ever the peacemaker. "Eli, maybe you could just leave your jacket off? Then it won't be quite so noticeable."

Reluctantly, he removed his jacket, and I had to admit it did make a big difference. Our ties were different enough that we no longer looked completely similar. Getting used to having someone around who shared my face was still taking some getting used to; there was no need to dress alike too.

Elijah tossed his jacket back into his room and the four of us headed downstairs together, heading for the hall where the ceremony would be taking place. By far the biggest room in the packhouse, the hall had been built to hold the whole pack, and it seemed like everyone was here tonight. The Alpha taking a new mate was kind of a big deal.

Abby and I still hadn't had our formal ceremony. We figured it made sense to do it at the same time as our Alpha and Luna investiture, which wouldn't be for another year yet. We didn't need a showy ceremony to prove our commitment to each other: I was one hundred percent devoted to her, and she to me. Since the moment she accepted me, our bond was never in any doubt.

Abby, Elijah and Liz all took their designated seats at the front of the room while I stepped up onto the small raised platform, next to my dad who had just arrived too. He wore suits much more frequently than I did, whenever he was on pack business, so he looked less out of place than I did. His expression was as serious as always, but I could see the new light in his eyes that had appeared over the last few weeks since Storm arrived, and it made me genuinely happy.

After everything my dad had been through — dealing with my mom's illness and losing her, hiding the truth about my parentage and raising me on his own, then having the whole deception outed by his Beta — he deserved this chance at happiness more than anyone else I knew.

"Are you ready?" I asked him, simply to make conversation since I was sure he was.

He nodded, his lips twitching a little in amusement. "I'm only worried that she's going to walk in wearing her leather biking gear and give all the elderly wolves a fright."

We both glanced out at some of the older members of the pack, and I bit back my smile too. "You don't have to worry about that. Abby told me they went shopping and that we'll be surprised, in a good way."

My dad's expression took on an affectionate hue as he looked over at my mate. "I really appreciate how supportive she's been to Stephanie."

He was the only one who could get away with calling Storm by her real name, but I agreed with the rest of the sentiment completely. "Abby's the best."

Music began to play, a song that Storm herself had chosen: a soft piano version of a heavy metal song, just classical enough that no one who didn't know the song already would ever guess its origins. As the door opened and his mate walked in, my dad's eyes widened in such amazement that this time I couldn't hold my smile in. When I glanced down at Abby, she had tears of happiness in her eyes.

The dress Storm was wearing was completely perfect: just formal enough to satisfy the traditionalists in the pack, and just different enough for the younger wolves to think it looked cool. Storm wouldn't tell any of us exactly how old she was, but my best guess was that she was about ten years younger than my dad and ten years older than me. She definitely brought out his younger side, anyway. My dad couldn't take his eyes off her for the whole ceremony, and there were knowing glances exchanged among many of the mated pairs in attendance. I suspected several of them were taking bets on how long it would be before the Alpha and new Luna disappeared for the night.

When the mating ceremony was complete, the elders performed the additional rites to initiate Storm as the official Jade Moon Luna. The ceremonial blade was drawn down my dad's palm, and then Storm's, and as they pressed their hands together, their blood mingling, she became a part of our pack, and just as instantly, a strong and instinctive urge to protect and defend her swelled up within me.

Abby, Elijah and Liz were the only ones in the room that wouldn't have felt it since they weren't members of the pack. Abby and I were linked to each other through our bond and our marks, but until we had our mating ceremony, she was still technically a member of her old pack. Since we'd been living on campus most of the time we'd been together, it hadn't caused any issues so far. Elijah was still a member of his old pack too, even though he was no longer Alpha, and Liz wasn't a member of any pack, since she'd only gained her wolf recently. She wasn't a rogue either, though; her royal blood seemed to give her some kind of independent status that overruled any pack alliance.

Despite all that, I wished Abby could have felt it anyway when Storm joined the pack. She still had doubts about whether she was going to be a success as Luna of the pack, but there wasn't a doubt in my mind. My bond with her would predispose the pack to love her, just as they were welcoming Storm now, and our blood link would confirm it. Abby didn't need to change a thing to get them to accept her; she just had to be herself.

The double ceremony was followed by a reception with food and music and dancing. It had been a long time since we had a reason for the whole pack to celebrate like this, and everyone was having a great time as Abby and I mingled among the crowd, chatting to everyone we came across as she tried to remember everyone's names.

"This is Richard Erickson, right?" she whispered to me as yet another couple headed our way.

I shook my head. "Close. Trent, and his mate Elizabeth."

Disappointment flashed across her face, but that was a tough one as there were a lot of Erickson brothers and they all looked alike. I squeezed her hand to reassure her, and once we were finished talking with them, I pulled her out onto the dance floor so we could have a moment to ourselves.

"Relax, Heels," I whispered to her as I pulled her body close to mine. "You'll get there. You're doing amazing, you just need to give it time. They're going to love you. They'll love you because I love you."

She melted into me as our mate bond helped to soothe her. "You know, I think your dad's getting a second wind now with Storm here. Maybe he wants to be Alpha for another twenty years or so."

As always, she made me laugh. "Nice try. I think he's going to want us to take over as soon as possible so he can go and enjoy his retirement with his new mate. Hopefully, in another twenty years, it'll be us retiring when our son or daughter takes over."

Although I knew there was no rush for us to have pups, the idea had been crossing my mind more and more lately. I couldn't wait to have a family with Abby and build our life here. Being here this summer, and being around my dad and Storm and Eli and Liz had only made that feeling stronger. I was even considering not going back to campus at all in the fall and finishing my degree long-distance, though I hadn't discussed that with Abby yet. That was definitely a decision we were going to have to make together.

"Oliver? Abby?"

We didn't even get to finish our dance before being interrupted and I couldn't completely hide my frustration as I looked over at my dad's Beta. "What?"

"I'm sorry to interrupt, but there's a phone call for Abby on the Alpha's line. They said they tried to reach her on her cell, but there was no answer."

Of course there wasn't; Abby had left her phone in her room. Who would be calling her here at the pack anyway?

She was obviously as stumped as I was, but she pulled back from me. "I better go see who it is."

"I'll come with you." I didn't want to let her out of my sight in that dress. Maybe if we played this right, we could even sneak back upstairs after she'd taken her phone call, without anyone noticing we were gone.

The pack house hallways were empty and quiet as we made our way to my dad's office. A button was flashing red on his desk phone, so Abby picked up the receiver and pressed the button to connect the call. "Hello?"

With my strong wolf hearing, I could make out the voice on the other end, but I didn't recognize it. The person also seemed to be crying, which made it harder to make out what they were saying.

"Mom?" Abby said, her voice filled with worry. "Slow down, I can't understand you. What's going on?"

There was a sob, and my stomach sank even before the words came out. No good news ever accompanied a sound like that. "It's your father, Abby. He's... he's dead."

~Abby~

Staring out the window of the car as we sped down the dark, empty road, it felt like I was in some kind of nightmare. Any second now, I was going to wake up, snug in my bed with my mate beside me, and this day would start all over again. We'd go through Alpha Patrick and Storm's mating ceremony again, the Luna ceremony, the party, all of it, but this time it would end with Oliver and I going back up to our room together the way we planned.

That phone call would never come, and my dad wouldn't be dead. *He couldn't be.*

My mom said there was no warning. He woke up early this morning, the same as always, and put in a full day of work as the Forest Ridge Beta. He was in his mid-50s and getting close to retirement, but he wanted to wait until Alpha Easton was ready to retire before he took that step. He'd served the Alpha ever since they were both young men, and he intended to finish what he'd started. That was the kind of man he was.

He was the kind of man who always snuck me books from the pack house library even after my mother said I had read enough, and the kind who always asked how my day had been at school, like it could have been anything other than awful. I couldn't bring myself to tell him how much I was bullied because it would have broken his heart.

He was the kind of man who let me go to college in the human town over my mother's objections, knowing that I wanted to go more than anything.

Whenever I was down, feeling I didn't belong, he always told me the problem wasn't that I didn't fit in but rather that I just hadn't found the right place to fit into yet. He couldn't have been happier when I met Oliver, and I knew his joy was not just because my mate was a future

Alpha, which was what impressed my mother, but because he saw just how happy Oliver made me.

My mom wasn't mean to me or anything like that; we were just very different people and she found it easier to connect with my sisters than she did with me. My dad, however, was my one true ally, the one person who always believed that I was meant for something important and that I was going to make a difference, despite all the evidence to the contrary.

When he didn't show up for dinner, my mom went looking for him and found him in his office, still sitting behind his desk, his head resting against the back of the chair as if he were just having a nap. She said his heart just stopped. The doctors couldn't find any other reason for it.

"How're you doing?" Oliver's voice was as warm as his hand that came over to rest on top of mine. He was driving my car, taking me back to Forest Ridge to be with my family. I didn't know what he told his own father or the rest of the pack. After I hung up with my mom, Oliver left me in the Alpha's office under the Beta's care while he went back to the party, and then he led me out to the car to take me to my old pack, all without me having to say a word.

"I just can't believe he's gone." My voice sounded strangely flat, even to my own ears. "There was so much I never got to talk to him about."

The last time I talked to him was two weeks ago, not long after the events surrounding Liz and Eli finding each other and the source of power. We found out that Liz descended from a line of royal were-wolves at the same time I discovered my family was not so distantly related to hers and that it had been our job to guard the source from people who would try to take it from its rightful owners.

I told my dad all about this, and the news was just as surprising to him as it had been for me. He offered to look into it more, and I promised to come and see him soon so he could share his findings with me.

Now, that was never going to happen. I would never see him again, and my eyes welled with tears as the gaping emptiness opened inside me again, just as it had when my mom first said the words, the wound caused by his loss ripping open all over again.

"What can I do?" Oliver pleaded, his grey eyes darting over to me before returning to the road ahead, illuminated only by our headlights. "It's killing me to see you so sad, Abby."

Nine times out of ten, he used my nickname, Heels, which he'd given me shortly after we met. When he actually called me Abby, it meant things were serious.

"There's nothing you can do besides being here with me," I told him. "I don't need to tell you how it feels. You already know."

Oliver had lost his mother a long time ago, so he understood the pain of losing a parent better than anyone.

But he shook his head at me now, not satisfied with my response. "It's not the same thing, Abby. I want to know how it feels for *you*. I want you to tell me everything, always."

He clearly meant that, and so, I started to talk. I told him stories from my childhood I hadn't even realized I recalled, all the things I remembered about my dad. I was the youngest of six children, and I was naturally a bit of an introvert anyway, so I flew under the radar a lot of the time. My dad, however, always made time for me, always sought me out and made me feel special, even when there were a million different things going on in our family and the pack that needed his attention too.

He was an amazing grandfather to my nieces and nephews, but he wouldn't get to see them grow up, and he'd never get to meet my pups at all. My tears started anew as that realization hit me too.

Oliver listened to it all, laughing with me when I remembered something funny, and holding my hand supportively as I cried. As always, I was so grateful for his presence, and I couldn't imagine going through this without him. He really was the best thing that ever happened to me.

The dashboard clock was nearing midnight as we pulled up to the Forest Ridge pack house. Despite the late hour, the lights on the ground floor were all on and there was a steady flow of people in and out.

The death of the pack's Beta was a big deal, not just for his family, but for the whole pack. As tradition dictated, his body would be laid out in the hall for two days and two nights, so anyone who wanted to could come and pay their respects.

Oliver held my hand tightly as we walked together up the wide steps to the door and into the entrance hall. We'd already been cleared at the border, and although Oliver's scent attracted some attention, no one questioned us as we went straight to the main assembly room. Earlier tonight, we'd been celebrating in the Jade Moon hall, and now, we were here in the corresponding room at Forest Ridge to mourn.

My three brothers and my brother-in-law, Grant, all stood guard around the platform where the coffin rested. Their faces were stoic as they looked straight ahead, not making eye contact with anyone who stopped by to pay their respects. That job was left to my mom and my sister, Maddie, who were sitting nearby, holding hands as they accepted the pack's condolences.

My other sister, Evelyn, wasn't here yet but I expected she would be soon. Her mate had recently been appointed Beta of his pack, which was based a few hours away from here.

"Good evening, Abby. Oliver." The deep voice behind us made us both turn, and I bowed my head in respect.

"Alpha."

Alpha Easton's face was drawn and there was sympathy in his eyes as he smiled sadly at me. My dad had been not only his Beta but his close friend for most of their lives, and he was obviously feeling the loss as much as any member of our family.

"Thank you for coming," he told us both. "I know it would mean a great deal to him."

Oliver gripped his arm in a show of support. "We are sorry for your loss, Alpha Easton. My father sends his condolences."

Alpha Easton nodded. "Of course. It's unfortunate that this sad occasion should draw you away from such a happy one, but that's the nature of life sometimes, isn't it?"

Oliver and I both nodded in confirmation. Taking the bad with the good was indeed something we all had to deal with.

And speaking of the bad, my whole body tensed as Alpha Easton stepped aside to reveal two other people who I had not seen in a long time.

"Abby." Though Jerrod's voice was warm, it still sent a shiver down my spine. I had managed to avoid him whenever I came to visit my family over the last few months, though Maddie always made a point of telling me how he was doing. She blamed me for Jerrod's diminished leadership role within the pack as if his unhealthy obsession with me had somehow been my fault.

Oliver's hand tightened around mine as he pulled me slightly closer to him. "Jerrod," he said, returning the greeting far more coolly than it had been offered. "Marissa. We're sorry for the loss to your pack. The Beta was a good man."

I had barely even noticed Marissa standing next to Jerrod, but she was indeed there. They didn't touch each other or show any outward sign of affection; if anything, Jerrod had his back turned to her ever-so-slightly.

Maddie also told me that there were plenty of rumours amongst the pack that Jerrod and Marissa's mating was not a happy one. That was my fault too, naturally, since I was the one who suggested they give their relationship another try after Jerrod had rejected their mate bond in an ill-advised attempt to remain available for me.

I had genuinely hoped they would find happiness with each other, the same kind that I had found with my fated mate. I didn't wish any harm on either of them; I just didn't particularly want anything to do with them either.

"He was a great man," Jerrod agreed, glancing towards the coffin in the centre of the room. "And a fixture of this pack. I can't remember a time when he wasn't around. I have a lot of fond memories."

He looked over at me, inviting me to join his reminiscences, and I knew what he meant. We had spent a lot of time together growing up, him as the son of the Alpha and me the daughter of the Beta. His parents were almost like surrogate parents to me, and vice versa. I would be truly sad when Alpha Easton died, so I did my best to take Jerrod's comments at face value, and offered him a small nod.

"I always loved the scavenger hunts he set up for us. At the time, I thought he wanted to develop our hunting skills, but now, I think he was probably just getting rid of us to have some time with my mom."

Jerrod's face lit up at the memory. "You're probably right. Some of those things were impossible to find. It must have been on purpose."

He smiled at me, and for just a moment, I could remember how close we used to be before he started treating me so poorly. We were friends once, and we could have still been friends now, if he hadn't pushed me away.

"I should go talk to my mom," I said, and Jerrod quickly nodded.

"Of course. We won't keep you." He reached out a hand to Marissa, but she stepped away without looking at it, or without sparing a glance for me either. It appeared I was far from being on her good side yet. Jerrod's face tightened at the slight from his mate, but he still gave Oliver and me one further nod before following his mate from the room.

With my hand still holding Oliver's, we went over to my family and to look at my father one last time.

~Marissa~

My blood was boiling as I left the hall. Oliver had only looked at me for a moment, and Abby for less than that. I was the future Luna of this pack, and they treated me like some kind of unsightly stain that might go away if they pretended I wasn't there.

All I wanted was some kind of recognition, some kind of acknowledgement, but apparently that was too much to ask for. Everything was about Abby, as it always was. I didn't know why I expected anything different, but for some reason, I had let myself get my hopes up anyway.

When Jerrod told me the Beta was dead, it immediately brought back memories of my own father. He'd been the Beta at my former pack, and he died not very long ago too. He was murdered, actually, by his own Alpha. Though I understood my father had done some things that weren't quite right, his intentions were good. All he'd been trying to do was protect the bloodline of our pack, and help me become Luna at the same time. Weren't parents supposed to look out for their children's interests?

He was the only person who ever put my needs first, and I was beginning to think he was the only one who ever would.

My mate certainly wouldn't, that was for fucking sure. As soon as he delivered the news of the Beta's death, he smiled that sickening smile that he reserved for one person alone. "That means Abby will be coming here soon, maybe even tonight."

Abby. I had never hated anyone as much as I hated her. Not only did she steal the man and the position that I had always wanted, she then forced me and Jerrod to be mated, against both our wishes, and everyone acted like she was some kind of saint for suggesting it.

Like I needed her pity or her cast-offs. Like I *wanted* to be mated to a man who didn't want me, someone who had already rejected me and would happily do so again if she gave him the slightest bit of encouragement.

I hated Jerrod, but I still hated Abby more.

"Oliver will probably come too," Jerrod continued, giving me an appraising look. "It's been a while since you've seen him, hasn't it?"

It definitely had. The last time I saw him was the day my father died, the day that my whole pack abandoned me here, discarding me like I was an embarrassment, when all I had done was come here with the other warriors, ready to defend the honour of the Jade Moon pack. I found out about my father's betrayal at the same time everyone else did, but for some reason, his actions were my fault too. As punishment,

I was forced to stay here and accept the man who had rejected me and clearly didn't want me. My situation was humiliating and demeaning, and no one acted like there was a fucking thing wrong with it.

"Try and dress appropriately," was the last thing my mate said to me on his way out the door. "I'll come and get you when they arrive."

In his wake, a scream of frustration left my lips, echoing around our large bedroom. When did I ever not dress appropriately? What he really meant was: be more like Abby. That was what he *always* meant. If I dyed my hair the same mousy brown as hers and started wearing glasses, he'd probably lose his fucking mind.

I really couldn't understand what the big deal about her was. With Oliver, it made a little bit of sense. The mate bond does crazy things, and it blinded him to the kind of person she really was and her obvious physical defects. I didn't blame him for it, not when I still looked forward to going to bed each night and to those moments of pure need when Jerrod's hands lit up my skin. Even though I hated him, for those few minutes, it felt special. *I* felt special.

If Abby gave Oliver that same feeling, I could see the appeal of it, although it didn't fully explain why he was so besotted with her the rest of the time too. And from what my friends in my former pack told me, he truly was. They hardly ever saw one of them without the other.

That used to be me and him. Back in high school, we were always together. I could still feel his arm casually draped across my shoulders as we walked the halls together, or see the way he'd smile at me after a football game as he took his helmet off, sweaty but satisfied. I was the envy of all the girls in the pack, and I loved it. High school was the best time of my life.

Our relationship wasn't all one-sided either. I taught him things. He was a virgin when we started going out, nervous and unsure, and I quickly showed him the ropes. Eventually, he got pretty good at it too. He owed me for that, and Abby did too. She was the one enjoying the fruits of my instructions.

When he broke up with me before he went to college, I wasn't particularly surprised, or upset for that matter. A long-distance relationship was never going to be my style. There were plenty of other men in the pack I could spend my time with, and I did. I heard the talk among the guys in the pack that Oliver was making a name for himself on campus as a bit of a player, and honestly, it made me proud. Once again, he had *me* to thank for giving him that confidence and those skills.

Only after I met Jerrod the first time, when he rejected me without knowing anything about me at all, did I begin to think maybe Oliver and I were meant for something else. And then Alpha Patrick, Oliver's father, told me that Oliver had asked to see me, that he wanted me to go and watch his football game and spend time with him afterwards.

It would be just like old times, and that was just what I needed for my wounded pride and broken heart.

But when I went to talk to him after the game, Oliver acted like he didn't want me there at all. He went to talk to some other girls instead, one of whom was a werewolf. He was acting so strangely, and when that same girl showed up on our pack land a few days later, I knew. They didn't say anything to anyone, but I knew it anyway: this completely unremarkable girl was Oliver's mate. Dreams I hadn't even realized I still had, dreams of Oliver realizing he couldn't live without me and choosing me to be his mate and Luna, all of those ambitions died a cold, painful death as I saw the way he looked at her.

The next day, I learned that Jerrod had rejected me for that same girl, and *then* she forced me and Jerrod back together with the Alphas of both packs deferring to her and praising her for her suggestion like she was making some kind of selfless, gracious gesture, and honestly, who could blame me for hating her?

Not to mention the fact that Jerrod was still in love with her, no matter what he tried to convince everyone else. I saw it in the way his eyes lit up whenever she was mentioned. He never acted that way when it came to me.

I had my position as his mate and I had his body, which brought me far more pleasure than I wanted to admit, but I had never had his heart. That belonged to Abby.

The only two men I'd ever felt anything for were both in love with the same woman, and that woman wasn't me.

And she couldn't even spare me a glance when I went to offer my condolences on her father's death, nor had she ever offered me any sympathy when *my* father died.

I really didn't get it: what was so fucking special about her?!

"Where are you going?" Jerrod's voice hissed from behind me as I reached the stairs.

"To bed," I shot back at him. "They didn't even notice I was there. I'm not going to stand around and be ignored all night to pay tribute to some guy I didn't even know."

I tried to keep going up the stairs, but Jerrod's arm shot out to stop me. "It doesn't matter if you knew him or not. It's part of your position to be at functions such as this. You have to act like you've got a heart, Marissa, even if you don't."

"You don't know a fucking thing about my heart," I sneered, trying to pull my arm loose, but he held me firmly. I hated how strong he was, and I especially hated how my body reacted whenever he got forceful like this. There was no good reason I should find it so sexy.

His nose twitched, letting me know he was completely aware of my arousal. "That would make it the only part of your body I don't know, then."

We stared at each other for a second longer, lust and disgust battling for control, but as it so often did, lust won out.

This time, when I tried to go up the stairs, he was right behind me, following me back to our room where we could both find a bit of pleasure in each other, if only for a moment.

Chapter Three

~Oliver~

In the months since we met, Abby and I hadn't spent much time with her family. That was partly my fault: as the future Alpha, I was needed at my pack whenever I had spare time, and since I was my father's only child, that was an additional reason for us to go there, so he wouldn't be alone without any family on special occasions. Abby, on the other hand, was one of six children, and she always assured me that no one would miss her if we spent the time we had off from college at the Jade Moon pack instead.

Perhaps I should have insisted more often, even if she said making the trip wasn't necessary. I really only got to speak to her dad a handful of times, and now he was gone. Tears fell down Abby's cheeks as she looked down on his lifeless body, and it killed me to see her looking so heartbroken and not being able to do anything about it. He looked peaceful, at least. Whatever happened, he didn't seem to have suffered.

After a few minutes, Abby leaned down and whispered something in her dad's ear, so quietly that not even my wolf hearing could pick it up, and then she gave each of her brothers a quick, rather awkward hug, with a handshake for her brother-in-law Grant. I shook hands with them all, offering my sincere condolences, and then we moved over to where Abby's mother sat with her sister, Maddie.

Abby's mom always treated me well, but I suspected that deference was due to my position rather than because she liked me as a person. Right now, after I paid my respects, I left the three of them alone so they could speak freely amongst themselves.

Let me know when you need me, Heels.

She nodded in response to my mind-link, her eyes still filled with tears, and my heart constricted again as I moved away. Fuck, I wished there was something useful I could do.

A table with food was set up at the far end of the hall, so I made my way over there as my stomach rumbled. We hadn't had a chance to eat much at my dad and Storm's reception since we'd been so busy speaking to all the different pack members before the phone call that brought us here. Abby was probably hungry too, but I would wait until she was finished talking to her mom before I insisted that she eat something.

For now, I focused on filling up my own plate, until my ears pricked up at a hushed conversation not far from me.

"The doctor wants to do a full autopsy, but the family's resisting."

"I thought the cause of death was a heart attack?"

I glanced over at the two men, trying to remain inconspicuous. They were both men in their late 30s, half-way between Abby's age and her parents. Quickly, I returned my attention to the food in front of me so they wouldn't notice me, though I was still listening intently.

"The doctor says there was no preexisting condition, nothing that should have caused it. He thinks it might have been something unnatural, made to mimic a heart attack."

I could hear the confusion in the second man's voice as he replied. "Then why doesn't the family want it looked at? Or the Alpha could insist? Surely if someone's managed to kill the Beta, that's a security risk for all of us."

"I wondered that too. Doesn't make much sense, unless the Alpha knows about it?"

This time, I couldn't stop myself from looking up at them in surprise. They weren't seriously suggesting that their Alpha had been involved in Abby's father's death, were they?

The sudden movement attracted their attention, and as soon as they saw me there and realized I was a stranger, they moved further away. If their conversation continued, I could no longer hear it, but the amount I heard already had ruined my appetite, so I put the plate back down on the table. I had no idea if what they said was just idle gossip or if there was something to it, but either way, I was going to have to find a way to bring it up to Abby. If there was even a chance that her father's death wasn't natural, her family deserved to know about it. Was it true that they had declined the autopsy?

"Is something wrong with the food?"

I'd know that voice anywhere: it belonged to Jerrod, the slimy Alpha's son who had nearly killed Abby a few months ago. Since then, he'd kept his distance from her, and tonight, he had been nothing but respectful. There was nothing in his conduct I could fault him for, but he still rubbed me the wrong way anyway.

I gave him what I hoped wasn't too fake a smile. Since we saw him ten minutes ago, his complexion had changed; now, he looked a bit flushed, like he'd just gone for a run or something. Marissa was nowhere in sight.

"The food's fine, I guess I just wasn't as hungry as I thought."

He smiled in return, almost to himself. "Sometimes we bite off more than we can chew."

What the hell was that supposed to mean? My stomach sank as I thought back to the conversation I'd just overheard. Was he talking about Abby's dad? Did Jerrod have something to do with that? He was reckless enough that I wouldn't put it past him. Maybe the Alpha was covering up for his son, and that was why he didn't want it investigated?

"I hear you'll be at the Alpha conference next week," he continued as if he hadn't just said something ridiculously creepy. "I'm attending, along with Marissa, of course. Perhaps the four of us could have dinner together. I understand you'll be taking over your pack soon, and so will

I. There might be ways we could collaborate for the benefit of both our packs."

Having dinner with Jerrod and Marissa sounded like nothing short of torture, but putting my personal feelings aside, I had to admit he had a point. Our packs were geographically close to each other, they had historically been friendly with each other if not exactly allies, and now, we were both mated to a woman from each other's pack. The opportunity for collaboration had never been stronger, and my pack's wellbeing had to come first; that was what being an Alpha was all about.

Besides, there was that old saying about keeping your friends close and your enemies closer. It might not hurt to find out what was going on in his head.

And maybe it wouldn't be so bad if I brought along a little backup, which I suggested now. "My brother Elijah and his mate will also be there. We could all have dinner together."

A flash of annoyance crossed his face, as if that wasn't what he wanted, but he quickly covered it up. "Of course, that sounds perfect. I'm curious to know more about him. It's such an... interesting... family you have, Oliver."

"It is," I agreed, choosing to take that as a compliment even though that obviously wasn't the way he meant it.

Oliver? I think I'm ready for a break now.

Abby's voice in my head was a relief since I was definitely ready for a breather too.

Jerrod must have seen my eyes glaze over as I received the link, as his gaze immediately moved over to where Abby was still sitting with her mother.

I gave him one last nod of acknowledgement as I picked up the plate of food I'd put together earlier. Maybe she would eat it, even if I couldn't. "Excuse me, my mate needs me."

"Of course." Though he tried to smile, he looked like he'd swallowed something rather bitter. "We'll see you at the conference, then."

"See you then."

Abby had done her best to put the Forest Ridge pack behind her over the last few months, but as I moved back towards her now, I couldn't help thinking that things weren't going to be quite that simple. Right now, it felt like there was still some unfinished business we would need to take care of first.

~Abby~

Oliver and I spent the night at Forest Ridge. When we left the wake at nearly one o'clock in the morning, we were taken to a guest room within the pack house, and after almost a year away, waking up in the same house where I grew up was very strange. I used to dread each new day when I had to deal with the bullying and the microaggressions and the people who simply pretended I didn't exist, and I used to dream of getting away and getting a fresh start among humans who wouldn't treat me like dirt simply because an Alpha's son told them to.

Now, I woke up next to a different Alpha's son, one who would protect and defend me to his dying breath, and I couldn't help thinking how quickly things could shift. Life could change irrevocably with one meeting, or with one parting.

It broke my heart to speak to my mother the night before. However I felt about our own relationship, she loved my father with all her heart, that was never in doubt. His death was a huge blow to her, and as someone who naturally empathized with the people around me, feeling her loss was overwhelming. I couldn't help imagining how I would feel in her place, and I held Oliver a little tighter this morning as a result, needing to know he was still there and he was okay.

"Is there a reason you don't want me to breathe, Heels?" he teased me as I squeezed him again. Despite his words, his arms wrapped tightly around me too, filling me with warmth.

"I'm just glad you're here," I told him honestly. "Thank you for coming with me."

"Of course. You never have to go through anything alone, Abby. But listen, there's something I want to talk to you about."

He sat up, pulling me up with him so that he could look into my eyes as the morning sun filtered in through the guest room curtains. He was a little blurry without my glasses on, but I could still make out the look of love and concern on his face.

"I didn't say anything last night because you had enough to deal with, but there was some talk in the room that your dad's death might not have been natural."

My stomach sank, making me feel a little nauseous. Who would want to hurt my dad? He never had a bad word to say about anyone. Sensing my distress, Oliver quickly placed a firm kiss on my forehead.

"I don't know if it's true, but they were saying that your family refused an autopsy, which doesn't make sense to me. Wouldn't it be better to find out? If the rumours are wrong, then it could put your mind at rest. And if they're right, well, I imagine you'd want to get to the bottom of it."

I hated even considering that it might be true, but I could see Oliver's point. Knowledge was power, we both believed that, and if an autopsy was going to be done, the sooner, the better, before any potential evidence disappeared.

"I'll talk to my mom about it," I promised, though the idea of causing her even more distress was not at all appealing. He nodded, but there was still something lurking in the back of his eyes, something he wasn't telling me, and I pressed him for an explanation. "What else?"

That made him smile, just for a moment. "I can't hide anything from you, can I? Something else was said, suggesting that the Alpha might be covering something up. Again, I have no clue if it's true, but there was talk."

Believing that Alpha Easton would be involved was even harder than imagining someone wanting to hurt my dad in the first place, but I knew Oliver wouldn't tell me anything that wasn't true. People must be talking about it, at least.

"I guess we better get going then."

Once we were dressed and ready, we headed to the dining room where breakfast was already underway. There was no set time like there was for lunch and dinner, the pack house inhabitants ate whenever they wanted, but my family was already there, including my sister, Evelyn, and her mate, James, who must have arrived after we went to bed.

Oliver hadn't met them yet, so I made the introductions and left the three of them to chat while I went to sit down next to my mom. "How are you today?"

Though she had her usual makeup on, her face was still pale and her eyes red. "When I woke up this morning, I hoped everything was all a bad dream," she admitted, her voice shaking. "But obviously, it's not."

Instinctively, I reached out and took her hand, and she squeezed mine back gratefully. A rare moment of connection passed between us, at least until Maddie piped up from across the table.

"I've been going over the seating plans for the funeral, Abby, and now that Evelyn and James are here, there isn't enough room at the front for you and your mate too. I hope it's okay that I've put you a little further back."

Seating charts? A flash of annoyance went through me that she was focused on something like that, but I tried to be understanding. Maybe worrying about that was what she needed to help her cope, and the truth was I couldn't care less about where I sat, so I simply nodded. "That's fine, Maddie."

Turning my back to her, I focused entirely on my mom.

"Did the doctors say anything to you about doing an autopsy?"

Immediately, my mom's expression turned more guarded. "They did, but I told them not to."

"Why?" I wanted to find out exactly what she'd been told and why she'd made that decision before I tried to convince her otherwise.

"He's gone, isn't he? What good is it going to do? And I don't want them to cut him up, he deserves more dignity than that…"

She trailed off, her eyes filling with tears again, and this time I put my arms around her. We rarely hugged, that wasn't the kind of relationship we had, but in this case, I couldn't stop myself. The pain in her voice was so raw.

"Nothing can hurt him anymore," I pointed out as gently as I could. "They could do it after the funeral if you want, once everyone has seen him. You wouldn't have to see him again afterwards if you don't want to. You can remember him just as he was, but if the doctors are suggesting it, there must be a reason."

"She already said no," Maddie interjected from across the table. I hadn't realized she was still listening to us, but when I turned to look at her, she was watching us closely. "It's her choice."

That was true, but there was more to it than that, which I tried to explain now without upsetting my mom even more. "It might affect the whole pack," I pointed out gently. "If there's a chance that something happened to him, they need to know about it."

"Why would anyone hurt him?" Maddie demanded, and my mom flinched beside me.

"I didn't say anyone hurt him," I countered. "I said something might have happened to him. Maybe he ate something that stopped his heart, purely by accident. If it came from the pack house kitchen, others might be at risk."

Those within earshot all looked down at their half-eaten breakfasts uneasily, and I grimaced. I wasn't doing a very good job of this.

"You think there might have been some kind of accident?" my mom repeated, looking up at me in confusion.

"I don't know," I admitted. "But the only way to find out for sure is to go ahead with the autopsy. I think you should."

"You don't have to, Mom," Maddie quickly added. "Remember what Dad said about moving on. He never wanted us to dwell on the past too much."

I knew what she was talking about, but she was twisting his words too. Whether she was misrepresenting them intentionally or if she had just truly missed the point, I couldn't say.

"He said not to dwell on things that we couldn't change," I reminded her. "But he also said we need to understand a situation as fully as possible before making a decision."

Maddie ignored that, addressing herself directly to my mom. "They'd have to take his heart out. Is that what you want?"

My mom flinched again, and I glared at my sister. She was tactless at the best of times and, clearly, this was not one of those times.

"Maddie's right, Abby," my mom said, to my frustration. "He would want us to move on."

I still disagreed, but there was nothing else I could say without upsetting her more, so I got back to my feet and returned to where Oliver was still chatting with Evelyn and James. As I walked up, the couple excused themselves to get some food, and Oliver turned to me curiously. "Any luck?"

I shook my head. "She's convinced herself she doesn't want to do it. Now what?"

Oliver's eyes moved to the door, where Jerrod and Marissa had just entered. Just like they had last night, they neither looked at nor touched each other as they came into the room.

"The Alpha has the authority to order the autopsy even without the family's approval," Oliver pointed out. "Maybe you could ask Jerrod to do it."

"Jerrod?" I repeated in surprise. Why wouldn't I ask the Alpha himself?

Oliver nodded in confirmation. "He seems eager to get on our good side, and I want to test a theory."

"What theory?"

He grimaced just a little. "If either he or the Alpha are involved in covering it up, their reaction might give us some clues. I think we should start with Jerrod."

I really didn't know what reaction we would be looking for, but I trusted my mate enough to do as he said, so I headed over towards Jerrod now with Oliver close behind me. A smile crossed Jerrod's face when he saw me, though he quickly pulled it back, seeming to remember this was still a sad occasion.

"How are you this morning, Abby?" he asked, sounding almost sympathetic. In my peripheral vision, I thought I saw Marissa roll her eyes.

"I'm okay, thank you, but I have a favour to ask of you, if that's okay."

His eyes brightened in anticipation. "Of course. What is it?"

"Don't say 'of course' until she tells you what it is," Marissa interjected, her voice dripping with disdain. "You sound like an idiot."

That seemed a pretty harsh reaction for what he'd said, and Oliver and I exchanged confused glances. Jerrod, however, ignored her entirely, his attention still on me. "What do you need, Abby?"

"I'd like an autopsy done on my father. My mother has refused it, but I think the Alpha can overrule that..."

I didn't even have to finish the sentence before he was nodding. "Of course. If that's what you want, I'll take care of it right away."

"And I'd like to be there for it," Oliver added from behind me.

That made Jerrod's brow furrow, for just a second. "I thought you were a chemist, not a biologist."

I didn't realize he knew that much about Oliver at all, but Oliver didn't miss a beat. "That's my focus, yes, but I know enough about all the sciences that I could follow along."

Jerrod's lips tightened but he nodded anyway. "Fine. I'll speak to my father about it now, and they can do it immediately following the funeral."

Well, that was all a lot easier than I expected, and despite everything else between us, I was grateful. "Thank you, Jerrod. I really appreciate it."

The simple thanks brightened his whole expression again. "I'm happy to help."

He moved off to speak to his father, Marissa following behind him at a distance.

"I forgot to tell you one other thing," Oliver said as we watched them go. "I agreed we'd have dinner with the two of them at the Alpha conference next week."

"You did what?"

My stunned reaction made him laugh. "I know. It must have been a moment of temporary insanity, but we'll bring Elijah and Liz too and maybe it won't be so bad."

Remembering the way Marissa and Jerrod interacted with each other, not to mention the history between all of us, I wasn't so sure about that, but I wasn't going to stress about it just yet. We still had a funeral and an autopsy to get through first.

~Liz~

Eli looked so disappointed when I asked him to sit in the front seat with Oliver on our way to the conference that I nearly changed my mind right there and then.

"You can still talk to me," I quickly pointed out. "And it's not like we could do anything else anyway, not with Oliver and Abby right there."

"You underestimate me, Liz." His smirk sent a rush of heat through me even as I shook my head at him. His ability to turn me on, no matter the circumstances, was both frustrating and sexy as hell.

"Please, Eli." I resorted to begging before he could change my mind, which he almost certainly could if he tried hard enough. "I really want to talk to Abby. We haven't had a chance to catch up properly since she got back from her dad's funeral."

I'd never seen my usually optimistic friend as subdued as she'd been the last few days, and I wanted to find out what was going on. We weren't only friends now, we were going to be sisters-in-law, and if there was something I could do to help her, I wanted to do it.

Despite the mask of indifference he sometimes wore, Eli cared about Abby too, so he reluctantly agreed, and he even took the lead on asking Abby if she would mind sitting in the back with me so that he could talk to Oliver about the conference.

Thank you, I said to him through our mind-link. *I owe you one.*

I will definitely be collecting on that later.

Even his voice in my head sent shivers of excitement down my spine.

Abby gave me a smile as we both buckled up in the back seat, but her smile was missing its usual spark, and that was just what I wanted to talk to her about.

"I know things have been busy since you got back," I began as Oliver pulled out from the pack house parking lot. Next stop was the Alpha conference where I had no idea what to expect, but Eli insisted my attendance was important. "What happened when you went to your old pack? Is everything okay?"

Abby pressed her lips together and for a moment, I thought she might not answer, in which case this was going to be a very long, awkward trip. But finally, she blurted out something I never expected her to say.

"My dad was murdered."

"What?" I gasped in shock. "I thought he had a heart attack."

That was what Oliver told us the night of the mating ceremony, when they had to leave suddenly in the middle of everything. He asked us not to tell Alpha Patrick and Luna Storm until the next morning, claiming he didn't want to put a damper on their evening.

"That's what we thought too, but there were a few things that were suspicious when we got there, so we insisted on an autopsy, over my mom's objections. Now, she won't even talk to me."

I tried to follow all of that. "So, the autopsy showed he was murdered?"

Abby nodded. "At first, the doctors couldn't find anything, they were ready to rule it as natural causes, but then Oliver insisted that they test his hair and that's when they noticed something strange."

"His hair?" I repeated curiously. This was way over my head. Abby and I were literature majors and there was a good reason for that: science had never been my strong suit.

She smiled, completely understanding my confusion. "I know, I didn't get it either. But apparently, your hair can show if you've been exposed to something over a long period of time. Oliver said he learned about it from cases of chemical poisoning that took place in labs."

He really is smart, I thought, as I gave Oliver an appreciative glance. He and Eli were deep in their own conversation, though I had no idea what they were talking about. Eli was smart too, I quickly added in my head, but in a different way. Definitely not the bookworm way.

"So, your dad was exposed to some kind of chemical?" I asked, hoping I had that right.

"It looks that way. Oliver is still running some tests to try to figure out exactly what the chemical was, which might help us pin down who was responsible for my father's death. Nevertheless, he's convinced it didn't happen naturally. If the whole pack was exposed to it, it would have affected the children first, but my dad is the only one who died."

Things were making more sense to me, but I was still missing something. "If the autopsy showed all that, then why is your mom angry with you? Wouldn't she want to know that her husband was murdered?"

"Not her husband, her mate," Abby reminded me, her usual smile flashing through for just a second before her face returned to its more serious expression again. "And she's angry because she doesn't know what we found. Oliver wants to keep it secret until he can get more answers. He figures if the murderer knows we found out about it, they might try to do something to throw us off. As far as she knows, the autopsy showed nothing, and we went against her wishes for no good reason."

"Wow." This all sounded like some kind of TV show. I didn't know things like this happened in real life, but then, I didn't know were-wolves were real until a few weeks ago either. "And you couldn't even tell your mom and ask her to keep it a secret?"

"Not when we don't know who might be involved," Abby explained. "It would probably have to be someone pretty close to him. The only people who know the truth are us, the doctors, and the Alpha's son. He's even keeping it a secret from his father."

My brow furrowed at that new revelation. "Wait, the same Alpha's son we're supposed to be having dinner with this week? The one who was obsessed with you?"

Oliver had filled us in on some of the history since we were supposed to be having dinner with this guy and his mate sometime in the next few days. I'd had no idea Abby had gone through half the stuff he told us about.

"That's the one," she confirmed with a grimace.

"And you trust him with this? What if he's the one who killed your dad?"

"It's crossed our minds," she admitted. "But since he's the only one who knows, if we do find out that evidence has been tampered with, that will only make him more suspicious. Oliver's formulating a plan, we just have to get through this conference first."

With all of that going on, I was surprised they were still coming to the conference at all, and I said so now: "Why didn't you guys just stay home?"

Abby grimaced again, this time glancing up at the front seat before leaning in closer to me. "Don't take this the wrong way, but Oliver's a little bit worried about Eli. He thinks he might try to take matters into his own hands at this conference, so he wants to be there and make sure he doesn't get carried away."

Now, I was completely lost, even more so than when we were talking about chemicals in people's hair. "Take what into his own hands? What are you talking about?"

Abby leaned in even closer, speaking almost directly into my ear. "Eli thinks you're the rightful queen, even though we haven't had a king or queen in hundreds of years. Oliver's just a little afraid that he might try to claim some kind of power on your behalf in front of the other Alphas. With good intentions, obviously, but it could cause problems anyway. Please don't say anything to Eli. It's not that Oliver doesn't trust him, it's just that..."

She didn't have to finish that sentence. "He was ready to sacrifice anything to get that power for himself just a few weeks ago," I filled in for her, and Abby nodded, grateful that I was on the same page. "I understand that, Abby, but I really don't think there's anything to worry about. He's changed. I almost can't believe how much."

"It sure looks that way," she agreed, but I could hear the tiny bit of doubt lingering in her statement. "But just in case things go sideways, Oliver figured it would be better if we're there. And with Jerrod coming too, we might be able to get more information about my dad. So even though we've got other things on our mind, it's really the best place for us to be."

It certainly did sound like there was a lot going on. No matter how this conference turned out, I had a feeling it definitely wasn't going to be boring.

Chapter Four

~Oliver~

It had been a long, stressful week. Since we got back from Forest Ridge, I'd been busy preparing for the conference with my dad while trying to run my own tests on the hair samples I'd taken from the autopsy. Add in the usual business of running the pack plus trying to spend some quality time with my mate, and it all made juggling college classes with football start to look like a piece of cake.

Although I'd been doing my best to give Abby what she needed during this difficult time, it didn't feel like enough, so as soon as we arrived at the conference, I told Liz and Elijah that we would see them in the morning. We were already planning to have breakfast with my dad and Storm, who were arriving separately, so we could catch up with everyone then. For now, I had a hotel room with my beautiful mate and I intended to make the most of it.

"How was your talk with Liz?" I asked Abby as we stepped inside the room where we'd be staying for the next few days. The conference was being held on neutral, human territory so that no pack had an advantage over the others. The hotel, however, was werewolf-owned, belonging to one of the biggest packs in the state who specialized in luxury hospitality venues.

Each pack handled their financial assets in different ways. My pack, for example, was focused on scientific pursuits, which was what led me to study the sciences in the first place. By lucky coincidence, I seemed to have a natural aptitude for it. Also coincidentally, I had learned recently that my biological father was also a chemist, but given his overall personality, our shared traits weren't something I was particularly proud of.

"Our conversation was good," Abby replied, placing her suitcase on the bed and starting to unpack. "I filled her in on what happened at Forest Ridge. I figured she might as well know, especially with Jerrod and Alpha Easton being here for the conference too. Maybe she'll pick up on something they say when we're not around."

As usual, we were on the same page. "I told Elijah for exactly the same reasons."

That made her smile, but only for a second, and it made me miss her carefree smile more than ever. It had been absent too much of the time lately. There had to be something I could do that would make her feel better, at least for a little while.

Looking around the room, my eyes fell on a brochure on the table advertising the hotel's spa services. The picture on the front was of a woman's back, and it immediately brought to mind the last hotel we'd stayed in together, back in San Francisco, when I was abducted by the men who thought I was Elijah, and how Abby had given me an amazing massage afterwards to help calm and relax me.

That was definitely something I could do.

"Okay, Heels, time to take your clothes off."

Abby stopped in mid-motion, a stack of clothes in her hands. "Excuse me?"

"You heard me. The next few days are going to be stressful, so right now, I want you to relax. Unpacking can wait. Lie down and I'll rub your back."

I could practically see the tension leaving Abby's shoulders at the mere mention of it. "That sounds really good."

"Then what are you waiting for?" I teased, reaching over to pull her half-empty suitcase from the bed. "Let me take care of you."

As she took off her glasses and started to undress, I went into the bathroom to find some lotion or oil I could use. Thankfully, the hotel was fancy enough that I was in luck. With the bottle of lotion in hand, I came back to find my mate topless and getting settled on the bed.

"Not just your shirt," I protested. "All of it. I'm going to rub every inch of you, Abby."

A shiver ran through her body, just as I hoped. If she only wanted a massage, I would stop there, but I was certainly hoping for more. I always was when it came to her.

She complied, getting back to her feet and removing the rest of her clothing too before lying back on the bed, face down with her arms beneath her head. I got up on the bed too, straddling her but trying not to put too much weight on her. Just the sight of her naked was enough to have the blood rushing to my groin; adding friction to the equation wouldn't help. Squirting the lotion into my hands, I started on her back, pressing down as I rubbed up to her shoulders and rolling my fingers across the top of the tight muscles there.

Abby's moan of pleasure made my pants even tighter as my fingers continued to knead at her skin, and I had to push up higher on my knees so she wouldn't feel just how hard I was getting.

After massaging her back and shoulders, her body growing looser with each pass, I moved lower, shuffling down the bed while I ran my hands over the curve of her ass and down her legs. There wasn't a part of her that I didn't find sexy, nothing about her that didn't turn me on, and as my hands came back up her legs, I couldn't stop myself from letting my thumb slip between them, and the heat and the wetness I could feel there, combined with the intoxicating smell of her arousal, was almost more than I could take.

"How are you feeling now?" I asked, my voice tight as I tried to repress my longing just in case she wasn't in the mood.

"That was perfect," she assured me, before turning her head and giving me a wink that sent another rush of heat straight to my cock. "But I could be feeling even better."

That was definitely all the invitation I needed. My hands went between her legs again, spreading them apart as she lifted her hips for me. The fingers of my right hand pressed into her slowly as my thumb found her clit, and I leaned down to nip at the soft curves of her ass with my teeth.

"Oliver." The simple way she sighed my name was enough to draw a groan from me too. I really needed to get my pants off, but I couldn't stop what I was doing, not while she was whimpering like that.

"Have I told you lately just how good you feel?" I asked, my fingers pushing into her again, faster now and deeper, curling against her g-spot.

Abby gasped, her hands reaching out to grab onto the pillow as her body writhed against me. "You... uh, you might have mentioned it once or twice," she managed to stutter.

"Good, because you should never forget it. The way you take me in, and the way your clit feels as I play with it, the feel of your skin beneath my lips, it's all amazing, Abby. You're amazing."

My words were getting her closer to her release, so I didn't let up.

"I never knew I could be jealous of my own body, but whenever my fingers are inside you, my mouth wants to be there, and my cock too. Every part of me wants every part of you, Heels, every minute of every day."

Her legs began to tremble around my hand as I pumped my fingers into her harder, and when I scraped my teeth across her cheek again, it pushed her over the edge. Her body gripped my fingers tightly, contracting around me, as her wetness coated them even more.

As soon as she'd finished, I was on my feet, pulling my own clothes off and breathing a sigh of relief as I released my cock from its zippered prison. In no time at all, I was back on top of her, straddling her while my cock took the spot my fingers had just vacated, and when I pushed into her, she moaned my name again.

"I want you every day too, Oliver. Always."

That was just what I needed to hear. There were no more words spoken other than the odd curse or sigh as I thrust into her repeatedly. Her legs were tight around me and my hands held onto her shoulders, continuing to rub them with my thumbs as my hips worked against her.

"Yes, Oliver!" Abby's control broke once again, and that was enough to break me too as I came deep inside her, our bodies pulsing in perfect sync, as usual.

As I lay down beside her, pulling her into my embrace, there was only one clear thought in my head: everything was going to be okay. No matter what challenges we had to deal with, in the next few days or for the rest of our lives, as long as we had each other and this connection between us, everything would always be okay.

~Elijah~

Oliver looked a lot happier when he walked into the hotel dining room in the morning, which I had to assume meant that he had a good night with his mate. No matter what was bothering me, a little one-on-one time with Liz never failed to make me feel a lot better.

How much I'd come to rely on her in such a short time was truly unbelievable to me. She was my everything, quite literally. I'd given up my pack and my home to be with her, though she didn't ask me to. She would never ask for anything for herself; that wasn't the kind of person she was.

And that was what made her the obvious choice to be the new werewolf Queen.

If people didn't like the word, we didn't have to call her a queen. She could be a president, or the Alpha of Alphas, or the fucking Grand

Poo-Bah of Wolfville for all I cared. The title wasn't important. What *was* important was the power that she had and the personality tied to it. I'd been an Alpha long enough to know all about the petty squabbling and maneuvering that went on between packs, and though the council tried to enforce their rules, it often came down to which pack played the dirtiest that determined who came out on top.

The council was like the United Nations in the human world: a great idea in theory but toothless in reality. They were never going to really hold an aggressor to task, not if one of the most powerful packs was involved.

Sure, I had been a little selfish in wanting the source's power for myself, but my motivations weren't entirely about me. The werewolf world was in desperate need of someone strong enough and impartial enough to impose some real order on our inter-pack relations, and I truly believed that Liz could be that person, perhaps in a way I never could have been.

Liz was different. Seeing the way she relieved my father of his wolf, I had no doubt she was powerful and had the ability to wield that power. And the grace with which she'd handled the whole situation — finding out she was a werewolf, and of a royal bloodline — and how she handled me too — giving me another chance to prove myself to her after our shaky start as mates — I believed that she would be fair in general.

She was exactly the leader we needed. I just had to make everyone else see it too.

"Good morning, everyone." Oliver held out Abby's chair for her before taking a seat himself, looking around the table with a smile. "Are we all ready for this?"

Alpha Patrick and Storm both smiled back at him. "As ready as I ever am for three days with a bunch of other Alphas," Patrick said wryly. "Anyone wanting to place bets on who loses their temper first?"

These conferences never passed without a fight. I'd been to enough of them on the west coast during my time as Alpha to know.

"You've got an advantage there since I don't know the local Alphas," I pointed out. "But I can usually spot the troublemakers a mile off. Like that guy, for example."

I pointed to the buffet table where a man close to my own age was arguing with the hotel staff over something to do with the food. That was his first mistake. A true Alpha never argued; he didn't have to. He commanded instead.

Abby grimaced as she followed my gaze. "That's Jerrod from Forest Ridge. He's the one we told you about."

Ah, so that was the Alpha's son we were having dinner with later. Oliver had given me the background and honestly, I didn't understand it. He had tried to kill Oliver, had nearly succeeded in killing Abby, and for some reason, he was not only still alive, but still in line to become Alpha too. Oliver called it mercy, but I thought it sounded more like weakness. Some people deserved second chances, and some didn't.

The hard part was knowing the difference.

As we all watched, a blonde woman came up to join him, adding her two cents to whatever the argument was about, and once the employee finally got away, the two of them bickered with each other for a while, if their body language was anything to go by.

"Is that his mate?" They seemed well-matched, at least in temperament.

"That's Marissa," Oliver confirmed. "She used to be part of the Jade Moon pack, her dad was Beta for years until he betrayed us."

Oh, right. I'd heard that part of the story before too. *What a fucking mess.*

"Well, dinner with them is going to be a delight," I said sarcastically as the couple went to sit down at a table with a few other people, and Liz gave me a nudge.

"We should keep an open mind," she reminded me. "Maybe they're not as bad as they seem, and people do change. Give them a chance."

And that was exactly why she was more suited for keeping the peace between packs than I was.

After breakfast, we all went to the opening remarks, and afterwards, Abby and Storm left to attend some kind of workshop about the evolving role of the Luna. Liz had thought about going with them, but I reminded her that she wasn't a Luna nor was she likely to be, unless something significant changed in our lives. Besides, I wanted her to come with me to the meeting that Oliver, Patrick and I were attending, looking at the future of the Alpha Council. That was exactly what I had come to this conference to talk about, and Liz was the reason why.

As we walked into the meeting room, our arrival attracted more than a little attention. The first reason was basic sexism: there weren't a lot of female Alphas and Liz stood out in the crowd. The second reason, however, was more nuanced. Even at breakfast, some of the other Alphas took notice of her, though they probably couldn't have explained why. There was a power that exuded from her that was subtle but significant. People felt her authority even if they didn't know why, and I hoped that would help the point that I was about to make.

First, though, I needed to get a feel for what priorities the other Alphas had, so for the first hour or so, I simply sat back and listened.

Some of them wanted to replace the specific members of the council, while others had ideas for tweaking the responsibilities and the way that packs reported into it, usually in a way that would benefit their own packs. Nobody was focused on the big picture; all their concerns were almost pathetically small.

Finally, I couldn't stay silent any longer. All eyes turned to me as I got to my feet, including my brother's and my adoptive father's, both of whom were watching me a little warily. I would appreciate their support, but I didn't need it. My responsibility to Liz was greater than to anyone else. She was watching me too, her gaze full of trust, and that trust was what I needed to honour now. "You can make all the tweaks and minor changes that you want, but until real action is taken, nothing is ever going to change."

A whispered sound of unrest ran through the room, both at my words and my presumption. "Who are you?" someone called out.

I had anticipated that question. "At the moment, I'm no one. I used to be an Alpha, but I recently relinquished control of my pack."

That brought even more consternation as more questions were shouted out.

"Why are you here, then?"

"What gives you the right?"

"Why should we listen to you?"

Again, their reaction was just what I had expected, and I had my answer prepared. "I'm here to represent the descendent of the Alpha King, who has just been identified. Some of you will have heard the rumours of the source of power that was stolen from the King and brought to this country. All of those stories were true, and that power has now been reclaimed by its rightful heir."

I had their full attention now, and Liz's too.

What are you doing? she asked me by mind-link.

Trust me, please, I replied. She might not think she was strong enough for this, but I knew better.

"The source is a fairy tale," one of the men called out.

"Is it?" I shot back. "You don't have to believe me, but you can ask Alpha Patrick of the Jade Moon pack. He has seen it in action."

All eyes turned to Oliver's adoptive father, who grimaced, obviously not pleased at being put on the spot. Despite his discomfort, I knew he would tell the truth, and he did.

"I have seen it," he admitted. "It's real."

That set off another round of whispers until one of the members of the council stood up to address me directly.

"What is the point of this? What do you want?"

That was exactly what I wanted to explain. "I want a system of government that actually works for the benefit of all werewolves. We all know it could be better; that's why we're all here, and I think the way to make it better is to embrace some of our ancient traditions while we keep moving forward. Power was given to the King for a reason, and if we accept that and his heir's authority, it will free us to focus on what's truly important."

Some of them were intrigued, I could tell, and others were resistant. So far, things were all playing out pretty much exactly as I expected.

"And who is this heir?" the same man asked, sneering at me. "You, I suppose?"

I shook my head. "No, it's not me. But if you all stop and focus, I believe you'll figure it out for yourselves."

Many of the Alphas exchanged confused glances, but others did as I said, looking around the room as they tried to identify the person in question.

And one by one, their eyes all moved to Liz.

~Jerrod~

Well, this meeting just got a whole lot more interesting.

Up until now, there had only been tedious discussions about procedural points, most of which made absolutely no difference to my everyday life. This was my first time at one of these conferences, and if this was what the whole thing was going to be like, I was beginning to regret coming along at all. Only the thought of seeing Abby later kept me going.

Just as I had glanced at my watch, trying to figure out how much longer this could possibly go on, Oliver's clone stood up and started talking about royal bloodlines and power. My ears immediately perked up, especially as I noticed the reaction of the other Alphas around me. Some of them were suspicious and beginning to grumble as Elijah kept talking, while others sounded intrigued and maybe even hopeful.

Rising tensions usually resulted in people taking sides, and that meant opportunity. I had played people off each other often enough in my own pack to know just how useful a tactic it could be.

When Elijah asked us to figure out who the heir was, my focus instantly went to the people next to him, figuring it would be someone he was with since he said he was representing the person. For a brief, terrible moment, I thought he might be talking about Oliver, and I was ready to lose it if that was the case. The guy already had everything any man could possibly want; could he be the royal heir too? The mere idea of it made my blood boil.

Luckily, however, I picked up nothing from him. Instead, my attention was quickly drawn to the woman who sat between the two brothers, and who also bore a significant resemblance to Abby, at least when Abby wasn't wearing her glasses.

She wasn't quite as appealing as Abby, of course, since no one was, but there was a definite likeness. Was she Oliver's brother's mate? That was kind of bizarre. She wasn't from our pack, obviously, and I wondered where they had found her.

What was even more strange, though, was the power I could feel emanating from her, even from the other side of the room where I was seated. As soon as I really noticed it, it became impossible to ignore.

Maybe Elijah did have a point. Maybe there really was something special about this woman. That was very, very interesting.

But even if she was powerful, not everyone in the room liked the idea.

"Who is she?" the head of the council growled at Elijah, having obviously zeroed in on the same person I had. "What pack is she from? What's her position?"

Oliver's brother answered the questions calmly and in order. "Her name is Elizabeth Langford and she's not from any pack, nor does she have a position. Until she claimed the source of power a few weeks ago, she thought she was human. It seems that when the King lost the source, his wolf was silenced, and that was passed on to his heirs too. Eventually, his descendants forgot their heritage entirely since they had no communication with their wolves. Now that the source has been returned to her, her wolf has returned too, as you can tell."

That was for sure. Her wolf must be very strong to be giving off as much authority as she was.

The next words out of Elijah's mouth were the tipping point, though: "She's also my mate."

Instantly, the room erupted into protests and arguments as people debated not only the idea of the royal bloodline but Elijah's motivations in bringing her here at all. He obviously stood to gain quite a lot if his mate was recognized as someone of authority, and we all knew it. My father quickly fell into discussion with the man next to him, but I said nothing, preferring to sit back and listen instead, trying to pick out the important parts of the chaos surrounding me.

"This is ridiculous," a large, angry-looking man across from us shouted. "We haven't had a king in hundreds of years. Why the fuck would we want one now?"

There were shouts of agreement, but they weren't unanimous. There were those who took the opposite view.

"The royals were chosen by the Moon Goddess," someone else pointed out. "If she's returned their power now, there must be a reason for it."

That obviously appealed to some of the more devout, traditional packs, but not to the stronger, more progressive ones.

"I'm not taking orders from some tiny, weak, human female!" was a common refrain, in one variation or another.

Everyone got louder and louder until one voice roared out above the din: "Quiet!"

That came from the head of the council, who growled loudly as he looked around the room, his face red with frustration.

"Obviously, this is news to all of us. I would like to speak to Ms Langford in private, along with the other members of the council and the Alphas of our four largest packs: Silver Crescent, Jade Moon, Seven Hills and Gold River."

More protests rang out from the other Alphas, including from my father, who wasn't pleased about being excluded.

"We will report back to all of you and you'll all have a chance to ask questions," the council head promised. "But first, we need to get some basic information. In the meantime, carry on with the rest of your day."

The people he'd identified all got to their feet, along with Elijah, Elizabeth, and Oliver too. Of course he'd be right in the middle of this, even though he wasn't an Alpha or a member of the council. He was always sticking his nose in where it had no right to be.

Once they were out of the room, the other Alphas resumed their own arguments, and I quickly began compiling a mental list of who was on which side. Though I wasn't sure exactly how yet, I had a feeling that information was going to come in handy.

Somehow, I was going to be able to use this to my advantage.

Chapter Five

~**Liz**~

Eli told me to trust him, but that was getting harder to do with every second that went by, especially when there was a roomful of very large, very angry-looking werewolves shouting at each other, all because of me.

Well, to be more precise, they were shouting because my mate had told them that they should all be answering to me.

Me! A woman who hadn't even known I was a werewolf at all until a few weeks ago, and still had a long way to go to figure out everything that came with the territory, never mind the rules that governed their society and the way they all interacted with each other. I was about the last person who should be in charge of any of them.

No wonder they were angry.

Abby told me that Oliver was worried Eli would try something just like this, and it looked like he was right. Which made me wrong, given that I had truly believed he wouldn't make any major decision like this without talking to me about it first. I had never given him any indication that I wanted to be in any kind of position of power. Why would he think I did? Was this about me, or him?

It didn't help that my wolf seemed to be completely on his side. *You were born for this, Liz,* she told me in my head. *We both were. Our mate is simply fulfilling his role by helping us. Embrace it.*

Embrace it? How was I supposed to embrace being thrust into the spotlight, into a role I was incredibly unprepared for and didn't even want? This wasn't who I was. Maybe my ancestors were rulers, but that was a very long time ago.

I was just Liz, and I thought Eli was okay with that.

So, when we all stood up to go into another room, surrounded by a contingent of the very largest and strongest-looking of all the very large and strong-looking men from the first room, I quickly mind-linked my mate furiously.

What do you think you're doing, Eli? I didn't ask for this.

He took my hand, looking down at me with eyes full of affection, but it didn't make his reply any less condescending. *Of course you didn't. You never would, and that's why I have to do it for you. I will fight to get you everything you deserve, Liz. Always.*

Did he even hear himself right now? *What gives you the right to decide what I deserve? That's not how a relationship works.*

He didn't get a chance to answer me before we reached our destination: a smaller conference room just down the hall. This one had a round table that everyone sat down around. I sat between Eli and Oliver, just as I had in the other room, while Alpha Patrick sat on Eli's other side, providing a buffer between him and the others. Oliver's expression was stoic, like he was prepared for a fight, Alpha Patrick looked equally grim, and the other men were all guarded. Only Eli looked excited, with that passionate fire burning in his eyes that I normally loved so much.

Now, it began to frighten me.

The man who had questioned Eli in the other room turned to me, his expression full of suspicion. "You obviously have some powerful blood in you, that can't be denied, but what makes you think you're qualified to lead?"

"She is qualified *because* of her blood," Eli quickly replied. "We've seen hints of the power she has, and it's truly impressive. Not to mention she..."

The man glared over at him. "I was talking to her, not you. Let her speak for herself."

Alpha Patrick put a hand on Eli's shoulder, trying to keep him calm, while the man looked at me again.

"Answer the question. Why should you have authority over us?"

Just tell them the truth, Eli said in my head. *Tell them what happened with the source.*

The truth? I could do the truth, though I suspected my truth wasn't what he had in mind. "I'm not qualified, not at all. I didn't come here for this, and I'm sorry that my mate is wasting your time."

Eli's brow furrowed in confusion and disappointment while the other men exchanged glances. That clearly wasn't the answer any of them had been expecting.

The man in charge looked even less impressed than before. "Is this some kind of joke? We don't have time for games."

This time, Oliver stepped in on my behalf. "It's not a game. My brother is a little over-enthusiastic on behalf of his mate, which I'm sure we can all appreciate."

There were a few knowing looks exchanged around the room. Imagining these big, intimidating men being as devoted to their mates as Eli was to me wasn't easy, but I had learned enough to understand that things usually worked out that way. The mate bond overruled most other considerations for werewolves, and perhaps for Alphas more than anyone else.

It even overruled common sense, apparently, at least in the case of my mate.

"Liz does have unusual power," Oliver continued. "And perhaps there is a role for her, once she's had time to acclimate to the new situation in which she finds herself. But I don't think a complete change of government is in order, especially since Liz herself doesn't seem to want it."

That sounded entirely reasonable to me, and some of the other men nodded in agreement.

Eli, however, was not one of them, as he scowled at his brother. "She's not a performing monkey that the council can control. She was meant for greater things than that. Word will get out soon to the rest of the councils and the rest of the world that the royal bloodline has returned. How will it look for all of you if you were the first to discover her, and you didn't accept her?"

The world? My stomach sank even lower as I listened to Eli speak. Just how big were his ambitions? And why hadn't he told me about any of them before taking matters into his own hands?

"I think we understand the situation now," the first man answered, nodding at the others. "The three of you can leave now while the rest of us discuss it."

The 'three of you' he was talking about was me, Eli and Oliver, and that was absolutely fine with me. I wanted to have a few words in private with my mate right about now anyway.

As we got to our feet, however, one of the other men called out. "Wait. I want to see a demonstration of her power first."

A demonstration? I didn't have the first idea what I could do, and Eli growled next to me, clearly not happy about the request either.

"What did I just say? She doesn't have to perform on command for you. You can feel her power, I know you can."

"I feel something," the man admitted. "But it could be a trick. I want proof, real proof."

All eyes in the room came back to me, and I had rarely wanted to disappear into the floor quite as much as I did now.

But then, unbidden, my wolf spoke up again. *I've got this.*

I had no idea what she was doing, but a wave of heat and energy seemed to flow through my body, and the next thing I knew, everyone in the room – Eli, Oliver, the man in charge and all the Alphas, were all bowing down to me, whether they wanted to or not. All I could see was the tops of their heads.

Okay, that's enough, I begged my wolf. *Please, stop.*

She listened to me, thankfully, and the power inside me receded while the men each raised their heads, looking around at each other a little sheepishly, as though they couldn't quite believe that just happened.

"Anything else?" Eli demanded smugly, beaming down at me with pride.

That look made my stomach lurch again, and I quickly looked away, not meeting his eye. I didn't want his pride over that. It hadn't been my idea, no more than what he'd done.

"That's fine for now," the man in charge said, his tone a little less harsh than before. He was obviously taken by surprise too. "You may go."

That was all I needed to hear to head straight for the door, and as soon as we were out in the hall with the door closed firmly behind us, I turned to my mate angrily.

"What the fuck was that, Elijah Reynolds?"

~Abby~

The Luna workshop started off just as badly as I expected it to. When Storm and I first walked in, it felt like high school all over again. There were titters among some of the perfectly-styled women around my own age, and disapproving looks from some of the older ones. It didn't matter whether they were directed at me with my glasses, ponytail and simple clothes, or if they were for Storm with her leather, tattoos and piercings. The end message was the same: we simply didn't fit in, and part of me was ready to turn around and head back to my room right then and there.

But Storm held onto my arm firmly as she muttered into my ear. "I know that look, Abby, and you're not going anywhere. I promised Patrick I'd do this, and there's no way I'm doing it alone. We'll suffer together."

That made it a little easier to take, so with a deep breath, I held my head high while we made our way over to some empty chairs.

Another round of giggles burst out, and though I wanted to ignore it, I couldn't help glancing over in the direction they came from. My heart sank a little further as I saw Marissa in the centre of the group, with her bleached blonde hair, designer blouse and skirt and heavy makeup, blending in perfectly with the women surrounding her. They all looked like they were variations on the same template, and I couldn't help wondering how she'd made friends with so many of them so quickly. That was a skill I had never been able to master. People usually liked me once they got to know me, but rarely did anyone take to me right away, Oliver being the obvious exception.

"Don't pay any attention to them," a new voice said from behind me, and I turned around to find a rather cute man settling in behind us. He was thin with dark hair and glasses, and a knowing smile on his face. "Trust me, every second you spend worrying about what they're laughing about is time you'll never get back. I'm not even sure they know what's so funny themselves."

His assured, sarcastic tone made me smile too as I introduced myself. "I'll definitely keep that in mind. I'm Abby."

I held out my hand to him and he shook it firmly. "Daniel. I haven't seen you two around before. Is this your first Luna meeting?"

I nodded while Storm gave the newcomer a curious look. "Did you take a wrong turn somewhere to end up in Barbie hell with us?"

His eyes twinkled with amusement. "Some days it feels that way, but technically this is where I belong. I'm a Luna too. My mate is Alpha Marcus at the Blue Valley pack."

I recognized the name, though I hadn't met the Alpha before. They were a smaller pack from the other side of the state, but they were friendly with ours so I dropped our pack name too. "We're from the Jade Moon pack. Storm is Alpha Patrick's mate, and I'm mated to Oliver, his son."

"Storm? That's a kickass name, and it suits you perfectly." Daniel nodded at Storm in approval before turning to me. "I know Oliver, but only a little. Marcus used to have the biggest crush on him when they were younger."

"Really?" He had never mentioned anything like that to me. "Did Oliver know?"

"Oh, Goddess, no, and please don't tell him now. Marcus will kill me if he finds out I told you."

Daniel's conspiratorial wink made me like him even more, and soon, he called over a few other people he knew and we were introduced to them too. They all seemed like genuine and interesting people, and I began to have a little hope that maybe I would find a place to fit in among the other Lunas. Maybe they weren't *all* like my old pack's Luna.

That feeling of pleasant surprise continued throughout the meeting when we started discussing the role of a modern Luna within the pack's hierarchy. There were some, like those sitting with Marissa, who argued the traditional role was ideal and didn't need to change, but there were plenty of others who spoke passionately and intelligently about the other ways that a Luna might support her pack besides simply throwing parties and looking good.

I kept quiet, simply taking in everything that was being said, until Marissa herself piped up. Someone else had just said that there was too much pressure on a Luna to always have a perfect appearance, and Marissa quickly spoke up.

"It's the Luna's responsibility to set a good example for the pack. She should be someone they aspire to be like and that starts with her appearance and the first impression she makes. Anyone can roll out of bed and throw their hair back in a ponytail. A Luna needs to stand out."

Even if her eyes hadn't moved over to me as she mentioned the ponytail, it would have been clear enough that she was talking about women like me, if not me specifically.

The words came out of my mouth before I even had a chance to fully think them through. "Wouldn't it be a better example to let other members of the pack know they don't have to be perfect all the time? That there are other contributions they can make to the pack besides the way they look?"

Marissa's eyes narrowed at me as those around me nodded in agreement. "I didn't say their appearance was the *only* thing they could contribute. I just said it's important to keep up a certain level of professionalism."

"That's exactly the problem," I shot back. "What kind of a message is it for our children if we give them the impression that you can only be professional if you look the part? Why not focus on what they can do instead?"

Others jumped in to take both sides, and I leaned back in my chair, my heart racing. I didn't usually speak in front of big groups of people like that, and I wasn't quite sure what had possessed me to do it now.

"A friend of yours?" Daniel guessed, leaning over to whisper in my ear.

I could hear the laugh in the question, making it clear he was teasing me. "There's a bit of history there," I admitted.

"No kidding."

He was obviously curious to know more, but before I could say anything else, I received a mind-link from Oliver.

Any chance you can sneak out, Heels? Liz could use some backup.

Backup? I repeated curiously in my head. *What's going on?*

I'll explain when you get here.

That sounded serious, so I quickly leaned over to Storm to let her know I was ducking out. I thought she might jump at the chance to come with me, but she told me she'd stick around to hear the rest of the discussion. It seemed she found it more interesting than she expected to. I whispered a quick goodbye to Daniel and the others before sneaking out of the conference room as quietly as I could.

Once outside, I mind-linked Oliver to find out where they were and arrived at the end of the hall just in time to see Oliver, Eli and Liz coming out of another meeting room. They looked safe and well, but as I walked up to them, it became clear that something had happened, especially as Liz's question rang out down the hall.

"What the fuck was that, Elijah Reynolds?"

~Elijah~

From the corner of my eye, I could see Abby walking over to us, but my attention was entirely focused on Liz and the angry, unimpressed look she was giving me. After what she just did in the room, forcing the strongest Alphas in the region to bow down to her, I had hoped she was beginning to embrace the destiny that was so clearly hers, but the question she asked me quickly tempered that optimism.

Obviously, she wasn't quite on board yet, but that was okay. I could win her over, just like I would convince the others. This was what was best for everyone; they just didn't know it yet.

"That was you demonstrating your power in no uncertain terms," I answered, deliberately misunderstanding her question. "That was them realizing that you are stronger than all of them put together. That was the beginning of you claiming your birthright."

"None of that was me!" she exclaimed, growing more agitated by the second. "That was all my wolf, who seems to be on the same wavelength you are, but I can assure you that I most definitely am not! I don't want any of this, Eli. Why would you think I do?"

Her voice broke on the last question, turning from anger to hurt, and pain rushed through me at the thought that I'd upset her. The last thing I wanted to do was hurt her, but I needed to help her reach her potential. Finding that balance was a fine line to walk, and apparently, I wasn't doing a great job of it right now.

"I think that because you were born for it," I tried to explain. "What else would you do?"

She stared at me in disbelief. "I'm a college student, remember? I've still got three years to go before I need to figure out what to do with my life, and just a few weeks ago, I didn't even know that being a werewolf was an option. I need some time to figure all of this out, Eli, and I need you to respect that."

Oliver cleared his throat, giving us a slightly sheepish look, as though he didn't want to interrupt but couldn't help himself. "Actually, now that everyone knows who you are, Liz, I don't know if going back to college is going to be possible. It certainly won't be easy. For Abby and me, being off our pack land wasn't such a big deal because, in the grand scheme of things, we're nobodies. Our packs have no real enemies. But now that people know what you can do, you'll probably need extra security whenever you go off pack land, and that could make living on campus difficult. I don't know how it will play out exactly, but it's not going to be as simple as just going back in the fall like you were planning."

Liz's face fell as she listened to Oliver, and when she turned back to me, there was even more indignation in her eyes than before. "So, you just completely changed my life, upended everything I've been working towards, and for what? So you could look good in front of a bunch of men you've never even met before?"

Her anger was slicing into my skin and piercing my heart, but I couldn't back down; this was too important. She might not thank me for it right now, but eventually, she would see that I was right. They all would.

"This isn't about me, Liz. It's for you, and it's for all of us. We need better leadership than we've got, and you're the one who can provide it. I thought I was going to be the one to make those changes, but now I know it's you. You don't need to go back to school. You've already got a job that you were made for, and I'll be there right beside you to help you learn and grow into it. You don't have to do any of this alone."

She just shook her head sadly at me while Abby put a comforting hand on her shoulder. "You just don't understand, Eli, and that makes it even worse. I think you honestly believe you are doing this for me, and it frustrates me that you can't see why that's not true. If you really cared about me, you'd be asking me what I want instead of telling me."

She couldn't really mean that. "*If* I cared about you? You're all I care about! I gave up my pack for you. For this. For *us.*"

"And I didn't ask you to do that!" she shot back. "You can't make a decision completely on your own and then use it to blackmail me into something I'm not ready for."

"Okay, let's all take a breather," Abby suggested, putting her arm around Liz more fully. "It's almost time for lunch, so Liz, why don't you come with me and Storm? You can both take some time to think this over and talk about it again once everyone's a little more calm, okay?"

Part of me didn't want to let Liz go, not while she was still this angry with me, but I could see the logic behind Abby's suggestion too. Liz was still caught off guard by everything that had just happened, including the power that her wolf had shown. With a bit of distance, hopefully, she would see that I really only had her best interests at heart.

I love you, Liz, I told her through our mind-link as she walked away from me. *No matter how much we might disagree, please remember that.*

I'm trying, she replied just before she and Abby disappeared around the corner.

When I glanced back over at Oliver, he was giving me a look that was half sympathy and half reproach. "You probably could have handled that better."

"Probably," I agreed, but I still wasn't sorry I'd done it. Whether Liz meant to or not, she had completely proven my point with that display of her authority. "You felt what she did in there though. Word's going to travel fast, so we need to get as many people as possible on our side before the council makes any kind of move."

"*Our* side?" he repeated. "Right now, there isn't an 'our' side. You and Liz aren't even on the same page."

"We will be," I promised him. "We'll get it all sorted out soon, but there are other things we need to be doing in the meantime..."

He shook his head, not letting me finish. "There's no 'we', Elijah. I totally agree with you that Liz is powerful, but I also completely agree with her that it's up to her how she wants to use that power. I'm not taking any sides or taking part in any kind of plotting until that's all straightened out."

"You're my brother," I pointed out, stating the obvious. "I need your help."

What was the point of family if they weren't going to support you?

"And you'll have it, once you confirm with your mate that this is what she wants. Until then, I'm siding with Abby on this one. The best thing you can do right now is just take a step back and give Liz some space to come to terms with all of this."

Of course I wanted Liz on the same page as me, but there wasn't time right now. Factions would already be starting to form, we had seen that as soon as I brought up the mere idea of the royal bloodline's return. I needed to corral the people who were on our side and get in front of the curve before they got any ideas of their own.

Liz's agreement would come later, I was sure of it. Until then, there was no time to waste.

Chapter Six

~Oliver~

Things were going from bad to worse. Leading up to this conference, I'd been afraid that Elijah would do something reckless, and now, that was exactly what he'd done. If there was a way to tackle him when he started speaking in the Alpha meeting and stop the words from coming out of his mouth, I would have done it, but unfortunately, things didn't always work out in real life as they did on the football field. The opportunity never presented itself, so I had to just sit there along with everyone else, hoping he was going to turn it around and it wouldn't be as bad as it seemed.

Now, after Liz's display of power in front of the other Alphas, that hope was definitely dashed. This was looking like a fucking disaster.

Liz was understandably furious, all the other Alphas were in an uproar, Elijah was asking for my help, and in the middle of everything, I got a text from the lab where I'd sent some of the hair samples from Abby's dad for further analysis.

They were able to identify the exact chemical which must have caused the Beta's death; that was the good news. The bad news was that in order to progress to the next stage of my investigation, I was going to need to ask for help from inside the Forest Ridge pack, and I still wasn't sure who could be trusted. Jerrod already knew about the preliminary results from the autopsy but I didn't trust the guy as far as I could throw him.

Less, actually, since I was pretty sure I could throw him pretty far if I really wanted to.

It looked like Alpha Easton was going to be my best bet, so when we ended up back in the dining hall for lunch, I left Elijah with my dad and headed over to where Alpha Easton was sitting with Jerrod and a few other local Alphas who I also recognized.

Giving them all a friendly nod of greeting as I walked up to their table, I addressed myself to the Alpha. "Could I trouble you for a few minutes of your time, Alpha Easton?"

He gave me a wary look. "If this is about what your brother is proposing..."

"It's not." I quickly cut him off, not wanting to go down that road. "It's got nothing to do with that."

"Very well." He got to his feet and Jerrod immediately did too. The Alpha must have caught my look of dismay since he turned to his son and held out a hand to stop him. "Jerrod, you can stay here. I'll just be a moment."

Jerrod's jaw tightened, making it clear he didn't appreciate being excluded, but he did as his father said, sitting back down while the Alpha and I made our way over to a quieter corner of the room, away from the sensitive ears of our fellow werewolves.

"What's going on, Oliver?" he asked, getting straight to the point.

"It's about Abby's dad," I answered equally bluntly. "You know the autopsy that we had done?"

He grimaced. "Of course. Kathryn Flintoff has been giving me the cold shoulder ever since. Though I didn't want you to find anything, I almost wish you had just so I could prove the autopsy was justified."

That's interesting. It seemed Jerrod really hadn't shared the results with his father, as I'd asked him not to. It could mean a number of things, though, including that he was simply trying to cover his own tracks, so I didn't want to read too much into it. "Well, that's what I wanted to talk to you about. We actually did find something: it looks like Abby's father was murdered, and someone in your pack must have been involved."

The look of shock on his face would be hard to fake, making me more convinced than ever that Jerrod really hadn't told him anything. "That's a very serious accusation, Oliver. Are you absolutely certain?"

"Completely." Pulling out my phone, I showed him the results from the tests I'd had done. "That chemical is not a naturally occurring compound. There's no way it could have got into his system unless someone put it there deliberately, or if he was secretly working on a nuclear fission project that he never mentioned to any of us. It also couldn't have been delivered all at once, or there would have been other signs in the autopsy. It must have been administered in small amounts, over a significant period of time."

The Alpha's lips pressed tighter together as he reviewed the information on the screen. "If it's not a natural element, I'm assuming it's not something that can be picked up at the corner store then?"

I had to smile at his sarcastic yet completely accurate comment. "Hardly. It would almost certainly have been secured online since it's not manufactured anywhere locally. This is where I need your help, Alpha. We'll need to get access to online records for anyone you think might be a suspect, but without knowing your pack dynamics, I don't have a clue where to start. Who would have wanted Abby's father dead?"

He shook his head sadly. "Honestly, no one jumps to mind. The Beta was well-respected and well-liked. If anyone had a problem with him, they certainly never talked to me about it. He was a good man and my best friend."

A pang of sympathy went through me, and I tried to soften my rather clinical tone. In my eagerness to get to the truth on behalf of my mate, I'd forgotten that the man in front of me had lost someone close to him too.

"Could it have been directed at his position rather than him as a person?"

The Alpha thought that over for a moment. "I suppose that's possible, though I'm not sure why it would have been necessary. He was planning on stepping down as soon as I passed the Alpha position to Jerrod, but that's been... delayed, as you know."

I certainly did know that, and I knew why too. "Is there an obvious successor to the position, or is it up for grabs?"

"It's not confirmed," Alpha Easton admitted. "I've given it to his eldest son, Keaton, on a temporary basis, but I was leaving the final appointment to Jerrod since the person will be his Beta longer than they'll be mine. I believe he has a few different candidates in mind."

That was hardly conclusive, but at least we had a place to start. "Can you put together a list of those candidates, and anyone else that you can possibly think of who might have had a reason to target either Abby's dad specifically or the Beta position in general? You might even want to consider that the poisoning was an outside job, that someone was trying to weaken the pack by attacking your Beta. If you'd like, I can run a test on a sample of your hair too, just to make sure you aren't being given the same compound."

His face paled slightly at that thought, and he quickly reached up and yanked out a few strands of his own hair. "Here. I'll have a list of potential suspects by tomorrow morning."

"Thank you, Alpha. It's important to me that we get to the bottom of this, for my mate's sake."

That earned me a small smile. "You're a good mate, and a good man too, Oliver. I hope that you don't get too caught up in whatever crazy schemes your brother has planned. I can tell you, there is a lot of unhappiness over what he said this morning, and some of it is directed at your pack since you seem to be at the centre of it."

That was not a surprise to me. Elijah had not only put a target on Liz, he'd also drawn attention to the Jade Moon pack, and not in a good way. All I could do now was hope we could mitigate any problems before they got out of hand. "I'm hoping we can reach an agreement that's acceptable to everyone, Alpha."

"I hope so too. I'll be in touch."

With that, he returned to his table, where he was immediately accosted by Jerrod who was no doubt wondering what we'd just been talking about. I hoped the Alpha wouldn't share it, simply because I hadn't ruled Jerrod out of my own list of suspects yet, but in the end, I couldn't control what the father and son talked about, no more than I could control what came out of Elijah's mouth.

All I could control was myself, and right now, I was doing my best to simply keep all the balls I was juggling in the air without letting anyone down.

~Marissa~

Over the lunch break, I got my first hint of the controversy that was brewing. At the time, I was still fuming over the morning meeting and how Abby tried to make me look bad in front of all the other Lunas. We were both new here, both of us at our first conference, and when I arrived, I was thrilled to find a group of other women who were just like my friends in high school. Things were definitely looking up.

They immediately recognized that I was one of them and invited me to sit with them. There was a queen bee in the group already, but that didn't worry me too much. She was probably almost thirty and her mate's pack wasn't even one of the most powerful packs. Her time was clearly coming to an end, and someone new would be needed to take her place; I was sure that I could be that person. If I played it right, I could even be in that spot by the end of this conference.

There was a lot of snickering in the group when the tattooed, red-haired woman walked in, and I was happy to join in with it until I saw Abby at this woman's side. Of course she would find a way to make herself stand out. She always did, even though there was absolutely nothing remarkable about her in the first place.

Of course she was here; that was the whole reason Jerrod wanted to come. I wasn't an idiot. I'd figured it out the second he mentioned to me that we'd be having dinner with Abby and Oliver, and I thought, not for the first time, that he must be insane.

"What do you really think is going to happen?" I sneered at him. "That all it's going to take is one meal and she'll realize that you were the love of her life all along? You're pathetic."

Putting him down was the only way I could get any reaction out of him, the only way to get that fire to flash in his eyes, as it did now.

"You let me worry about Abby. You can focus on Oliver."

Yeah, right. I was a lot more realistic than my mate was. There was no way Oliver was going to give me the time of day while Abby was around. After seeing him at the Beta's funeral, that much was perfectly clear to me. The only chance I would have was to give him some kind of love potion, but unfortunately, those didn't exist in real life.

Or did they?

The day before we left for the conference, I was getting a manicure done in the pack's salon when I overheard one of the other women talking to some of her friends. "I always thought science was stupid, but my mate has been learning about all of these different drugs that can affect the body in different ways and even change the way people behave. It's so interesting and powerful, it's almost like magic."

The word 'magic' definitely made my ears perk up, as did the idea of changing someone's behaviour. Later that afternoon, I cornered her in the pack house when we were alone. "What kind of drugs were you talking about?"

She bowed her head to me politely. "There are all kinds, Luna. My mate has a lot of connections, he can get just about anything. If there's something you need, I can ask him to find it for you."

The way the woman spoke to me helped to soothe my bruised ego. She was one of the few who gave me the respect I deserved, even calling me Luna though the title wasn't mine just yet. I liked that.

Describing what I wanted without giving too much away was tricky, but I did my best. "Is there something that could make someone attracted to me? Even temporarily?"

Her eyes widened in surprise and dismay. "You would be the last woman who would need something like that. All the men in the pack adore you. I've even had to slap my mate's wrist a couple of times when I caught him staring at you."

I couldn't help feeling a little flattered at that. What she said *should* be true. I was beautiful, and I worked hard at it.

But I knew it still wasn't enough for Oliver. When it came to him, I was going to need something stronger.

"It's not for me," I lied. "It's for a friend. She's had a crush on someone for years, and she just wants one night with him."

I hadn't really thought this out in advance, but as I spoke, a plan was quickly taking shape in my mind.

One night should be all I need. Abby didn't seem like the kind of girl who would get over being cheated on. It would crush her confidence, as it should, and then Jerrod could swoop in and pick up the pieces by offering his support and affection. Jilted by both our mates, Oliver and I could find comfort in each other, and then I could go back to my home, to the place that should have been mine all along.

It made sense to me and it might actually work, as long as I could get him to give me that one night in the first place.

The woman in front of me quickly thought things over. "Well, there's one thing he told me about that might work. It won't make the man attracted to your friend, necessarily, but it can create hallucinations in his mind, like an illusion. If she dressed up like someone the man *is* attracted to, he wouldn't be able to tell the difference."

I almost had to laugh. Maybe I would end up having to make myself look like Abby after all. Jerrod would fucking love that.

"How quickly can your mate get it here?" Since we were leaving the next morning, time was of the essence.

"First thing tomorrow," she promised me. "He would do anything to help out his Luna. That's what a good Beta does."

That message could hardly be clearer. Her mate was one of the men who wanted the position of Jerrod's Beta, and by doing me a favour, she hoped I would put in a good word with my mate. I understood how the game worked.

"I'd be sure to let my mate know how grateful I am," I promised, and her eyes lit up.

Having reached an understanding, she hurried off to make the arrangements, and, sure enough, the next morning she sought me out with a small packet.

"It's in liquid form," she explained. "Your friend just needs to slip it into the man's drink."

"How quickly will it work?" I didn't want to take any chances of messing this up.

"It will take about half an hour. Apparently, his pupils will dilate and take on a slightly yellowish hue, that's how you'll know for sure that he's ready. But my mate also said to let her know that it will affect the man's memory, so even if they sleep together, he won't remember it."

That was fine. He didn't need to remember. I could arrange for other evidence that would be far more useful anyway.

"I won't forget this," I promised, taking the package from her. "*If* it works, the Alpha and I will both be in your debt."

She couldn't hide her ambitious smile. "I'm sure it will. Enjoy the conference, Luna Marissa."

On the drive that afternoon, I told Jerrod my plan, and he was completely on board. "I'm actually impressed," he said, sounding surprised. "Who was the wolf who got it for you?"

That was my secret for now, and my advantage, so I shook my head. "I'm not telling you until we know if it works."

Although that made him scowl, I could tell he respected it too. "We'll play it by ear to figure out the best time to use it."

And now, with the vial still safely tucked into my purse as Abby shot down my ideas in front of the whole Luna conference, backed up by her little gang of misfits, I was more determined than ever to make sure it worked. I couldn't wait to wipe that smug, self-satisfied look off her stupid, plain face.

Almost immediately afterwards, she ran out of the room, and only over lunch did I find out why. Apparently, Oliver's twin brother had tried to make a power move and take over the whole council on behalf of his mate. The power grab was ballsy, I had to admit, and everyone was talking about it. The Lunas were eating separately from our Alpha mates, but everyone was getting updates from their mates via mind-link, so I quickly checked in with Jerrod, even though he hadn't bothered to share the news with me himself.

What does this mean for us? I asked him bluntly. *Is it going to be a distraction for Oliver? Are we still on for dinner?*

I don't know yet, Jerrod admitted. *I'm still figuring it all out, but there might be a way we can use it. Just keep an eye on Abby and Oliver's brother's mate. Her name is Elizabeth. Find out anything about her that you can.*

My eyes immediately went to the door where Abby was just walking in with a girl who looked an awful lot like her, minus the glasses. She was equally plain and unimpressive. *This* was the woman everyone was in such an uproar about? When did the world go so crazy?

I didn't understand it, but I did as my mate suggested, keeping an eye on them both. Elizabeth seemed upset and Abby was trying to calm her down. They weren't paying attention to anyone else, so I had no problem watching them openly as I studied them both, their mannerisms and the way they moved. If I was going to pretend to be Abby later, I would have to be as convincing as possible. The last thing I wanted was to go to all this trouble and not have it pan out.

I was only going to get one shot at this, and I was determined to make it count.

~Liz~

As Abby and I sat down for lunch, I was feeling a little calmer, but not much.

"You can say 'I told you so'," I stated as I tried to ignore all of the other women in the room, most of whom were openly staring at us. It seemed word was spreading fast about what Eli had done, and what I had done too. I supposed that was what happened when everyone around us could communicate with their partners telepathically. "You said you guys were afraid he'd do something like this, and you were exactly right."

That might be what was upsetting me most of all, though there were certainly a few contenders for the title. I was upset with what Eli had said and I was upset that he'd said it without talking to me about it first, but perhaps I was most upset that I'd been so certain he wouldn't do it and now I'd been proven wrong.

I didn't exactly have the best track record when it came to knowing which men to trust, but I thought this time was different. I thought *Eli* was different, and now, I was not only doubting him, I was doubting myself all over again. Not only had Eli let me down, my heart had too.

"I didn't want to be right," Abby said, refusing to take the opportunity to gloat even a little. "I still believe he loves you and that he honestly thinks he's doing this *for* you."

That didn't make it much better. What did it say about how well he understood me if he really thought this was what I wanted?

"Is what Oliver said true? I won't be able to go back to school?" I hadn't been entirely sure how things were going to play out between Eli and me once I returned to college, but I thought we would figure it out together. He was enjoying working with Oliver's pack, so I thought maybe he'd keep doing that and we could see each other on weekends. It wouldn't be easy to be apart, but people made it work when they were in love.

They did *not* volunteer their partner to take over the world when she was clearly unqualified to do so and had no interest in it in the first place.

"I'm afraid that's probably true," Abby admitted. "But it doesn't mean you can't finish your degree. I was already thinking about doing remote learning in the fall anyway, so maybe we could do it together. It might be fun."

She was always looking on the bright side, always trying to find a solution that made everyone happy, but right now, I didn't want solutions. I just wanted to be angry for a while, and luckily, someone soon joined us who matched my mood entirely.

"What the fuck is Eli doing?" Storm demanded as she sat down to join us. "I thought he was over all of this source nonsense."

I had hoped so too, but apparently, he couldn't let it go that easily.

"Have you spoken to Alpha Patrick?" Abby asked. "What happened after Liz left the room?"

"The Alphas are spooked," she told us. "Some of them want to support Liz after what she did, but others are digging in against the idea. It's not going to be easy to come to a consensus, and whichever way it goes, someone's not going to be happy."

At this point, I was pretty sure that someone was me.

"What would you do?" I asked Storm. "If you were me and your mate tried to force something like this on you, how would you handle it?"

She couldn't help smirking. "I'd hold his balls to the fire until he was begging for forgiveness and promising to never, ever pull this kind of shit again."

I believed she would, but that really didn't sound like me, and it didn't solve my bigger worry either. "Do you think I jumped into this too fast? Maybe Eli and I aren't right for each other after all."

It hurt my heart to even think that, but I didn't know what else to think right now. Maybe I had been fooling myself all along, just like with Liam. My former professor had convinced me he wanted one thing when he was really after another, and right now, it felt like Eli was doing exactly the same thing. He said he wanted to support me, but it seemed that meant only if I did what he wanted me to do in the first place.

Why was it never about what I actually wanted?

Abby did her best to reassure me, as usual. "I know it feels fast, but honestly, for werewolves, this is just how it goes. We accept each other first and we figure the rest out later. I truly believe you and Eli have something special. You just need to work through this together."

Just the thought of sitting down with Eli and trying to talk through this exhausted me. I didn't even want to think about it right now, let alone deal with his passion and determination when it came to my 'birthright'.

Luckily, Storm seemed to be on the same page as me again. "Do you know what we need? A girl's night out, with absolutely no Alphas around."

I thought Abby might protest, saying I needed to hash things out with Eli, but instead, she nodded in agreement. "I think that sounds great. A night to himself might be just what Eli needs to come back to his senses. Oliver and Alpha Patrick can talk to him while we go out dancing."

"Dancing?" Storm repeated in dismay. "I meant finding a gun range and blowing off some steam."

Abby's eyes widened in return, and we all laughed as Abby gave me a sheepish grin. "Maybe we can find a compromise somewhere in the middle? And we could ask Daniel and some of the others to come too. What do you think, Liz?"

In the end, I agreed that a little time away from Eli was probably a good idea. Whether I'd be able to keep my mind off things was another matter, but I was willing to try. "Let's do it."

They both looked pleased with my agreement, and they soon invited another small group of people to join us and I was quickly introduced to everyone. Daniel, the only male in the group, sat next to me. "So you're the all-powerful Queen, huh?"

The question made me wince. Word really was spreading fast. "Something like that."

His smile immediately turned sympathetic. "Sorry, I didn't realize the title was a sore spot. But personally, if it has to be anyone, I'm glad it's someone like you. The fact that you're not shouting it all over the place is a really good sign for all of us. Can you imagine if the heir was one of the blonde squad over there? We'd never hear the end of it."

I glanced over in the direction he gestured, where there was indeed a table of cookie-cutter blondes sitting together, with one of them staring right at me.

What the hell is her problem? Refusing to be intimidated, I stared right back, holding her gaze across the room until, with a snort, she looked away, saying something to her friends, and they all burst out laughing.

Why did it feel like I was right back in high school again? Only this time, the popular girls' boyfriends weren't football players, they were strong and scary Alphas who weren't too happy about someone like me coming in and disrupting the status quo.

I spent the rest of the afternoon with Abby and Storm and the others in our new circle, attending some of the other meetings and trying to fly under the radar as much as possible, but I also paid careful attention to what was being discussed, soaking in as much as I could.

By the time the day was over, I had some new things I wanted to talk about with Eli, but I also wasn't quite ready to see him yet either. Tonight, I could hang out with the Lunas, and tomorrow, Eli and I could clear this mess up and figure out what our future looked like, assuming we had one at all.

Chapter Seven

~Elijah~

At lunch, Oliver left the table just as his father arrived, which worked out well for me. I wanted to get a feel for how Alpha Patrick was reacting to everything that had taken place without feeling like the two of them were ganging up on me. Oliver had made it clear where he stood; now, I needed to know about his father.

"What did they say after we left?" I asked as soon as the Alpha was settled. He had been allowed to remain in the room with the council leaders and the other Alphas when Liz, Oliver and I were asked to leave.

The look he gave me wasn't exactly approval, but it wasn't as discouraging as Oliver's expression either. "You've piqued their interest, certainly."

"You mean Liz has." This was never about me.

He almost smiled at that. "Right. There is some support for her, but I don't know how much of it is genuine. They recognize her power and they're interested in getting behind her, but I suspect it's only because she comes across as meek and easily manipulated. They think they can use her to promote their own interests."

I appreciated his blunt assessment, but I didn't understand it. "After feeling her power, why would they think they could manipulate her?"

"Because they see you doing it. She said straight out she didn't want this, and yet you pushed her and had her demonstrate her power anyway. They figure that makes her pliable and they can sway her too, either directly or through you. If I were you, I'd be prepared for either a lot of intimidation or a lot of ass-kissing from those who claim to be behind you."

"I'm not manipulating her," I protested. "I'm supporting her."

"You might need to take another look at what those words mean," he told me firmly, but then, having said his piece, he sighed, his expression softening. "Look, Eli, I understand how you feel, perhaps more than you think I do. I also know what it's like to lose a mate because she felt like I could never understand what she was going through. If I had been more truly supportive of your mother rather than assuming I knew what she needed, her life might have turned out very differently. It's not the same situation, of course, but there are similarities, and I don't want to see you make the same mistakes I did. Talk to Liz; *really* talk to her and listen to what she has to say. That's the only way to make her feel truly supported."

The reference to my mother, a woman I had only met very briefly in death, hit me hard, as he must have known it would. Since coming to live at the Jade Moon pack, I had learned a lot more about her and the relationship between her and Alpha Patrick, and also between her and my father. She and Alpha Patrick had both hidden things from each other, trying to protect the other, and it led indirectly to her death.

He said there were similarities to my situation with Liz, but I didn't really see them. Yes, I might have kept my intentions for this meeting a secret, but that was it. Now, everything was out in the open and we could work together going forward. I fully intended on talking everything through with her, just as soon as she agreed to talk to me again.

The afternoon passed quickly as the other Alpha meetings were all overshadowed by the events of the morning. Everywhere I went, people wanted to talk to me, wanting to know about Liz and to declare either their support for or their opposition to her. By my rough count, it seemed pretty even between those for and those against, but I knew there were many more who were keeping silent, biding their time to see which way the wind was blowing before they made a public declaration.

It must have been one of those people who sent me the anonymous text I received as the conference was wrapping up for the day.

I can deliver you the support you need. Meet me at 8:00 at the Bitter End bar on highway 47. Bring your brother.

Quickly, I glanced around to see if I could figure out who sent it, to see if there was anyone watching me to see my reaction, but there were more than a few people looking my way, just as there had been all day. That didn't narrow things down at all.

I hadn't given my phone number to anyone, so whoever sent it had to have the connections and insights necessary to get it, at least. That was a positive sign that he wasn't a total crackpot, but it didn't completely eliminate that possibility either. I had noticed the bar he mentioned on our way into town the previous day and it looked like a pretty rough place.

I sent back a quick reply: *The hotel bar is a lot closer.*

His response was nearly as fast. *We can't be seen together. If they know I've spoken to you, it will spoil the illusion of impartiality.*

Well, I was even more intrigued now. He wasn't asking me to come alone, which would have been suspicious. With Oliver as backup, I felt confident we could take on any of the Alphas here. And by going to a human bar in neutral territory, the chance of violence was limited anyway. Exposing the werewolf community was one of the quickest ways to get blacklisted, and starting a fight in the middle of a human bar would be risky at best and downright disastrous if it went wrong.

Overall, I felt confident he really wanted to talk, not fight, but was it worth my time? I still wasn't sure.

I'll see if I can make it, was my reply, and there was nothing further back from the other side.

We were supposed to be meeting up with our mates for dinner, as we had the night before, and my heart felt a bit lighter as soon as I laid eyes on Liz. She didn't look quite as angry as she had earlier, which I hoped meant that the time apart had done us good, as Abby had suggested.

But when I asked her if we could talk after the meal ended, she shook her head at me. "I've got plans for tonight with Abby and Storm. We do need to talk, Eli, but I think you need to take some time alone to really think things over first."

"When will you be back?" I was still thinking about going to this meeting tonight, but I wanted to make sure I was waiting for her when she returned.

"I'm not sure. Late, probably. I'm going to stay in Abby's room tonight, and Oliver can bunk with you."

That was hardly what I'd envisioned for tonight, but she'd clearly already made up her mind and it didn't seem worth the trouble to argue about it. We were already on thin ice, so I needed to pick my battles carefully. After she packed up a few things for the night, she left me alone in our room, and not long afterwards, Oliver appeared, carrying a small bag of his own and looking just as put out as I felt.

"This is not my idea of a good time," he announced as he flopped down on the bed next to me and picked up the TV remote.

"Trust me, you're not my ideal roommate either."

My sarcastic tone made him smile, but it quickly vanished as I took the remote from his hand and flipped the TV off again. "What are you doing?" he asked in confusion.

I had only just made up my mind, and I shared my decision with him now. "We're going out. I'm meeting with someone off-site about Liz, and I need you to come with me."

I showed him the messages I'd received, and Oliver's frown deepened as he read them over. "Why do they want me to come?"

I hadn't thought of it in exactly those terms; I had read it as a suggestion that I could bring Oliver along if I wanted to, but as I re-read it over his shoulder, I supposed it could be seen as an order rather than an offer.

"I don't know, but I'd like you there for backup anyway," I admitted. "You know the Alphas here better than I do, so you'll be able to tell me if this guy really has the influence he's claiming to."

Oliver's lips tightened, making it clear he didn't like the idea. "It smells funny to me, Elijah. I don't think you should be running off and getting involved in any other schemes until you sort things out with Liz."

As much as I was growing to like my brother, there were still times that his holier-than-thou attitude got on my nerves, and this was one of those times. "I'm not 'running off' or 'scheming'. I'm going to a business meeting and I've invited you to come with me. That's all it is."

He dug in deeper. "And I'm saying there's no point in meeting with anyone until you know what your mate wants."

"She'll be able to make a more informed decision if I find out what's possible for her in the first place," I argued back.

"I disagree," he said simply, making it clear we were at an impasse, and I had no more energy to waste on this.

"Fine. I'll go without you."

"I really don't think you should..." he started to say, but I wasn't interested. He'd made his position clear enough already.

"I would have your back if you asked for my help," I couldn't help pointing out as I grabbed my room key and wallet. "You don't always need to assume the worst of me."

Leaving him alone in the room, I found a taxi outside the hotel that would take me to the bar. Hopefully this meeting would help to turn things around because right now, it felt like everyone was against me.

~Jerrod~

Things were really falling into place now. I hadn't heard a word from Oliver all day about the dinner that we were supposed to have, and I suspected that with everything going on with Elijah and Elizabeth, those plans were probably going to fall by the wayside. Every time I saw him, he was glued to his brother's side, and he hadn't spared a glance in my direction all day. That could have upset me, but it didn't. In fact, it provided a new opportunity.

Separating Abby and Oliver if we all went out together was always going to be difficult, or at least to separate them long enough for Marissa to slip whatever drug she picked up into Oliver's drink and get him to mistake her for Abby instead. Ever since she mentioned the whole idea to me, I'd been trying to figure out how it would work, and I kept returning to the same problem: how did we get the two of them apart for any real length of time?

Now, that was taken care of for me. At her meetings, Marissa over-heard that Abby was going to be going out with Elizabeth and some of the other Lunas tonight, which was perfect. Actually, that arrangement was better than anything I could have pulled off. While she was occu-pied looking after her friend, Marissa and I would take care of her mate.

Next, we just needed to get him out somewhere where there'd be drinking involved. Given the history between us, it didn't seem too likely that he'd just agree to come out with me on his own, especially if we went somewhere off-site. I didn't want to do this where there were any prying eyes of other Alphas around or any chance that Abby might return early and find us before we accomplished our goal. We needed a place that was completely off the radar, and I had the perfect location in mind. On the outskirts of town, just off the highway, there was a dive bar that I'd noticed when we arrived, with a seedy-looking motel right next door. *Perfect.*

How did we get him there? As I watched him sticking close to his brother's side all day, the answer seemed pretty obvious: where one went, the other seemed sure to follow, and Elijah was going to be much easier to persuade than Oliver was. All I had to do was offer him the one thing he so clearly wanted — support for his rather fanatical scheme to take over the Council — and he wouldn't be able to stay away. Oliver would come with him, I'd get the drug into Oliver's drink and Marissa could take it from there while I kept Elijah busy talking about his grand ambitions. We'd already rented a motel room next door with several hidden cameras set up, though the cameras were hardly going to be necessary since Abby would feel the pain of his betrayal anyway. The video evidence was just for insurance.

Everything was coming together perfectly.

As we set up the last camera, Marissa lying on the bed so I could get the angle right, she looked over at me with a bit of curiosity.

"You know it'll hurt you too when Oliver fucks me, the same way it will affect Abby. That doesn't bother you?"

"You can fuck the whole town for all I care," I scoffed. "Doesn't make any difference to me."

That wasn't exactly true. In fact, the idea of my mate spreading her legs willingly for that arrogant jackass had been sticking in my craw all day, leaving a bitter taste in my mouth, but I wasn't about to tell her that. There was no reason it should matter to me. I knew that she and Oliver had slept together in the past, a fact she liked to remind me of frequently, and I didn't have any kind of real feelings for her. The mate bond was the only reason I felt jealous, and I could rise above that. Any physical pain I felt would be no more than I could handle.

It would all be worth it in the end.

And now, I was sitting at a table, waiting for Tweedledee and Twee-dledum to show up. Marissa was seated on a stool at the bar, near the back, so she could keep an eye on things and I could link her when it made sense for her to step in.

I glanced over at her now, just in time to see her smiling up at some inebriated human who was clearly trying to hit on her. My jaw clenched as I mind-linked her. *You're supposed to be staying focused, not flirting with anything with a dick.*

***He's** flirting with **me**, she quickly shot back. What's the matter, Alpha? Are you worried his is bigger than yours?*

I gritted my teeth even tighter. If we didn't have bigger problems to worry about, I would go over there right now and show her exactly who was in charge here.

Thankfully, the door opened just then and a familiar-looking blond head walked in.

Only one of them though. *Damn it.* Where was the other one?

I wasn't even sure which one I was looking at until he started scanning the room, his nose twitching as he searched out the scent of another werewolf, and finally, his eyes landed on me. There was a flicker of recognition in his gaze, but only a little, and that told me everything I needed to know.

This was Elijah. *Where the fuck was Oliver?*

Others moved out of the way as he walked over to me, naturally deferring to his ingrained authority. He was clearly of Alpha stock even though he no longer had a pack. I'd learned that much about him today: how he used to be Alpha of a pack over on the west coast but he'd recently stepped down, apparently to put his full backing behind his mate's grab for power. He'd made a huge gamble and he must be desperate to see pay off.

Desperation played right into my wheelhouse.

"You aren't exactly who I was expecting to find here," he growled as he pulled out the chair across from me and took a seat. "You better not be wasting my time."

"You know who I am?" I hadn't really expected him to; we'd never spoken to each other before. I thought Oliver would make the introductions, but there was still no sign of him.

"My brother's told me a little about you."

From the way he said it, Oliver clearly hadn't been speaking about me in a positive light, but I wasn't going to let that bother me. I didn't have anything good to say about him either, and besides, it gave me the perfect segue to what I really wanted to talk about. "Where is Oliver? I thought you would come together."

The muscles in Elijah's cheek tightened, just a touch, but enough that I noticed. Something was obviously going on between them, and I filed that piece of information away in case it came in handy later.

"He couldn't make it, but you don't need him here anyway. Tell me what you're offering and what you want."

Obviously, he knew I wasn't offering to help him out of the goodness of my heart, and that was a good thing. He seemed like someone who liked to get to the point, someone I could talk business with.

And maybe, in the end, he was right. He looked *exactly* like his brother, and that resemblance would only get stronger as his clothes started to come off. The substitution wasn't ideal, but to the cameras, it wouldn't make much of a difference.

Maybe I really *didn't* need Oliver.

~Oliver~

Not much more than ten minutes after Elijah left, I began to feel both guilty and a little nervous.

I still thought I was right: he shouldn't be continuing to pursue his agenda when Liz had made it pretty damn clear she wasn't interested. However, since he seemed determined to find out what this mysterious contact had to offer him, perhaps I should have gone with him. Not necessarily for support so much as to provide a cooler head if he got carried away, or if things weren't quite what they appeared to be. The last thing I wanted was for him to make things any worse.

And Elijah did have a point too, one that ate away at me the longer I thought about it: I didn't have to assume the worst. Ever since we met,

I'd been suspicious of him and his motives, and although at times I had pretty good reasons for feeling that way, my dad always used to say that people will live up to your expectations of them. Expect someone to succeed, and they will; expect them to screw up, and they'll do that too.

Abby assumed the worst of me when we met, so I knew what that felt like. Maybe Elijah would surprise me, just as I had surprised her. Maybe I just needed to make more of an effort to really understand where he was coming from.

With those thoughts swimming around my head, I grabbed my coat and my keys and headed out after him.

Luckily, I remembered the name of the bar where they were meeting from the text he'd shown me, so I drove myself over there. From the outside, it didn't give me a lot of hope. The place was rough-looking and so was the skeevy motel next door. It definitely didn't look like the kind of place someone would go if they had something above-board to discuss.

I had only just got in the door and started to look around when suddenly a hand clapped me on the shoulder. "Hey, are you Oliver West?"

A quick sniff of the air told me the voice didn't belong to another wolf, and I turned around to find a slightly inebriated human man, a few years older than me. He was wearing a baseball cap with his t-shirt and jeans, and he was with four other men who all looked pretty much the same as him, like variations on a common theme.

I was pretty sure I'd never seen him before in my life.

"Yes?" It came out as something of a question since I didn't have a clue where this guy would know me from or why.

"Aw, I knew it was you! We gotta buy you a drink! You crushed it the last time you were in town, and though I hate to see our Huskies lose, credit where it's due, man. You've got something special. You must have pro teams sniffing around, right?"

Without waiting for me to answer, he and his friends steered me towards the bar as I gradually clued in to what was going on here.

Football. These guys must be college football fans, and the Huskies were the local team, one that my team had beaten soundly in the playoffs this year.

I didn't often get recognized off the field outside of campus, so I couldn't help feeling a bit flattered even though the timing wasn't ideal. I still needed to find Elijah but in the state they were in, it didn't look like these guys were going to take no for an answer, and I didn't want to cause a scene. One quick drink wouldn't hurt.

They were soon asking me about specific games and quoting stats at me, making it clear they really knew their stuff. When I told them I wasn't likely to go pro, they were truly disappointed. Chatting with people who were just as into the game as me was a lot of fun, but I did have another reason for being here, so I was about to make my excuses and leave when someone else joined us, someone I definitely wasn't expecting to see.

"Hi, Oliver."

The men all stepped back to give Marissa room, exchanging appreciative glances. "I shoulda been a football player," one of the guys muttered to the group as he looked Marissa up and down.

"Hey, Marissa." What was she doing here? It didn't seem like the kind of place she should be on her own; did that mean Jerrod was nearby? Did this have something to do with Elijah?

I tried to look around the room for them, but she quickly stepped forward, blocking my line of vision. "Buy me a drink?"

The other men quickly recognized they weren't needed in whatever Marissa had in mind, so they wished me luck and left us alone as I turned to my ex-girlfriend.

"I'm not here to drink," I told her. "I'm looking for my brother."

She gestured to the now-empty beer bottle in my hand. "You just had a drink."

"I did, but one was enough."

She looked so disappointed that, despite myself, I felt a bit sorry for her. We really hadn't spoken at all since she left the Jade Moon pack to go live with Jerrod. I had no idea what was going on with her or how she was adjusting to everything, and right now, she didn't look particularly happy.

Against my better instincts, I decided to ask her about it. "What are you doing here? Where's your mate?"

Her nose wrinkled as if she'd smelled something foul. "My *mate* is busy with his own crackpot ideas, as usual. He's only ever interested in me when he needs something from me."

That was a little ironic, I couldn't help thinking, since she had only ever been interested in me because of what I could do for her too.

"You guys have been together for months now," I pointed out. "You must have had some good times."

"Not really. Not like you and I did."

Reminiscing about our relationship was definitely not on my list of priorities for tonight, especially because I remembered it rather differently. "You and I had nothing in common, Marissa. I remember you literally falling asleep once when I was talking about chemistry."

She gave a little shrug that was probably meant to be charming. "We had chemistry in our own way, though."

Her hand reached for my chest, but I quickly grabbed hold of her wrist and lowered it back to her side again. I wasn't sure how much she'd had to drink, but she couldn't possibly think anything was going to happen between us. Even she couldn't be quite that delusional.

My actions didn't seem to discourage her, however. "Besides," she continued, still smiling up at me. "I've become a whole lot more interested in chemicals lately. It turns out there are some pretty useful ones."

I had no idea what she was talking about, and I really didn't want to know. I tried to steer the conversation away from me and back to her and Jerrod.

"If you're really unhappy with your mate, you don't have to suffer, you know. Everyone thought because you and Jerrod were fated that you would be a good match, but if you're not, nobody's forcing you to stay."

"Where would I go?" she asked, and to my surprise and dismay, tears began to form in her eyes. "I couldn't stay at Forest Ridge if Jerrod and I broke up. My father's dead and the next Luna in my old pack hates me. I'm completely on my own."

For just a moment, I could see a flash of the vulnerable girl I had only seen a couple of times before. Those brief, unexpected glimpses of her humanity had made me stay with her as long as I had in high school. I always hoped it meant she would eventually grow into a more caring, complex person.

So far, it still hadn't happened, but maybe, just maybe, there was still hope.

"If it's really that bad, we could find a solution," I offered. "Abby doesn't hate you. She doesn't even know you, and I think there are maybe two people in the whole world she truly hates. You're not at that level."

Those two people were Liam and my biological father; they were the only people I'd ever seen my mate completely lose empathy for. I had a feeling she would be sympathetic to Marissa, given the situation. She was just that kind of person.

"Really? You would do that for me?"

She blinked up at me hopefully, the tears still clinging to her eyelashes, and I did my best to give her a supportive smile. "If you needed it, of course I'd help. But it's not really that bad, is it?"

"It's hard to be objective sometimes when you're in the middle of it," she said, surprising me with her insight. She wasn't usually that philosophical. "It might help just to talk it over with someone who's not from Jerrod's pack. I don't really have anyone I can confide in."

Shit. I could hardly blow her off after that, after I was the one who asked the question, but I still needed to find Elijah too.

"Just one drink?" she suggested. "Please?"

That shouldn't take *too* long. How much more trouble could Elijah get into in the next ten minutes?

"Alright," I agreed reluctantly. "One drink."

Chapter Eight

~Marissa~

There were few decent men in the world who could resist a woman in tears; I'd learned that a long time ago and used it to my advantage more than once. It didn't work on my mate, which was no real surprise since 'decent' was about the last word I'd use to describe him, but on Oliver, it worked like a charm, like it always had.

I guided him over to a table on the opposite side of the room from where Elijah and Jerrod were sitting. Oliver hadn't spotted them yet, and neither had Elijah seen Oliver, owing to the fact that he was too caught up in whatever nonsense he and Jerrod were talking about. Keeping them apart seemed like the best course of action right now.

When I first saw Oliver walk in, I quickly mind-linked Jerrod. *He's here. He's going to the bar with some humans, for some reason, but he's here. I'll try to get him alone.*

I could almost hear the frown in my mate's voice in my head when he replied. *We don't need him now. I've already got the other one, don't complicate things.*

Are you an idiot? I shot back. *If we use Elijah, Abby won't feel any-thing, and Oliver will know he wasn't involved. How long do you think it'll take them to figure out it must have been his twin? Minutes, or just seconds? It has to be Oliver, and he's right here.*

But I've already given the drug to Elijah, he told me in frustration. *Now, what do I do with him? I can't just send him back to the hotel, someone might know there's something wrong and they'll get suspicious.*

That was a good point, actually, though I wouldn't admit it to him. *I'll get another room at the motel,* I suggested. *He can sleep it off there.*

Jerrod grudgingly agreed to that, so I quickly called over to the motel and arranged a second room before approaching Oliver. Though he tried to resist me, he was too polite to simply walk away, especially once the tears came. Even though I wasn't in his pack anymore, he still had that protective urge to make sure I was okay, and I was going to make it count.

Once we were seated, a waitress came over to take our drink orders, and she gave me a quick nod of confirmation before walking away. I'd already given her the drug to slip into his drink, along with a few hundred dollars to sweeten the deal. The money was Jerrod's, so I had no problem spending it, and once I explained to this woman just how badly Oliver's girlfriend had treated me, she was happy enough to help me get a little revenge. I promised her the few drops of liquid in his drink wouldn't hurt him, just loosen his inhibitions enough that he'd sleep with me, and not only was she willing to help, she told me she knew a few other women who'd be willing to pay through the nose for something like that.

That idea was tempting, but money wasn't my focus. I had plenty of that in my new position; what I didn't have was a mate like Oliver.

I kept him talking as long as I could once the drinks arrived, watching him swallow the liquid in his glass down.

To my surprise, it actually felt really good to get some of this stuff off my chest about Jerrod and living at Forest Ridge. Oliver listened sympathetically, as he always did. This was one of the few real conversations we'd had since he left for college three years ago, and I was surprised to find how much I missed having someone truly listen to me. He said we'd never had much in common, but I didn't believe that was true. Sure, I found his science talk boring, but otherwise, we had *everything* in common. We knew all the same people, had all the same memories growing up and especially of high school. We both loved the adulation of the crowd, me as a cheerleader and him on the football field. It would only be better when we were Alpha and Luna together.

I was sure we had far more in common than he and Abby did.

"What do you do with your time these days?" he asked me as he took another swig from his drink. "What do you and Jerrod do together?"

"I really only see him for an hour or two a day," I explained. "He's busy working with his dad so I help the Luna out. Jerrod and I don't do anything together other than eat and sleep."

And fuck, of course, but I didn't need to mention that.

"Maybe you just need to find something you enjoy doing together, even if it's not immediately obvious," he suggested. "Look at me and Abby: we have pretty diverse interests. She loves reading and writing, and I like experimenting in the lab. We could just go to separate rooms and do those things, but since we want to spend time together, she's actually started writing a book where the hero is a chemist. She comes and writes in the lab and asks me questions about how the character would do certain things, and I show her some experiments to help make it more real for her. It's something we both have a lot of fun with."

I tried my best to keep from gagging. That sounded both sickeningly sweet and incredibly boring all at the same time, not to mention that I really didn't want to talk about Abby right now.

Besides, there was literally nothing Jerrod and I liked to do that would work well together. Aside from working with the Luna, which was tedious, I spent my time maintaining my appearance, while Jerrod was obsessed with proving to everyone that he was ready to be Alpha. This scheme we were working on right now, trying to break Abby and Oliver up, was the first time we'd felt on the same page in all the time we'd been together.

Having someone to plot with *was* kind of fun, but in the bigger scheme of things, the goal was still the same: to end up with the people we should have ended up with in the first place.

As soon as Oliver swallowed the last mouthful of his drink, he got to his feet. "It's been good to catch up," he said, already looking away from me. "But I really need to find my brother now."

He turned around, and I quickly mind-linked Jerrod again when Oliver wouldn't see my eyes glazing over. *He drank it, but it hasn't been long enough. He wants to find Elijah. Where are you?*

We've just arrived at the motel. He's looking pretty out of it now. He keeps calling me Julian, whoever that is.

That was good news, at least: the drug seemed to be working. Now I just needed to keep Oliver occupied long enough for it to kick in for him too.

Call me on my phone in a few minutes, I instructed my mate.

Staying on Oliver's heels, I trailed after him as he searched the bar for his brother, growing more frustrated when there was no sign of him.

"He must have left already," he finally announced, giving his head a shake. "I've really messed this up. I better get back to the hotel and find him."

Just as he started to move towards the door, my phone rang. "Hang on," I told Oliver. "Let me get this."

He looked confused about why he needed to stay for that, but being the courteous guy he was, he did it anyway.

"Alright, I'm phoning you," my mate grumbled on the other end. "What's going on?"

"It's Jerrod," I said to Oliver, ignoring my mate. "He's with Elijah."

That got Oliver's attention, and the look he gave me was both curious and wary. "Where? Why?"

I ignored the second question to focus on the first, as I asked Jerrod the question and then relayed the answer to Oliver. "They're at the motel next door. He says they were talking and Elijah started to look unwell, so he took him over there to rest."

I was only stretching the truth a little bit. Most of that was entirely true.

"Shit," Oliver muttered. "Alright, can you take me to him?"

That was exactly what I wanted him to say.

~Abby~

It took a while, but we finally reached a compromise on what to do for our 'girl's' night out. The guest list wasn't entirely women since Daniel was coming too, but he promised us he didn't mind if we called it that.

"Trust me, I'm used to it by now," he told us with a laugh. "As the only male Luna on this side of the state, I always get lumped in with the ladies, but there are far worse places to be. I'm sure we'll have more fun than the Alphas will tonight since they'll just be sitting around missing us."

He gave me a wink, and I could imagine us having a lot of fun together at future events such as these, on occasions when we weren't quite as stressed as we were now. For tonight, Liz said she just wanted to get her mind off things, so when both dancing and the gun range were ruled out as being too 'extreme', we settled on visiting an escape room instead.

This was the idea of one of the other women, and she had to explain the concept to Storm, who had never heard of it before.

"We'll break into teams and they'll lock us into a room with a scenario about why we're there and clues on how to get out. You get a certain amount of time to figure it out, but the clues usually involve some kind of teamwork. It's a lot of fun, and afterwards, there's a bar where we can go have a drink and unwind."

That sounded just about perfect. Although trying to break out of a room we were locked in wasn't stress-free, the stress was a completely different kind from what we were dealing with right now. By giving us an immediate problem to focus on, it would help to take Liz's mind off the mess with Eli and my mind off what had happened with my father. Liz asked if she could stay in my room tonight since she was pretty sure that if we had a few drinks and she went back to Eli, she wouldn't be able to resist him, and she wanted to be sure that they talked things out properly before being intimate again.

"I don't want him to think he can flash that sexy smile of his at me and that's all it takes to be forgiven," she explained.

I could understand that, and I could hardly say no, even though the idea of spending a night away from Oliver wasn't ideal. I hated to be apart from him, and he wasn't thrilled about it either as he packed up a few things and headed out to go stay with Eli for the night.

"Don't do anything I wouldn't do," he teased before giving me a sweet good night kiss.

"You don't have to worry about me," I promised, even though he already knew that. We both had complete trust and faith in each other. No matter what else was going on, he was my rock. "Try to talk some sense into your brother, if you can."

He grimaced. "That might be a tall order but I'll try."

When he had gone, Liz and I got ready for the night together. We weren't getting too dressy since we didn't know what the escape room would involve, so my usual jeans worked just fine. On the way out of the hotel, we passed the group of Lunas that Marissa had been hanging out with all day, and they were all much more dressed up, in dresses and heels, hair perfectly done, obviously planning on having a very different night than we were. Marissa wasn't among them, though, and I wondered for a moment why not, but quickly pushed the thought out of my mind. I had enough things to worry about already; I definitely didn't need to add Marissa to that list.

At the venue, we split into two teams: Daniel joined me, Liz and Storm, while the three other women formed their own team. They already knew each other so they figured they'd work well together, while Daniel said he was curious to see the three of us in action. We made a friendly wager over which team would get out first, with the losing team having to buy the first round of drinks afterwards, and we headed into our room where the door was quickly and firmly locked behind us.

Inside, it looked like something from Star Trek: vaguely futuristic with a lot of electronic panels and controls, all of which seemed to be turned off at the moment.

"Okay, this should take us about five minutes," Storm announced, looking around the room and rubbing her hands together in anticipation. "Where do we start?"

"That's the first thing we need to solve," Daniel explained. "Look around the room for a clue."

Liz pressed the first button she could find, and immediately a video began to play on the far wall, making us all jump before we laughed at our own reactions. The video explained the concept of the room: we were on an alien spaceship and we needed to find the weapon that was aimed at Earth and disable it before the planet was destroyed. We also had to avoid alerting the aliens to our presence.

Liz grew more excited as the mission was outlined, and her enthusiasm made me grin. Sci-Fi was one of her favourite genres to read, so this was right up her alley. It would be the perfect distraction.

It took us a little more than the five minutes Storm had suggested it would take to solve the puzzles, but we still worked together very well. Storm had a lot of practical, hands-on problem-solving experience and was ready to take risks. Since Liz and I read a lot, we were best at the general knowledge parts, and Daniel was a great lateral thinker, looking for less obvious solutions. For the forty minutes it took us to complete the challenge, I completely forgot about everything else, and I was pretty sure Liz did too. We were completely in the moment.

It was just what we needed.

When we finally solved the final puzzle, saving the Earth once and for all, we exited through the now-unlocked door and were even more excited to see that the other team hadn't finished yet, making us the winners. Laughing and chatting excitedly about the whole experience, we settled down at the bar with a drink as we waited for the others to arrive.

"To kicking some alien ass," Storm toasted as we all held up our drinks, and I laughed once again as I brought the glass to my lips.

However, before I could take a drink, a sudden, searing pain ripped through me, like someone drawing a knife across my heart, and the glass slipped from my hand, spilling its contents all over the table. With a gasp, Liz quickly picked up the glass while Storm set about mopping up the liquid with some napkins, working together just as they had in the room. Meanwhile, I simply clutched a hand to my chest, praying for the pain to subside as I struggled to breathe.

What the hell is going on?

"Are you okay?" Daniel's brown eyes were watching me in concern from behind his glasses. Storm and Liz were both looking at me too, equally troubled.

"I... I don't know." Just as I got the words out, the pain did, thankfully, start to fade, leaving me relieved but even more confused. "What does a heart attack feel like?"

I meant it to be kind of a joke, trying to keep the mood light, but the worried looks on their faces told me this was no laughing matter. To be honest, it didn't feel like one to me either. I had never felt anything like it before.

"It's a tight, squeezing sensation," Storm supplied. "Your chest feels heavy, like something's resting on it. Is that what you're feeling?"

I shook my head. "No, it's not like that. It felt more like a cut or a tear, but internally. It seems to have stopped now though."

No sooner had the words come out of my mouth than I felt it again, and this time I cried out in surprise and distress.

Even through my pain, I saw Daniel and Storm exchange looks, looks that suggested they might know something that I didn't, and whatever they were thinking, it obviously wasn't good news.

"What is it?" I asked, taking a deep breath as the pain faded once more. "Do you know what this is?"

"I don't know anything for certain," Daniel said, almost apologetically. "But there's something we should eliminate first before we think about taking you to a hospital."

"What?" I was eager to get to the point. My own father had just passed away unexpectedly, and I didn't want to take any chances.

He looked over at Storm again, who nodded at him in encouragement. When his eyes returned to me, they held a new sympathy, one I didn't understand.

"Abby, do you know where your mate is tonight?"

~Oliver~

I had a bad feeling about all of this as I followed Marissa across the dark parking lot to the motel next to the bar. A streetlight above us tried its best to light the way, but it kept flickering on and off, making my vision blur even more than it had already started to.

Why was I feeling so lightheaded after just a couple of drinks? Werewolf physiology meant that our bodies metabolized alcohol faster than human bodies did, and two drinks shouldn't have been enough to even give me much of a buzz let alone make me as dizzy and disoriented as I was starting to feel.

Marissa said Elijah wasn't feeling well either and that was why Jerrod took him to the motel. It seemed a little too coincidental that we should both start to feel bad at almost exactly the same time unless there was something wrong with the bar itself... or the people we were with.

Knowing that Jerrod was the one Elijah met with and remembering that the text Elijah received told him to bring me along, the whole thing was beginning to feel like a setup, though to what end, I didn't know yet. Maybe I could figure it out if my head wasn't so fuzzy, but for now, all I wanted to do was find Elijah and get the hell out of there. Jerrod and Marissa and whatever shit they were trying to pull could be dealt with later.

"They're up on the second floor," Marissa told me as we reached the outside staircase at the front of the motel.

Since I was feeling a little dizzy, I went to grab the railing to help myself up, but as my hand reached for it, it suddenly seemed to transform into a snake instead. With a shout of surprise, I backed away, and Marissa looked over at me curiously.

"Is everything okay?"

Blinking hard, I stared at the railing until it turned back into the piece of metal it should have been and I simply shook my head, not wanting to give her any indication that there was anything wrong. "It's fine. Let's go."

We reached the door numbered 214, and as Marissa knocked, the numbers seemed to dance in front of my eyes. I could have almost sworn the number 4 winked at me. *This is not normal.*

She knocked again, and when there was no answer, she pulled a key out of her pocket instead. In confusion, I stared at it in her hand, trying to make sense of everything as she opened the door. If Elijah had simply taken unwell and Jerrod brought him over here on the spur-of-the-moment, why would Marissa have the key to the room? That didn't make sense, but in my current state, I couldn't work out what it meant.

Marissa entered the room first once the door was open and I followed in behind, wincing as she flipped the light on. Inside was a typical motel room with two double beds and a piece of nondescript art on the wall; nothing out of the ordinary, except that the room was completely empty.

"Where are they?" I demanded. "Where's my brother?"

Her eyes were almost comically large as she looked around, feigning innocence. Despite her attempts at acting, I was becoming more convinced by the second that this was all intentional. "I have no idea, this is where Jerrod said they'd be. I'll call him back."

She pulled out her phone again and held it to her ear before pursing her lips in frustration.

"There's no signal here. Let me try in the bathroom instead."

Without waiting for me to agree, she went into the small room and closed and locked the door behind her. I pulled out my own phone, intending to call Elijah myself, but the buttons on the screen didn't want to stay in one place. After jabbing at it uselessly for a few seconds, I sat down on the edge of the bed and put my head in my hands, trying again to clear my vision.

Something was very wrong here. This was more than just alcohol; something else was happening in my body, something completely unnatural. I should go and get help, but I couldn't just leave Elijah here if the same thing was happening to him. Maybe he was in even worse shape than I was.

It was hard to say how much time had passed as I sat there, but eventually I heard the front door open again, and when I looked up, my mind took in the dark hair and glasses that were my favourite sight in the world.

"Abby? What are you doing here?" As thrilled as I was to see her, I didn't understand how she could have found me. Was I dreaming now? Maybe I had fallen asleep without realizing it.

"I felt through our bond that you were in trouble," she replied, her voice sounding a bit strained and not quite like herself. "I came to help you. What's wrong?"

Before I could even reply, she was sitting on the bed next to me, her hand on my back, and when I turned to look at her, she pressed her lips firmly against mine.

It would have been so easy to fall into her kiss, as I usually did, but something still wasn't right. My brain was working slower than usual, but it hadn't entirely switched off, and a few things weren't adding up. Even if she had felt my distress, how would she have found me? At the bar, perhaps she would have, since my car was parked outside, but here at the motel, and in this particular room?

Unless she tracked my phone like she did back in San Francisco when I was abducted?

I supposed that was possible, but how did she get here so fast?

Unless her arrival wasn't fast at all? How long had I been sitting here?

As I tried to work it out, she continued to kiss me, her hands sliding across my chest as I tried to sort this all out in my head, and suddenly, I picked up on one very important thing.

There are no sparks.

Not on our lips, and not from her hands either. The sparks were one of the best things about the mate bond, the special way that my skin reacted to the touch of my mate and no one else.

And if there were no sparks, then this was *not* my mate.

I pulled back from her as quickly as I could, blinking hard as I tried to sharpen my vision. It really, really looked like her, but it couldn't be. I just felt it.

"What's wrong?" Her voice wasn't right either; the tone was too baby-ish, like someone trying to do an impression of Abby, but pulling it off badly.

"Who are you?" The words were heavy in my mouth, but as they came out, a new thought came to mind. "Liz?"

Maybe my brother's mate had got confused between us? It didn't make a lot of sense, but then, neither did any of this.

"Of course not. It's me, Abby."

She kissed me again before I could stop her, my reflexes slowed and dulled by whatever was happening to me. There were still no sparks, and her scent was wrong too, I realized.

There was one way to know for sure, without any doubt. Pushing her away once more, I staggered to my feet so she wouldn't be able to kiss me again until I confirmed my theory.

"Oliver? What's wrong?"

She sounded almost as confused as I was, and for a moment, I was worried that I was mistaken and I was really pushing my mate away. But I didn't think that was the case; I was pretty sure I was right, and I was pretty sure I knew how to prove it.

"What do I call you?" I asked her, looking down to where she still sat on the bed. "What's my nickname for you?"

She looked away from me, thinking it over, and that was when I was completely certain. This wasn't Abby. She wouldn't have to think about that for a second. Whatever the fuck was going on, this was not my mate.

"I don't know what this is, but I'm out of here," I muttered, heading towards the door. Though I had no idea what the game was, I didn't want to play anymore.

"Wait," she called after me. "You call me baby, of course."

"Nice try." I turned back to look at her once more as I pulled the door open, and in her frustrated expression, I finally saw the clues I'd missed before, in the tilt of her chin and the way she had her arms crossed, and the way her eyes glazed over as she spoke to someone else through her link. "Marissa? What the hell?"

That was the last thing I remembered before something hit me hard on the back of my head.

Chapter Nine

~Jerrod~

Nothing about this was going to plan as Oliver collapsed from the blow I'd just given him.

"What did you do that for?" Marissa whined at me as I lugged his unconscious body back over to the bed and dumped him onto it, face-first. "He's no good to us like this!"

"What was I supposed to do?" I countered in frustration. "You said the drug wasn't working and he was leaving. We couldn't just let him go."

We didn't want him getting anywhere near another person or, worse, a medical centre, until we were sure the drug was out of his system.

"I just meant to keep him here a little longer," my mate exclaimed angrily. "The chemical wasn't quite at full strength yet. He almost believed I was her; another few minutes and I would have had him."

Well, she didn't tell me that, and it was too late now. He was out cold and he wasn't waking up anytime soon.

"This whole thing has been a fucking waste of time," I muttered. "We've got one who's useless and the other one who's having some kind of breakdown."

At some point, Elijah lost track of who I was and started thinking I was someone named Julian instead. Whoever that was must be a friend of his because he started pouring his heart out to him about how he had messed things up with his mate and he didn't know how to fix it and how he'd have nothing if she left him. He was going round in circles, getting more worked up by the minute, and I had been tempted to knock *him* out just so I wouldn't have to listen to it anymore.

He only let me go when Marissa mind-linked me because I told him I was going to go and find his mate. The look of hope and gratitude on his face was truly pathetic. It almost made me glad I wasn't beholden to the mate bond that way. I may not have a mate I loved, but at least I still had my dignity.

"Our efforts weren't a total waste," Marissa offered. "I did manage to kiss him a couple of times so Abby would have felt that, I'm sure. But we didn't get any video of anything really incriminating, so I'm not sure it's enough."

It sounded like a lot of trouble to go through for a couple of kisses that Abby might just pass off as indigestion. I had felt it too, of course, and the pain wasn't that bad.

"We could strip him," I suggested, glancing down at the unmoving body on the bed. "Have him wake up in bed with you? If he doesn't remember how he got there, he might be convinced that he did more than he did."

Marissa thought that over for a minute. "That's not bad. I still wish we'd gotten some video though."

Before I could say anything to that, Oliver's phone began to ring in his pocket. Shoving him over onto his back, I pulled it out just in time to see Abby's picture flash across the screen before it went to voicemail. In the photo, her eyes were shining with happiness and her smile was bright as she looked into the camera, and my chest tightened painfully at the sight of it.

It had been a long, long time since she smiled at me that way. Maybe she never had.

"She's probably calling to check up on him," Marissa guessed. "After what she just felt, she must be suspicious."

That was a good sign at least, but we still had to be smart about this. "We need to get rid of his phone," I told Marissa, holding it up to her. "And Elijah's too. If we're keeping them here overnight, we don't want anyone tracking us down before the morning."

"Just throw them in the back of one of the trucks out in the parking lot," she suggested. "When the person drives off, they'll be taken somewhere totally random with nothing to track them to us."

That was rather clever. She was actually quite good at this kind of thing.

"Alright. I'll go get Elijah's phone then, but I don't know what to do with him after that. He's still completely conscious, unfortunately, and completely out of it. He doesn't have a clue where he is or what's happening."

As soon as the words were out of my mouth, a new idea crossed my mind, and from the spark in Marissa's eyes, I could tell she'd had the same one too.

"Now that Abby's felt the pain..." I started, and she quickly filled in the rest.

"... it wouldn't matter which of them was in the video. And if Oliver wakes up with me, like you said..."

"... between that and the video and what Abby felt, the evidence is a lot stronger."

It made sense to me, and it really could work. Elizabeth would feel something, of course, but there was no reason they couldn't have both hooked up with someone tonight. Finally, it felt like we were back on track.

"So we need to get Elijah in this room," she summarized, looking up to where I'd placed the overhead camera. "And take Oliver to the other one?"

"I'll take him," I offered. "You can lead Elijah here by pretending you're his mate. Honestly, I don't think you even need the wig. He was completely convinced I was someone else without me even trying. If you just tell him that's who you are, he'll believe you, and it's better for the video anyway if it looks like you."

For once, she took my advice without arguing, pulling off the wig and glasses she'd worn to pretend to be Abby and quickly checking her makeup in the mirror. To my surprise, she actually looked a bit better without all that stuff on, and a flash of desire and appreciation ran through me as I watched her run her hands over her body, smoothing out her clothes.

Where the hell did that come from? I was letting the thrill of victory cloud my judgement; that was all this feeling was, and I quickly pushed it aside.

When she was ready, I awkwardly lifted the unconscious Oliver from the bed. Fuck, he was heavier than he looked and I grunted as I got him upright. Half-dragging him out the door, I hoped no one would notice us as we walked along the outside hallway to the room a couple of doors down where Elijah was waiting. Thankfully, this motel wasn't the kind of place where people paid too much attention to other people. Everyone was caught up in their own business.

With Oliver still slung over my shoulder, I went to stand on the other side of the door while Marissa opened it. From where I was standing, I could just make out Elijah pacing the room nervously, mumbling to himself. He looked even crazier now than he sounded before.

"Elijah?"As soon as Marissa said his name, his head jerked up and he squinted at her while I held my breath, hoping this would work.

"I've been looking for you," she said, giving him a smile, and the look on his face melted from confusion into relief, though she looked nothing like his mate at all.

"Liz?"

"Yeah. Can I have your phone for a minute?"Obediently, he pulled it out without question and handed it to her. Smiling up at him from beneath her lashes, she blinked at him sweetly.

"Can you come with me? We need to talk."

Once more, he did as she said without question, following Marissa out of the room as she tossed his phone to me behind his back. He never even noticed me standing there, and I watched as she took him back down the walkway to the other room, the one with the cameras inside. Just before she went in, Marissa looked back at me and gave me a determined nod of her head, and an odd little feeling of pride settled in my chest. If there was any way to pull this off, she was going to find it. She was a little bit ruthless, just like me.

I still had things of my own to do though. First, I lugged Oliver into the now-empty room and dumped him onto the bed. Taking his phone and Elijah's, I went and deposited them into an open truck bed as Marissa had suggested, and when I got back to the room, though stripping him wasn't easy, or in any way pleasant, I managed to get Oliver's clothes off and strewn over the floor before covering him with the blankets from the bed.

With all that taken care of, I pulled out my phone and tuned into the camera feed from the other room to see exactly how my mate was getting on.

~Elijah~

Things weren't entirely making sense to me right now.

One minute, I was in the bar talking with Jerrod about my ambitions for Liz and surprisingly, he actually seemed to know what he was talking about. He had a list for me of all the major Alphas in the area and which side they were currently on based on what he'd seen at the meeting today. He knew the alliances between them and who I should target if I wanted to significantly change the balance in my favour. He even offered to help set up meetings between me and the Alphas in question.

"What's in it for you?" I asked him warily once he'd outlined his proposal. From my experience, most people didn't go out of their way for a complete stranger out of the goodness of their hearts.

To his credit, he didn't try to pretend he was acting out of anything other than self-interest. "I want a seat on the council when I'm Alpha, and I want to be Chairman of the council within the first year. My pack has always been shut out of the big decisions because we're not as aggressive as some of the others, but what we lack in brute strength, we make up for in cunning."

That seemed to be a good word for him, which only made me more hesitant. "The Council will have less authority once Liz is in power," I pointed out. "You won't be able to do whatever you want."

"I understand that, but she's not going to spend all of her time administering the day-to-day running of one local council. She's obviously meant for bigger things than that. She'll need to delegate, and I'm happy to take that responsibility."

If he really could deliver me what he was promising, it seemed a reasonable trade, but I knew I was already in enough hot water with her as it was so I didn't agree to anything right there and then. "My mate and I have a few things we need to talk over first, but I will definitely keep your offer in mind. I'll be in touch tomorrow."

Intending for that to be the end of it, I got to my feet, but the room immediately spun around me as I did so, and I had to hold onto the edge of the table to keep from falling over. *What the fuck?* One drink never affected me like that.

"Are you okay?" Jerrod was still sitting and watching me curiously.

"Fine." I wasn't about to admit any weakness in front of him. "I'm going to head back now. I just need a taxi."

I pulled out my phone to order one, but the icons on the screen swam in front of my eyes, not staying in one place long enough for me to select one.

"I can take you back to the hotel if you want," he offered. "I'm heading there myself."

Something about that didn't seem right. Didn't he say he didn't want to be seen with me, and that's why we had to meet way out here in the first place? Wouldn't people see us together if he gave me a ride back?

It didn't make sense, but then, my head was feeling strange in general. Right now, just getting back to the hotel, no matter how I got there, seemed like the best idea.

He told me his keys were in one of the rooms at the motel next door which, again, didn't entirely make sense. He was staying at the same hotel I was so why would he have a room at the motel? But that concern immediately disappeared as I followed him out the door of the bar, and everything seemed to change.

I wasn't sure how it happened, but suddenly I was back on my pack land in Oregon with the tall trees towering above me. When I looked to my side, Jerrod was gone, but my Beta, Julian, was there instead.

"Come on," he said to me. "It's this way."

I didn't know where he was taking me or why, but I trusted him and wanted to know what he had to show me, so I followed him willingly enough. A couple of minutes later, we walked into my office in the pack house and I took a seat behind my desk. Everything was familiar, but it felt odd too, and my stomach sank as I realized why.

"Where's my mate?" I asked.

Why was I here at all? I had given up my pack for Liz, so if I was here, did that mean Liz was gone? Had I pushed her away? Was it too late to fix this? Panic flooded my body as I tried to figure out what I was missing.

"She'll be here soon," Julian promised me. "Just sit there and be patient."

That wasn't how Julian normally spoke to me, but right now, I was too relieved that he said Liz was on her way to be upset about it. I hadn't realized just how much I missed having him to talk to, and soon, I was pouring my heart out to him about Liz and the declaration I'd made at the Council and what she'd said to me about how I was doing this for myself instead of for her.

He didn't say much in return but it felt good just to get it all out, and when he stood up to go, I was genuinely disappointed. I didn't want to be on my own.

"I'm just going to get your mate," he grunted. "I'll be right back."

He was going to bring Liz here now? That was wonderful news. That brief moment where I thought I had lost her made things a lot clearer for me, and I was more than ready to listen to her now.

Once he had gone, I tried to rehearse what I was going to say to her, how I could explain to her everything that I wanted for her and why, and when she arrived and asked me to go with her to talk, my heart soared. At least she was willing to hear me out and try to work things out. That was a good start.I followed her down the hall of the pack house, and when she opened a door for us to go into, I was surprised to see we weren't at my room at all, but the room she and I had been sharing at the Jade Moon pack house. How did we get here? Wasn't I just on the other side of the country?

It didn't make sense, but as she stepped into the room after me and closed the door behind her, I focused all my attention on her instead. It didn't matter how we got here; the important thing was that we were here, together, and I was going to do everything I could to make things right.

~Marissa~

The drug was definitely working better on Elijah than it had on Oliver. As soon as we got into the room, he turned to me with a look of such adoration that I couldn't help feeling a little guilty. I didn't know anything about this man other than the fact that he was Oliver's double, and I didn't wish him or his mate any particular harm. It was just his bad luck that he ended up in the middle of all of this with Oliver's face.

"Thank you for coming," he said to me, his expression eager and hopeful. "It means a lot to me that you're willing to talk this through with me."

I had no intention of talking with him any more than I had to. If he tried to engage me on anything specific, he could quickly discover that I wasn't his mate. As Oliver had already proven, though the drug affected perception, the effects weren't foolproof. And besides, I didn't want to know anything about him. It would make it easier if I didn't know.

With that in mind, I tried to steer him in a different direction instead. "Talking isn't what I'm interested in right now. I've missed you, Elijah."

As I wrapped my arms around him, he sighed happily. "I've missed you too, Liz. So much."

That was all it took. Men really were ruled by their dicks, it seemed.

He kissed me eagerly and willingly, nothing like the way Oliver kissed me a few minutes earlier. Clothing came off until we were both down to our underwear and then I pulled him over to the bed, in the perfect spot for the cameras to pick us up. His hands caressed my body, his mouth hungry and demanding against mine, and his cock firm against me, straining against his underwear.

And I...

I felt nothing at all.

I had slept with quite a few men before, and even when the sex wasn't great, I still got some pleasure out of it. Right now, however, it just felt awkward.

This man didn't want me; he never had. At least with Oliver, we had our past to go on, and I was sure he still felt something for me, no matter how deep those emotions were buried. You didn't spend years of your life with someone and not have any kind of leftover emotion. It didn't seem impossible to rekindle it under the right circumstances, so when I kissed him, there was hope there, hope and the memories we used to have together.

When I was with Jerrod, on the other hand, my body always burned brightly. Sure, it flamed with hatred rather than love, but at least there was fire.

The numbness I was feeling now was disconcerting, and so was the way Elijah looked down at me as he broke our kiss, his body still firmly pressed against mine.

"I know I'm not perfect," he whispered, looking at me like I held the answers to all of life's mysteries. "But I will try to be better, Liz. Thank you for not giving up on me."

Shit.

What was I doing? Here he thought he was making up with his mate, when in reality, she must be in pain right now, feeling him here with me. Maybe she could forgive him for whatever he'd done before, whatever he thought he was apologizing for, but would she forgive him for this? I hadn't really thought about that when Jerrod and I were laying out the plan.

Hurting Abby was one thing; that was simply payback for the pain she'd caused me. But the idea of putting this woman I didn't even know through hell and maybe even breaking her and her mate up, it didn't sit right with me.

This isn't who I am, is it?

It had been a long time since I'd even asked myself that question. I was so buried in my own grievances, so focused on my own heartache, that I lost sight of the fact that the man on top of me was a real person too and not just a prop in the game I was playing.

As gently as I could, I pushed him back. "I haven't given up on you, but maybe this is too fast. Maybe we should just go to sleep instead."

Dismay registered across his face. "Did I say something wrong? I love you, Liz. I want to show you how much."

He tried to kiss me again, but I pushed him back harder. "I know you love me, you don't have to show me right now. What would really make me happy is if you got some rest. Aren't you tired?"

The power of suggestion with this drug was incredibly strong. As soon as I asked the question, he began to yawn and his eyes immediately drooped. I pushed him all the way back until he was lying down, and he looked up at me once more, trying his best to keep his eyes open. "You love me too, right?"

He sounded so hopeful, so stupidly, delusionally hopeful, that I couldn't contradict him. "I do. Good night, Elijah."

His eyes closed completely, and a moment later, he was snoring as I let out a huff of disbelief. *Men.*

Getting up from the bed, I started to put my clothes back on, but I hadn't gotten very far when the door opened and my mate burst in, his face red with frustration. "What the hell just happened? You were almost there!"

So, he had been watching. I should have guessed. "The drug must have been too strong," I lied, knowing there was no audio on the video feed. He had no way of knowing what was actually said. "He just suddenly dozed off."

His jaw clenched, Jerrod looked over at Elijah's sleeping form, sprawled out on the bed in his underwear. "Well, at least we got *some* video. I can edit it to look convincing."

He rubbed at his chest with his hand almost absent-mindedly, and I couldn't help asking: "Did it hurt? Watching me and him?"

"Of course it hurt," he scowled back at me. "We're mates and we're bonded, that's how it works."

That wasn't what I meant. "That's not what I asked. Did it hurt *watching* me and him?"

He stared at me for a moment, an indefinable emotion flashing in his eyes, before he turned away, not answering the question. "Wait here."

Without another word, he walked out of the room, leaving me alone, and my indignation grew as I put the rest of my clothes back on. Did he really feel nothing for me at all? He said it wouldn't bother him to see me with another man, but there was a part of me that had hoped he was lying. Now, I really wasn't sure.

A few minutes later, he was back, and still saying nothing, he grabbed my hand and pulled me from the room, closing the door behind us. Along the walkway, we went until we reached another room, not the one Oliver was in but a completely different one, and he pulled a key from his pocket and opened the door.

This room was empty, and as soon as we were inside, Jerrod's hands were on me, and my body immediately responded with all the fire that had been missing when Elijah touched me. "No one will ever make you feel as good as I do," he growled into my ear as he pressed his hips against mine, his cock already hard in his pants. "You know that. It didn't bother me to watch you with him because I knew he wasn't pleasing you, not the way I can."

I didn't even try to fight it. The truth was that I didn't want to, not when he was right. No one made me feel like he did, for better or for worse, and if there was one thing this whole crazy night had proven to me, that was it.

My mate was the one man who couldn't resist me, no drugs required.

Chapter Ten

~**Liz**~

Not for the first time since I found out I was a werewolf, I was completely confused about what was going on. First, Abby was complaining of chest pain, then Daniel asked if she knew where her mate was, and now, she was placing a call to him, though from the look of growing unhappiness on her face, it didn't look like he was answering.

What did Abby's chest pain have to do with Oliver? Picking up on my confusion, Daniel leaned over to explain it to me: "Mates can feel when their mate is being unfaithful; that's the downside of the mate bond. The upsides are the connection and the sparks and the fantastic sex, of course, but when things go wrong, it's not pleasant."

Unfaithful? That didn't make any sense. There was no way Oliver would ever cheat on Abby. I had watched the two of them for months at college, being more than a little jealous of the relationship they had. I had never seen two people who were more devoted to each other than they were.

Abby lowered her phone and looked over at the rest of us with concern. "There's no answer. That's really not like him; even if he's busy, he'll answer to tell me he's busy."

That sounded much more like the Oliver I knew too.

Daniel and Storm exchanged looks again. "Well, if he's doing what it feels like he's doing, he might not want to answer," Storm pointed out bluntly, but not unkindly. Clearly, nobody at the table *wanted* this to be true, they were simply trying to be practical.

"It's stopped now, though," Abby told us, looking down at her body as if it might provide some answers. "This doesn't make any sense."

"I can call Patrick and ask him to check in on the boys?" Storm suggested. "At least he can see if they're in their room."

Abby gave her agreement so Storm pulled out her own phone. Her mate picked up immediately, and he told her to wait on the line while he went to Eli's room, where Oliver was meant to be spending the night. Storm put the phone on speaker so we could all hear it.

"No one's answering," Alpha Patrick announced. "Hold on, I'll break the door down."

"No, don't..." Abby and Storm cried out at the same time, but they were too late. The sound of splintering wood echoed through the phone speaker and we all winced, other than Daniel, who was trying not to laugh.

"Alphas," he whispered to me with a roll of his eyes. "Leave them alone for five minutes and they'll find something to destroy."

I smiled back, even though this whole culture was still strange to me. Who just went around kicking doors down?

"There's no one here," Patrick told us, presumably speaking now from inside the room. "They're both gone."

They must have gone somewhere together then, and Abby was clearly on the same page as me. "Maybe they're in the hotel bar?" she suggested.

"You could have checked there before ruining the door," Storm told her mate wryly.

"I was already at the door," Alpha Patrick pointed out, sounding completely unconcerned about the damage he'd just caused. "It would have been a waste of time to have to come back."

I couldn't help imagining what would have happened if Oliver really *had* been in the room with another woman; they would have had a heart attack when the door came crashing down. Although, if that was the case, maybe they would have deserved it.

A minute later, Alpha Patrick declared the bar to be empty too. "There's no sign of them. Should I be concerned?"

"We don't know yet," Storm told him honestly. "I'll keep you posted." Hanging up the phone, she looked back over at Abby. "What's your plan?"

"I could track his phone," she suggested, looking a little uncomfortable at the idea. "It's not that I don't trust him, I'm just worried he's in some kind of trouble."

"We understand, Abby," Daniel told her encouragingly. "If you've got a way to track him, let's do it."

Abby was just starting to pull up the tracking app on her phone when suddenly my own chest seemed to explode in pain, as though someone had cut right into it and was slowly ripping it apart. I couldn't have held in my cry of agony even if I wanted to, and the other three at the table all looked over at me in alarm.

"You too?" Abby asked, and I could only nod. Based on what she'd described, it seemed to be exactly the same kind of pain, a pain stronger than anything I'd ever felt before and not letting up at all; if anything, the torment was getting worse.

Daniel looked around as I cried out again. "We should go. We're starting to attract attention."

The humans around us were indeed starting to look over at us curiously, but I wasn't sure I could even walk right now. All my energy was focused on remembering how to breathe, since the pain seemed to have stolen all my breath away.

Without me needing to ask for help, Daniel picked me up and carried me out of the venue, asking the woman at the door to let the other Lunas know that we had to leave. "I've got a lock on Oliver's phone," Abby announced as we reached Daniel's car. "It's moving now, but it's not too far from here. Hopefully, Eli is with him."

"We'll catch up to them," Daniel promised as he placed me gently in the back seat of the car and gave me a sympathetic look. "Are you doing okay?"

I was not. The tearing sensation in my chest was only getting worse, like someone twisting a knife deeper and deeper, slicing more of me apart each time, and that was even before taking into account my emotional turmoil.

Eli couldn't really be with someone else right now, could he? We had argued today, of course, but he wasn't the kind of guy who would look for comfort somewhere else.

Or is he? In the long run, I really hadn't known him that long, and after what he did at the meeting today, I already knew that he could still surprise me. I had been sure he wasn't going to act without talking to me about it first, but he did. Maybe he *was* the kind of guy who would cheat on me too. I really didn't know for sure.

"I just need to see him," I managed to gasp, and Daniel nodded in understanding.

Storm climbed in the back seat with me while Abby got in front to give Daniel directions as they followed the tracker on Oliver's phone. We caught up to a green pick-up truck just as it pulled into the driveway of a tidy-looking bungalow in a residential part of town.

What were they doing here? Were they actually going to someone's house? It didn't make much sense to me, but as the door of the truck opened, the pain in my chest finally began to ease and my stomach dropped. Was Eli about to get out of the truck? Did the pain stop because he'd stopped doing whatever he was doing in there? Was there another woman with him right now?

However, Eli didn't get out of the truck, nor Oliver either. Instead, a large man in a baseball hat hopped down, slamming the door behind him, and then looked over at us in surprise when Daniel, Abby and Storm got out of the car to go talk to him. I stayed where I was; although the pain was lessening, I still wasn't sure I could walk yet. At least I could still hear what they were saying, thanks to my new and exceptional wolf hearing.

"Can I help you folks?" the man asked warily as my three friends walked up to him.

"Is there anyone else in there?" Abby asked, glancing over at the truck. "We're looking for someone and we thought maybe he was with you."

"I'm on my own," the guy answered. "But there are people just inside, so if you're thinking of trying anything…"

"We're not mugging you," Storm told him, rolling her eyes in exasperation. "We're just looking for two guys who look exactly the same. Abby, show him."

Abby pulled up a photo of Oliver on her phone and held it out to him. Recognition flashed across the man's face as he looked at it.

"That's Oliver West. My friends and I were talking to him at the bar earlier, but I don't know where he went after that."

"Bar?" Daniel repeated, and the man gave us the name of the place he'd seen Oliver.

"Are you a friend of his?" Abby asked, looking confused about why the man knew him by name.

"No, we're just fans. Would've loved to talk football with him all night, but a girl came over to buy him a drink and he ditched us to go with her."

From the way her jaw clenched, I could tell Abby wasn't thrilled about that, but she tried to keep focused. "Did you somehow end up with his phone? We're friends of his, and it looks like his phone is here. That's why we followed you."

The man's brow furrowed in confusion. "I don't think so. Don't know how that could've happened."

He checked his pockets and only found his own phone, so Storm gestured to the truck. "Mind if I take a look in there?"

He told her to go ahead so Storm hopped into the back, not even opening the tailgate, and sure enough, she soon emerged with two almost identical-looking phones.

"Give him a call, Abby," she instructed, and when Abby dialed Oliver's number, one of the phones began to ring. Storm nodded and looked over at me. "Liz, are you able to call Eli's phone?"

I felt in control enough to do that, so I placed the call, and the phone in Storm's other hand began to ring.

"That's what I was afraid of," she said grimly before turning to the man. "Thanks for your help."

Though he must have been confused, he simply nodded and headed into the house while the other three got back in the car with me.

"Looks like we're going to a bar tonight after all," Storm announced. "Let's go see what kind of trouble these boys have gotten themselves into."

~Jerrod~

There was something different in the way Marissa and I had sex this time.

She didn't make fun of me, for one thing. She barely said anything at all, not after she asked if it hurt me to watch her and Elijah. I told her it didn't bother me and that was mostly true, but only because she so obviously wasn't getting anything out of it. She looked stiff and stilted in his arms, not swept up in the heat of the moment like she was with me. Sure, she usually called me names and insulted me, but at least she was fully in the moment.

If anything, watching her with him only made me want to get her into bed with me instead, so I could make her feel like she was supposed to feel, and that was exactly what I did.

Without her taunts, I could actually focus more on what I was doing and on her reaction to it. I made her come first with my fingers, which was also strange for us. Usually, we both wanted to get this over with as quickly as possible, to give in to what our bodies wanted without wasting too much time, but tonight, our connection wasn't just about that. I wanted her to remember exactly how good I could make her feel.

Though she hadn't said so, I could imagine she was feeling a little bit rejected, after one guy had to be knocked out and the other fell asleep on her while being seduced. Despite everything, I didn't want her to feel that way. She *was* sexy, I'd never disputed that. That was the whole reason I couldn't stay away from her even when she made me feel like shit. Usually she wasn't lacking in self-confidence — some might say just the opposite — but her silence tonight made me suspect that belief in herself had taken a bit of a hit, and so I wanted to build it back up again.

When I went to grab a condom from my pocket after she came the first time, Marissa put her arm out to stop me. "You can skip it for tonight," she told me. "Just this one time."

I didn't ask why. I didn't want her to change her mind, and when I slid into her, feeling the sparks between us deeper and more intense than ever before, I realized why she had always insisted I wore one before.

This kind of connection was hard to resist.

In that dingy, backwater hotel, I had what might have just been the best sex of my life.

Even when I rolled off of her, both of us breathing heavily as we recovered from our mutual orgasm, she still said nothing, leaving me wondering if she had felt that in the same way I had. She had enjoyed it, that wasn't in doubt; her body made that clear. But did it mean anything else to her?

Was this her way of saying goodbye, our last hurrah before we put the rest of our plan into action and ended up with Abby and Oliver instead, as we were meant to?

At least, I used to think we were meant to. For some reason, that suddenly seemed a lot less clear to me.

At last, Marissa cleared her throat. "So, what's the plan now?"

Right, the plan. *Focus on that, Jerrod.* This was not the time for me to start worrying about my mate. We were in deep now, and we had to be careful not to mess up. If Oliver or Elijah ever figured out exactly what we'd done tonight and why, we could be in a lot of trouble. There was no way out of this now; we had to fully commit.

"I'm going to go back to the bar. I want people to see me there, to give me an alibi if I need one."

She nodded. "And I should go get into bed with Oliver?"

The idea of her being naked in bed with him, even with him unconscious, wasn't particularly pleasant to me, but that was, in fact, the plan. There was no way to change it now.

"Right. I'll edit the video and figure out when and where to release it."

I couldn't help noticing that neither of us was quite as excited about this as we had been earlier. Maybe we were just tired. It had been a long evening, with plenty of ups and downs. We probably just needed a good rest.

Once we were both dressed again, I watched her go back into the room with Oliver before heading back across the parking lot to the bar, where, despite the late hour, things were showing no sign of slowing down. Pulling out my phone, I got to work on editing the video, and this time, watching Marissa in Elijah's arms really did send a pang of jealousy through me.

What the hell was going on? Now that I was close to getting rid of her, just as she and I had both wanted for months, was I actually starting to care about her? Was this my problem? Was it just a matter of wanting what I couldn't have? That was one of the things the therapist had suggested when I had to talk to her about Abby, but I had dismissed it as garbage.

I really didn't know, but for the very first time ever, there was a small part of me that wished I could start this all over. Not just tonight, but all of it, right back to the moment I had first met Marissa and rejected her.

Maybe I should have given her a chance then.

Maybe, just maybe, we weren't as wrong for each other as I'd thought.

~Abby~

The worry in my chest was getting tighter by the minute. As we got closer to the bar we'd been told about, I tried to reach out to Oliver by mind-link but there was no reply. Without his phone, I had no idea where he was or what he was doing. He was still alive, I knew that at least, but I wanted a lot more than that. I wanted to know what the hell was going on.

What was the pain I felt earlier, and that Liz felt too? I couldn't believe either of our mates had been with other women; it just wasn't possible. I suspected that Storm and Daniel thought I was being naïve, but they didn't know Oliver as well as I did. Eli was more of a mystery to me, but over the time we'd spent together, I'd seen just how devoted he was to Liz. The problems they were having right now were *because* he valued her so much, not because he didn't.

Following our GPS, we found the Bitter End just off the highway. The parking lot was full so Daniel parked in the lot for the motel next door instead and the four of us walked over to the busy, dark and loud bar.

There were so many people and so many smells when we walked in that even though I sniffed the air deeply, I couldn't tell if there were *any* wolves in there, let alone my mate.

Oliver? Are you here? I tried to reach him once again, thinking that perhaps the distance between us had kept him from hearing me before, but once again, there was only silence.

"Let's split up," Storm suggested. "Daniel and Abby, you take the left side, Liz and I will check the right."

Men and women gave me curious looks as I peered closely at each table, making sure I didn't miss anything. It didn't matter to me what they thought right now, I was only concerned about Oliver. There were pool tables to one side of the bar where large, tattooed men and women in tight dresses were hanging out, but Oliver wasn't with them. Around the back, there were a few quieter tables and we came across a few couples making out, but none of them was Oliver either, which was obvious to me by the fact that I wasn't feeling any kind of pain. I didn't need to see their faces.

We had almost reached the end of our side of the bar when I spotted a familiar face; not my mate, but someone I knew well, and the fact that he was here instantly had me on high alert.

"Do you know that guy?" Daniel asked, noticing how I stopped to stare at Jerrod, who was looking down at his phone and hadn't seen me yet. "He's a wolf, isn't he?"

He could smell him and I could too, now that we were closer. The scent of my old pack was very familiar but there was nothing comforting about it right now. I only wanted answers.

"Yeah, I know him." With no further explanation, I went over and took a seat across from Jerrod, who looked up in surprise before quickly shoving his phone into his pocket.

"Abby? What are you doing here?"

I bluntly told the truth, watching his reaction carefully. "I'm looking for my mate. Have you seen him?"

A grimace crossed his face, for a fraction of a second, making it clear he knew *something*. "No. He was meant to come, but he never showed up."

I was definitely not expecting that answer. "Why was he meant to come? Why are *you* here?"

"I came to speak to Elijah. I told him to bring Oliver with him so he knew that everything was above board, but Elijah came alone."

Each word was making me more confused, not less. "Why were you meeting Elijah?"

"I wanted to talk to him about what happened at the conference today and offer my support."

That seemed to be the truth, at least, and fully in character with what I knew of Jerrod. If there was a way to weasel himself in somewhere, he'd take it. "So, Elijah is here?"

I quickly glanced around to see if I could see him, but there were only humans surrounding us.

"He was," Jerrod explained. "He left a little while ago, with a woman."

No. I didn't believe that, not from Jerrod's mouth at least. There had to be more to it than that.

"Start from the beginning," I instructed. "What exactly happened?"

As he explained the conversation he'd had with Elijah, Liz and Storm soon joined us, asking questions of their own. They hadn't found any sign of Oliver or Elijah either.

"Eventually he said he wasn't feeling well," Jerrod told us all. "I offered to get him a taxi but he said he was okay on his own, and then I saw him walk off with a woman. That was the last I saw of him, and Oliver, I never saw at all."

This wasn't adding up. Oliver *had* been here. The man in the truck told us that he spoke to him about football. I supposed he could have been here without speaking to Jerrod; maybe he had been here to watch Elijah from a distance and keep an eye on him? But then, if that was the case, why would he let Elijah leave with someone else?

There had to be more to the story than that.

"Why are you still here?" Storm asked Jerrod, her voice full of suspicion. Though she didn't know him personally, I could tell she wasn't trusting a word he said either.

Jerrod raised his glass that was sitting on the table next to him. "I stayed to try to ease my pain, actually. It seems like while I was busy here tonight, my mate was keeping herself busy in a different way."

My stomach sank even before my mind could make the connection. "What do you mean?"

He looked over at me with something like regret in his eyes. "I mean that she was with another man. I could feel it."

"When was this?" Daniel asked, and Jerrod gave a time frame that coincided almost exactly to the pain that I had felt.

That wasn't possible. It couldn't be. It must be a coincidence, or something else, because it absolutely could not be what it sounded like.

"And you just sat here drinking instead of doing something about it?" Storm demanded. "What kind of wolf are you?"

Jerrod turned his hard eyes on her. "The relationship my mate and I have is complicated. You wouldn't understand."

"No, I fucking wouldn't," Storm muttered under her breath before asking him another question. "Do you have any way of tracking her down?"

He thought about that for a second. "I suppose I could track her phone. I've never bothered to before."

"Do it," Storm ordered before turning to me. "If nothing else, it will put your mind at rest."

Was I that easy to read? Oliver always told me I had a terrible poker face.

Jerrod tapped away at his phone for a couple of minutes before making a surprised sound. "Huh."

"What?" we all asked at almost exactly the same time.

He looked up, his eyes travelling across all of us before they finally settled on me. "It looks like she's at the motel right next door."

~Oliver~

My head was aching as I tried to open my eyes. Everything around me was unfamiliar: the scratchy sheet beneath me, the musty air, stale with a hint of perfume, and there was an odd aftertaste in my mouth, something I couldn't place.

Where the hell am I?

It took a few tries before my eyes finally opened, but even when I could see, it didn't clear things up. The room was mostly dark other than the glow of a neon light filtering through the flimsy curtain on the window on a wall to my right. As I tried to pull myself up in the bed, another shot of pain went through my head, and when it faded, I realized that, for some reason, I was naked beneath the covers of the bed. The sheets were thin and cheap, and the scent of perfume grew stronger. I'd smelled that brand before, but I didn't find it particularly pleasant.

Putting a hand to my throbbing head, I tried to figure out what was going on. What was the last thing I remembered?

I was at the hotel with Elijah and he wanted me to go with him to a meeting. We had an argument, he left on his own, and then I followed him anyway. At the bar, I had a drink with the football fans and then I ran into...

My stomach dropped painfully hard as I realized where I recognized the perfume from. That was Marissa's perfume, a scent that had always felt unnatural to me, and I remembered having a drink with her at the bar and talking to her about her mate. We left together to try to find Elijah and then...

And then nothing. That was the last thing I could remember: walking across the dark parking lot towards the motel and seeing the neon sign in front of it, the same neon sign that was flashing through the thinly-covered window now.

No. No, no, fuck no.

This couldn't be happening. My heart pounded, amplifying the pain in my head as I tried to think of another reason, *any* other reason that I might be naked in a motel room with Marissa's perfume in the air. Maybe I was abducted by aliens? I didn't believe in alien abduction, but right now, it seemed infinitely preferable to the alternative. Dread filled my whole body, all the way down to my toes as I turned my head, hoping against hope that the bed next to me was empty or that, even better, somehow my sweet mate was beside me.

Those hopes were quickly and tortuously dashed.

Marissa lay next to me, fast asleep, her blonde hair splayed out on the pillow and her mouth hanging open. As I breathed in deeper, trying to catch my breath since it felt like all the air had been knocked out of me, I could smell her perfume even stronger, and I could smell sex on her too.

Oh, God, fucking no.

I wasn't sure I had ever wanted anything to be a dream as much as I wanted to wake up right now and find that my mind had invented this. Unfortunately, pinching myself didn't accomplish anything other than making my arm hurt as my fingers dug in deeper, trying to wake myself from this nightmare.

I couldn't have done this. It simply wasn't possible! I had felt a bit sorry for Marissa at the bar, but sympathy was all I felt. There was no possible path I could see that would have gotten me from the last thing I remembered to where I was right now, but I couldn't ignore the evidence in front of my eyes either. I was, first and foremost, a realist.

A knock sounded at the door, loud and urgent, and I winced as pain shot through my head again.

Next to me, Marissa began to stir. "Oliver?" she mumbled sleepily. "What's going on?"

That was what I wanted to know. *What the fuck is going on?*

Someone knocked on the door again, even louder, banging on it with their fist. "Marissa? I know you're in there."

I knew that voice, and obviously, so did the woman beside me. "Fuck, it's Jerrod," she gasped, as if I hadn't figured that out already. "What do we do?"

We? I didn't want there to be any 'we'. I didn't want to be here at all.

"If you don't open the door, I'm breaking it down," her mate warned from the other side.

Marissa sat up, wrapping the blanket tighter around herself, and I made a Hail Mary attempt, still hoping that somehow, this wasn't what it looked like. "Please tell me we didn't have sex, Marissa. Please."

For just a second, there was a flash of something in her eyes, something pained and haunted, but it quickly disappeared. "What are you talking about? Don't you remember?"

No, I sure as fuck did not remember. That was why I was asking.

A second later, Jerrod made good on his threat, and the door broke off its hinges as he kicked it in while Marissa shrieked and tried to hide behind me, pressing herself against my side.

Before I could get away from her, before I could do anything at all, Jerrod walked into the room, followed by several other people, but there was only one face I saw, only one expression that registered in my still-aching head.

Abby.

My mate stood just inside the door, her face frozen in disbelief and for a moment, it felt like nothing in the world existed outside the two of us. I had felt that way before, but usually in a good way. The only thing I had to compare to the way I was feeling now was the day that Abby nearly died, the day Jerrod shot her with the poisoned arrow, that feeling that I was going to lose her, and even then, the comparison wasn't completely accurate.

Because this was *my* fault. Though I didn't know how, somehow I had done this, and the look I could see on her face fucking broke my heart.

The incomprehension in her expression gradually gave way to disappointment and I felt it flow through me; the agony in my chest, ripping and twisting as the sting of the betrayal she was feeling came to me through our bond. Every doubt, horror and sorrow that flowed through her, I could feel them as if they were my own. And they were, because I didn't just do this to her, I did it to *us*. That was what was being torn apart right now, the trust we'd built and the future we'd created, falling to pieces in the devastation raging in her eyes.

"Heels."

That word was all I could get out: a plea, a cry for her from the deepest part of me, begging her to try to understand, to try to help *me* understand, but it didn't work. Tears filled her eyes before she turned and ran, followed by another pair of footsteps, but whose they were, I had no idea. I hadn't seen anything but her.

"I should have guessed," Jerrod was saying, his face red not with sadness like Abby's but with anger as he looked at me. "I tried to put the past behind us and make peace, but you just take whatever the hell you want, just like always."

"I didn't..." I tried to say, but I couldn't even finish that sentence. The truth was, I had no idea what the hell I had done.

"Oliver." That was Liz who spoke, and I noticed her there for the first time, wearing a look of disappointment that sent another wave of shame and recrimination through me. Storm was beside her, and the expression she wore was demanding answers, the same answers that I wanted too. How could I have done this?

"It just happened," Marissa claimed from beside me, and I realized belatedly that she was still holding onto me. "You know how it is with first loves."

What? That wasn't what this was. I had no residual feelings for Marissa, none at all, but I had no other explanation.

Desperately, I looked around the room, searching for something that might give me a clue what the fuck actually happened here, and that was when I noticed the room number on the door that Jerrod had just broken down: 218.

A memory flashed across my mind of standing outside the door while Marissa opened it, and seeing the number. It stuck out at me because the number seemed to move, and I remembered the 4 in particular. Two *four*teen, not two eighteen. I was almost completely sure of it.

Without a word to anyone, I got out of bed and grabbed my pants that were on the floor of the room. The state in which my clothes and Marissa's were spread across the room only added to the scene, making it hard to doubt what had gone on here, but doubt it, I did. Maybe I was grasping at straws with the room number, but if there was even the slightest chance that there was another explanation, I was going to hold onto it with everything I had.

I could go after Abby, but until I knew what I could say to her to ease the hurt she was feeling, there didn't seem a point. I needed answers first.

"Where are you going?" Marissa asked, sounding put out as she remained in the bed with the blankets wrapped around herself.

"I need to check something." That was all the explanation I gave as I walked past them all and down the hall, looking for some kind of salvation.

Chapter Eleven

~**Liz**~

There were a lot of different things going through my mind right now, but most of all, I was angry.

I was angry with Oliver for hurting my friend, I was angry with the woman next to him who was acting like what happened was no big deal, and I was angry with my mate who was still missing but, based on what I'd felt earlier, was probably in a situation very similar to this one. It seemed he and Oliver had more in common than just their appearance.

When Abby ran off, part of me wanted to go after her and make sure she was okay. She would do the same for me; in fact, she had, several times before. However, I also wanted to stay and see what Oliver had to say for himself. It could be important for Abby to know what happened next, so when Daniel took off after her, and I knew she'd be safe, I decided to stay where I was.

Oliver still hadn't offered any kind of apology or explanation. He'd given a half-hearted denial, which was kind of ridiculous given the evidence we could all see with our own eyes. Maybe he didn't mean for things to go as far as they did, but whether he planned it or not, he'd obviously screwed up. Just like with Eli earlier today, intentions only counted for so much. Eventually, you had to take a person's actions into account too.

And where *was* Eli now? I was growing more convinced by the second that he had cheated on me the same way Oliver had on Abby, since the pain I felt earlier seemed to confirm it, and he didn't even have the poor excuse of having a previous relationship to rekindle. It would have had to have been a complete stranger he took to his bed.

When Oliver pulled his pants on and set off down the hall, I followed after him and so did Storm and the guy from the bar, Jerrod. Oliver didn't go far, just down the hall to another door which he banged on loudly. A voice shouted from further away, telling him to be quiet, but Oliver didn't listen. He knocked again, and when there was no answer, he kicked the door in, just like Jerrod had done at the previous room.

What the hell was with these werewolf men and hotel room doors?

"I've got to teach them how to pick a lock," Storm muttered under her breath, clearly on the same page as me as we both followed Oliver inside.

Inside was a carbon copy of the previous room, right down to the handsome, shirtless man in the bed, who looked just like the one standing over him right now.

Eli.

There was no naked woman next to him, and I found myself almost disappointed. Based on what I'd felt earlier, the reason he was here wasn't too hard to guess, and the fact that he was alone must just mean that the woman had left already. At least if she'd been here, I could have given her a piece of my mind too. As it was, Eli was going to have to answer for all of it, and right now, I was in no mood to listen.

How *dare* he. How dare he break down my walls, convince me that he loved me and would never use me, and then do exactly that. First, there was the conference today and now this. Were all of his flowery words and promises just to get me to agree to seek power with him? *For* him? It seemed I was finally seeing who my 'mate' really was, and I didn't like the view at all.

Despite being the one to lead us here and break the door down, Oliver looked completely confused as he looked down at his brother in the bed. "What the fuck is going on?" he asked no one in particular before rounding on Jerrod. "You brought him here. Why?"

Jerrod's nostrils flared as he glared back at Oliver. "Really? You just screwed my mate and you're asking *me* to explain myself? Maybe you should be a little more worried about groveling to your own mate and begging her forgiveness. I know Abby; she isn't someone who'll get over something like this."

Oliver's face contorted beneath the truth of those words, but he kept talking anyway. "Marissa and I came over here to look for Eli," he explained, glancing over at me and Storm as if he was asking for our help. "I remember coming to this room, but that's the last thing I remember. I have *no* idea how I ended up in bed with her in another room. Honestly, I don't remember."

There was pain and confusion in every word, but my sympathy at this moment was entirely with Abby. Maybe being a convincing liar was a genetic trait that Oliver and Eli shared.

"How much did you idiots have to drink?" Storm asked him bluntly.

"I don't know about Elijah, but I only had a couple of drinks," Oliver told us. "Definitely not enough to black out. I don't understand how this could have happened."

"I know what I felt," Jerrod snarled at him. "And I'm sure Abby felt it too."

Oliver looked over at Storm and me again, looking for confirmation, and when Storm gave him a curt nod, his eyes closed and he honestly looked like he was about to cry.

"I've got to go and deal with my mate now," Jerrod continued. "But this isn't the end of this, Oliver."

When he'd gone, my attention returned to my sleeping mate, and Storm looked over at him too, snorting in disbelief. "How is he still asleep?"

That was a good question; we weren't exactly being quiet. Without a word, I went over to the bed and gave him a hard shove. As my hand connected with his shoulder, the sparks of our bond tingling between us, he finally began to stir.

"Liz?" His lips curled into a smile as his eyes slowly blinked open. There was only warmth and affection in his gaze as he saw me, until he looked around more and took notice of our surroundings. "Wait, where are we?"

"It must have been more than a couple of drinks," Storm announced, looking between Oliver and Eli. "More like a couple of bottles."

"Storm?" Eli sat up, rubbing his eyes as he looked around again. "Oliver? What's going on?"

He reached for my hand but I backed away sharply, going to stand next to Storm instead, and Eli's brow furrowed in confusion as he watched me.

Oliver answered his brother, still looking almost like he was going to be sick. "I was hoping you might have some answers, because I sure as fuck don't. We're in the motel next to the bar where you met with Jerrod."

"I don't know how I got here," Eli told us all, rubbing his hands over his face once more. "I thought... well, it doesn't make sense, but I thought Liz and I were at the pack house."

His eyes moved to me in hope.

"You forgave me, and you kissed me, and..." He trailed off as my expression made it clear that had definitely not happened tonight, and his lips pursed. "I guess I was dreaming."

He sounded so disappointed that I could have almost felt sorry for him, if I wasn't so sure the entire thing was bullshit. "You did kiss someone tonight, Eli, it just wasn't me."

That made his eyes go wide, and he immediately got to his feet. He was wearing his underwear, at least, not that it made much difference. "What? No! That didn't happen, that would *never* happen..."

I flinched as he moved closer to me, and Storm immediately stepped between us. "Okay, back off a second. I'm doing a blood test on both of you, right now."

That stopped everyone in their tracks. "What?" we all asked at once.

"If you drank so much that you both blacked out, there should still be traces of it in your system. It's no excuse, but at least we can try to understand how it happened."

Oliver immediately offered his arm. "Do it."

"Don't you have to have a proper needle and..." I started to ask, but before I could finish, Storm reached into the small bag she had over her shoulder and pulled out a needle and syringe. With all the steadiness of someone who had done this a hundred times before, she took a sample from Oliver, and then another from Eli, and I tried to peer into her bag as she tucked the samples away. "How many of those do you have in there?"

"Enough," she answered bluntly. "I'm taking them to a clinic right now. Liz, do you want to stay here, or come with me?"

I glanced over at Eli who was watching me with an almost desperate look in his eyes. There were a million things I wanted to say to him but I also didn't want to be anywhere near him either. "I'll go with you," I decided.

Storm gave me a nod before turning to the brothers. "I'll let you know as soon as I have any answers. In the meantime, I suggest you both take a good, hard look at yourselves."

With that, she headed out of the room and I quickly followed, eager to get far away from this entire mess.

~Abby~

I hadn't gotten very far away when Daniel's warm hard grabbed hold of my arm. "Abby, wait. Running away isn't going to help."

He was right, but I didn't know what else to do. Apparently, when it came down to fight or flight, my instinct was flight, at least in this particular situation.

"Nothing is going to help right now," I pointed out, my voice and my body shaking as I tried to hold myself together. "Nothing can make this better."

My whole world was falling apart. Oliver *was* my world. He was my rock and our love was the foundation on which everything else was built. My father's death had shaken me, but Oliver's support kept me upright through it all. Now, it felt like the walls were tumbling down.

Running might not help, but I needed to get away from that awful image burned into my head of Oliver and Marissa in bed together, her body pressed up against his. My worst nightmare had come to life.

When we met, I was convinced I wasn't Oliver's type. Guys like him weren't interested in girls like me; that was simply a fact. He dated girls like Marissa and my cheerleader roommate, Whitney. Hell, he dated half the cheerleading squad. Our being mated had to be a mistake.

Gradually, with patience and kindness and good humour, he proved me wrong. Only now, it felt like we'd taken a huge leap back, not just to that point but further, to a point where he could put aside everything we'd built between us for a moment of pleasure with someone who was my total opposite.

How could that happen? How could the man I knew and loved do something like that?

"They were drinking," Daniel said as I twisted around to face him in the parking lot beneath the glow of the motel's neon sign. "It's not an excuse, but I'm sure he didn't mean for it to happen."

Drinking *wasn't* an excuse, that much was true, but it wouldn't be the first time that Oliver drank too much. He'd told me the story of how, before we met, he got so drunk that he caused an explosion in his dorm room *and* let it slip to his friends that he was a werewolf. Of course they didn't believe him, but that wasn't the point. He lost control and he had no memory of what happened. Was that what happened here?

But even if that were the case, when Oliver was blackout drunk that other time, he still didn't do anything out of character. He did a chemistry experiment and he spoke the truth, both of which were part of his character, he just did them both without any proper forethought. Did that mean that deep down, being with Marissa was something he still wanted, and when his inhibitions were lowered, that truth came out? Maybe he didn't even realize it himself on a conscious level?

That didn't make it any better, but I saw the desperation in his eyes a moment ago too. I felt his pain, even through my own.

"I know he didn't *want* to hurt me," I managed to say, even though my voice still wobbled as the words came out. "I have more faith in him than that."

After everything we'd been through together, I owed him the benefit of the doubt, no matter how my heart was breaking. One thing I loved about my mate was that he never jumped to conclusions, and I had to try not to either. I would think this through logically, just like he would do if the situations were reversed.

Just like he *had* done, I reminded myself. He was once sent a video that seemed to show me in an intimate situation with another man, and instead of blowing up at me, he took the time to analyze it, to think it through, and to talk to me about it before he reached any kind of conclusion.

Though my gut instinct was to respond emotionally, maybe in this case, I needed to be a bit more like Oliver.

Taking a deep breath, I pushed the image of Oliver and Marissa out of my head and went back to the beginning of the night.

"Jerrod said he invited Eli to the bar to talk to him," I reminded Daniel. He had been at the table when Jerrod told us that, but I needed to repeat it, to say it out loud again to make sure I wasn't missing anything. "He said Oliver was invited too but didn't show up, but that's not true. We know Oliver was at the bar because the man whose truck we followed earlier said that he had a drink with him."

"Could that have been Elijah instead?" Daniel asked. The question wasn't accusatory, he was just trying to cover all the bases.

Trying to keep an open mind, I considered that, but ultimately, I shook my head. "I don't think so. He said they talked about football, and Eli doesn't know anything about football. I heard him and Oliver talking about it once, Eli said he never understood the appeal of the game and had never bothered to learn it. He wouldn't be able to have a conversation about it."

Daniel nodded. "Okay, so that puts Oliver at the bar. That doesn't mean Jerrod's lying though; maybe he never saw that he was there?"

"That's possible," I had to agree. "Maybe he went to keep an eye on Eli from a distance?"

"That's what I might have done," Daniel agreed. "Okay, so we've got Jerrod and Eli talking, and Oliver watching them and/or having a drink with these football fans. Then what?"

My stomach twisted as I recalled the next part. "The man said that after having a drink with them, Oliver went off with a woman. That could have been Marissa."

"So she was at the bar with her mate? If that was the case, why weren't they sitting together?"

I could only shrug. "He said their relationship is complicated. There could be a lot of reasons they weren't together."

Daniel had to concede that. There was no way for us to know. "So, Oliver and Marissa have a drink, one thing leads to another, and they wind up over here. That must have been when your pain started."

With a wince, I nodded. Whether I wanted to think about it or not, they definitely *had* ended up over here since we'd just found them together, but as soon as Daniel mentioned the pain I felt, I frowned. It seemed indisputable at this point what the pain had indicated, but although the sensation was intense, it was also very short. The whole thing had probably lasted no more than a couple of minutes.

In all the times Oliver and I had sex, it had never been that quick. His stamina was a lot better than that.

And if he had been really drunk, so drunk that he wasn't thinking about me or the consequences of what he was doing, wouldn't that have an effect on his 'performance' in the first place?

Trying to be delicate, I voiced that thought out loud to Daniel. "I thought that when men drank too much, it makes things a little... floppy."

Daniel snorted in amusement. "That's true. A few drinks won't make a difference, but if he was totally shit-faced, getting an erection would be harder, so to speak."

That was what I thought. If he was sober enough to come over here with Marissa, to rent the motel room, which he wouldn't have done for any other reason than to sleep with her, and to have sex with her for less than two minutes, he would have been sober enough to remember that he was mated to me.

And if he was that aware of everything, there was no way he would have done it. That was my emotions speaking now, taking over from my logical brain, but in this case, I trusted them completely. Oliver wouldn't hurt me on purpose; I believed that with all my heart and soul.

Something did happen in that room, but with each passing second, I was growing more convinced that things were not exactly what they appeared.

Something very strange was going on here, and I intended to get to the bottom of it. To do that, I needed to talk to my mate.

~**Elijah**~

Once Liz and Storm had left, I turned to my brother in total confusion. "What the fuck is going on?"

It looked like he was ready to laugh and cry at the same time. "Your guess is as good as mine, quite literally. I can't remember how the hell I ended up here, and I'm guessing you don't either."

I really didn't. I remembered being at the bar with Jerrod, and after that, my memories were just vague snippets, like parts of a half-forgotten dream. I thought I remembered being back in my pack in Oregon, and I was almost certain I had been with Liz. I could almost feel her body beneath mine, but based on what she just said and the cold, detached way she'd been looking at me, that didn't really happen.

But why did she say I had been with someone else instead? That simply wasn't possible, and it killed me that she even thought for a second that it could be. Hadn't I proven to her just how much I loved and wanted her? I had certainly tried to. Had my actions at the conference today done more harm than I thought they had, to the point where she would believe something like that of me?

"At least you woke up alone," Oliver added, still looking like he'd just lost his best friend. "Abby just walked in on me waking up next to another woman."

My jaw dropped open in complete disbelief. "What?"

Oliver wouldn't cheat on his mate. There were a lot of things I still didn't quite understand about my brother, but that was something I would bet my life on. He was utterly devoted to Abby, just as I was to Liz, and I knew that I would never do anything like that either.

So why did Liz think I had?

"I don't remember doing anything with her," he told me. "But I don't remember anything at all, and apparently, Abby was in pain through our bond. I just can't…"

His eyes squeezed tightly closed as he thought about it, even the idea alone too painful to go on, and for once, I knew just how he felt. And as I thought back over what he said a new, sickening thought came to me.

Was Liz in pain too? Was that why she thought I had been with someone else?

How the fuck is that possible?

Suddenly, Oliver's expression completely changed, hope dawning across his face as his eyes glazed over. My guess was that Abby was linking with him, and he quickly confirmed it. "Abby's on her way here," he told me when his eyes cleared again. "She's willing to talk to me, at least."

The relief in his voice was almost palpable, and again, I completely understood it. All I wanted right now was to be able to talk things through with Liz, even though I had no idea what I would say. I still didn't understand a thing that was going on.

That news seemed to revitalize Oliver and he began looking around the room, pulling the covers off the bed and looking under it, and peering behind each piece of furniture.

"What are you doing?" I asked curiously as I watched him.

"Looking for clues," he explained. "Anything that might explain how you ended up here and why."

I didn't know what kind of clues there would be, but I took the opportunity to pick up my clothes off the floor and put them back on, my chest tightening painfully as I did. Why were my clothes off in the first place? It couldn't have been because I was with another woman.

It couldn't have been.

As I did my pants back up, I raised my eyes to the heavens, hoping for some kind of divine intervention, and that was when I noticed the small black square on the ceiling above the bed. "What's that?"

Oliver immediately followed my gaze, looking up, and his brow furrowed. In a second, he was up on the bed, reaching for it, and when he pulled it down, his jaw tightened in anger. "It's a camera."

"What?" It felt like that was the only word I was capable of uttering right now, but this was getting more and more bizarre.

His fist clenched tight around the device, Oliver quickly scanned the room and came up with two more identical devices attached inauspiciously to the wall, where they never would have been noticed if we hadn't been looking for them.

Just as he pulled the second one at the wall, Abby appeared in the doorway next to the splintered, broken door, along with a man I'd never seen before. He was a wolf by the smell of him, and Abby quickly introduced us.

"Daniel, this is Oliver and his brother, Eli. Guys, this is Daniel, he's the Luna at the Blue Valley pack."

I had no idea what this guy was doing here, but at the moment, he was the least of my worries, so I simply nodded my head at him politely while Oliver did the same before stepping closer to his mate, somehow eager and tentative at the same time.

"Abby, we just found some cameras placed around the room. I think it means there was some kind of set-up going on here. I don't know yet exactly what the point was or who's behind it, but it made me think of..."

"...your dad setting up the cameras in Liam's office," Abby finished for him, giving him a small smile. "Yeah, it crossed my mind too."

I didn't know what they were talking about, but Abby was definitely extending her mate an olive branch, offering to hear him out and consider what he was saying, and I was both happy for him and incredibly jealous at the same time.

I wish Liz could have done the same, but we didn't have all the history that Abby and Oliver did to fall back on. All she had from me was a few weeks and the memory of what I'd done earlier today. No wonder she wasn't interested in hearing me out.

More footsteps sounded down the hall outside, and a moment later, two uniformed police officers appeared. They looked at the broken door and then into the room at us. "We've had reports of noise and damaged property here," one of them told us. "Are you responsible for this?"

Shit. That was the problem with being on human territory; we had to deal with unimportant stuff like this. Who really cared about a broken door right now?

Oliver quickly stepped up. "That was me. I'm happy to pay for the damages, and we'll leave right away."

"What about the other door?" the officer asked, pointing down the hall, and though I didn't know what he was talking about, Oliver seemed to.

"I'll pay for that one too. The whole thing was simply a misunderstanding."

Oliver pulled out his wallet to show that he had the means to back up his offer, and the officers asked him to go with them to the motel office to sort everything out. He was still barefoot and only wearing his jeans so I heard him ask if he could go get the rest of his clothes as they walked down the hall.

Left alone with Abby and Daniel, I blurted out the question that had been at the top of my mind ever since Oliver mentioned it. "Was Liz in pain tonight?"

I didn't want to know, but I had to. I needed to understand exactly what made her look at me in that cool, distant way.

The looks on their faces told me everything I needed to know before they said a word, and I felt like I was going to be sick. "She was really suffering, Eli," Abby told me warily, but not completely without sympathy. "Are you saying you don't remember anything either?"

I shook my head vigorously. "Nothing about any other woman, I swear."

She and Daniel exchanged glances. "Why would someone want to set *both* of you up?" Abby wondered out loud as she looked back at me.

I had no idea, but if I found out that someone had messed with my relationship with Liz on purpose, there was going to be hell to pay.

Without her, I had nothing left to lose.

Chapter Twelve

~Marissa~

From the front seat of our car, hidden in shadows in the darkest part of the parking lot, Jerrod and I watched in silence as people went in and out of the motel rooms we'd vacated. I had still been pulling my clothes back on when Jerrod appeared back in the room where Oliver and I were discovered.

"We've got to go," he announced as he did a quick look around the room to make sure I hadn't forgotten anything, which was unusually thoughtful for him. "They found Elijah and Oliver's about to have a meltdown. It's best if we just leave them to it."

Though he didn't say he was concerned, I could hear the touch of worry in his voice, and he only grew more tense as we watched Abby and the guy she was with go back inside and the police officers show up. His hands were gripping the steering wheel even though we weren't moving, and I could see his knuckles growing white as he clamped down harder, his jaw clenching at the same time.

Finally, he looked over at me with an expression I'd never seen on his face before: vulnerability.

"I think we might have screwed this up," he admitted.

I had, unfortunately, come to the same conclusion. "Abby didn't seem to stay mad at him for very long. And if the police do a blood test..."

"They shouldn't jump straight to that," he said, but his tone was lacking its usual confidence. He knew a blood test was a possibility. "With werewolf metabolism, the drug should be out of their bloodstream soon. The effects of it were already gone by the time they woke up. Hopefully it will disappear entirely before they can get to a clinic."

The part about the effects wearing off was true. When Oliver woke up, he was no longer confused. He just looked genuinely horrified to see me in bed next to him, begging me to tell him that we didn't have sex, sounding like sleeping with me was the worst thing he could possibly imagine, which did not help my bruised ego in any way.

No one had paid me any attention when they all burst into the room either. I wasn't sure Abby even glanced at me; her eyes had been entirely fixed on her mate. I could have literally been anyone, and Oliver left without a backward glance, making the idea that he would seek comfort from me, as I'd hoped, seem like a ridiculous pipe dream.

It felt like we might have misjudged this, and along with what happened with Elijah and my growing guilt over having dragged another couple into the whole scheme, not to mention the way it felt when Jerrod and I had sex afterwards, my emotions were all over the place. I didn't know which way was up or down right now, but there was one thing that was starting to become pretty clear to me.

"I kind of wish we could start this night over again and do it differently."

My words were quiet, but I expected Jerrod to jump on them anyway. He always had in the past if I said something he disagreed with, but now, to my real surprise, he simply looked over at me with something that might almost be called sympathy.

"It's no use wishing for that," he said, and though his words were blunt, they weren't unkind. They were simply a statement of fact. "What's done is done. We just have to spin it the best we can now."

"Have you ever had any big regrets before?" I asked him with genuine curiosity. I'd never cared about getting to know more about him or his past before, but it seemed like it might be prudent now. How did he usually react in this kind of situation?

He stared at me for a long moment before answering. "Yeah, there are some things I would do differently if I could."

"Like what?" I pressed, wanting specifics.

"A few different things," he replied vaguely, but seeing I wasn't satisfied, he begrudgingly went into more detail. "Well, like the way I behaved towards Abby in high school, for one. I was told I had to stay away from her, so I made sure no one else went near her either. There were a few times when she looked sad or lonely that I wished I could change it. But it had gone too far by then, you know? I had to dig in or it would have made the whole thing pointless."

I could understand that, and I wondered if my father felt the same way when he betrayed his pack. He wasn't a bad person and I'm sure he didn't actually *want* any of the pack's wolves to get hurt. He probably just got in so deep, he didn't see any other way out.

Was I repeating his mistakes?

"What is so great about Abby?" I asked. Jerrod immediately tensed, so I hurried to explain myself, trying to keep my tone non-confrontational. "I mean it, I'm really curious. Why have you been in love with her all these years?"

Tentatively, he looked over at me, trying to gauge if I was setting him up, but I really wasn't. I genuinely wanted to know. There had to be *some* appeal I was missing, and after everything that had just gone down, I was more curious than ever. Why was Oliver *so* devastated at the idea of losing her?

"Growing up as the next Alpha isn't easy," he explained hesitantly, his eyes flicking between me and the motel where Oliver was coming out of the office and heading back towards the room where the others were waiting. It seemed like he wasn't getting arrested, at least. That should mean no blood test, which was one lucky break. "Everyone always had these expectations of me or wanted to be friends with me because of my position, but Abby wasn't like that. She never did what was popular or what everyone else did, just to fit in. She had her own little world, and in it, I could just be me."

I could kind of see the appeal of that. If anyone knew how much work it took to stay popular, I did. There were times I wished I didn't have to, but I'd been doing it for so long now, maintaining that image was simply who I was. I didn't know how to be any other way.

"She used to make up these stories about us," he continued, an almost wistful smile appearing on his face as the girl in question came out of the motel room along with her mate, his brother, and the other man. She and Oliver weren't touching, but they didn't look like they were fighting either. "Her imagination was incredible, and being the hero in her story was pretty addictive. So when my parents told me I had to stay away from her, I didn't want anyone else taking my place. Maybe I was her villain instead, but at least I still had a starring role."

We watched together as Oliver held the car door open for Abby and she gave him a small smile as she got in. *How* could they be making up already? Even if she could eventually forgive him, if their bond really was that strong, how could it only take a few minutes? Was everything we'd done really for nothing? I just couldn't understand.

"She definitely has a new hero now," Jerrod said, mirroring my thoughts in his own way. "The villain never gets the girl, does he? Maybe I should have known that. Maybe I've been fooling myself all this time."

This was definitely the most self-aware I had ever heard him be and though I could have pounced on his weakness as I usually did, for some reason, beneath the dark night sky in the run-down motel's parking lot, I didn't want to. "Maybe he doesn't get the girl in that story," I agreed. "But hers isn't the only book on the shelf."

Jerrod's eyes returned to me, cautious and uncertain, but before either of us could say anything, Oliver's car started and they pulled away.

In silence, Jerrod started our car too and we followed at a safe distance, parking a few cars away from them back at the hotel and watching as they went inside, still not holding hands, but walking side-by-side and speaking to each other quietly. Elijah and the other man were just behind them, and as they all disappeared through the front door of the hotel, I let out a long sigh.

"Well, we're fucked if they figure out what really happened tonight," I pointed out to my mate, though I was sure that thought had already crossed his mind. "And your dad will never make you Alpha if he hears about it."

Jerrod's jaw clenched, but his anger wasn't directed at me this time. He was simply as frustrated as I was. "We'll just have to hope they don't find out, then. He hasn't seen the video yet, and sending that to them might help stop this reconciliation."

Part of me really just wanted to let it go now. It didn't seem like the video was going to do any good, but I didn't say anything as he pulled out his phone and tapped out some kind of message. With a grim look on his face, he hit send and shoved the phone back in his pocket.

"There. It's done."

It didn't sound like he felt great about it, and I didn't either.

We were still sitting there silently when we heard another car door slam shut nearby, and we both looked out to see Elizabeth and the red-haired woman with all the tattoos heading for the hotel entrance. I wasn't sure where they'd gone when they left the motel, but they seemed to be in a hurry to get inside now.

"What do you think that's about..." I started to ask, but I didn't get a chance to finish. Before the women reached the front door, they were suddenly ambushed by a group of large men, all dressed in black, and quickly shoved into the back of a nearby van which took off out of the parking lot.

The whole thing took a matter of seconds. If we'd have blinked, we could have missed it.

"What the fuck was that?" I muttered as Jerrod restarted the car and pulled out after them.

"I have no idea, but I think it's worth finding out."

~Liz~

The stale, sterile scent of the 24-hour medical clinic nauseated me as Storm and I sat silently next to each other in the waiting room. When she burst through the doors a few minutes earlier, the woman behind the desk looked like she was afraid they were about to be robbed. Storm wasn't here to take money, though; she was offering it. She promised a huge donation to the clinic if they processed the blood tests immediately and completely off the record, and the manager on duty quickly agreed.

"Will Alpha Patrick be upset that you're spending so much on this?" I couldn't help wondering as she handed over the vials and we sat down to await the results.

"It's none of his business," she pointed out. "The money's mine, and even if it wasn't, it's to help the men he considers his sons. He would do the same thing."

She was so sure of that, so certain of the trust and support between them after such a short amount of time together, it only made my own uncertainty seem even bigger in comparison.

"Even if it turns out Eli was drunk and not fully in control, it doesn't mean you have to forgive him," Storm said after we'd both sat quietly for a while. "That's totally up to you. Don't let anyone else decide for you, and remember, you've got people who are here for you and will support you no matter what you decide. We're your family now, Liz, whether you're with Eli or not."

"Thank you." That was all I could manage to get out, but I appreciated it far more than I could express. It had been a long time since I had any kind of family to rely on, and I was grateful that she wasn't trying to sway me one way or the other in how to respond to all of this, unlike my own wolf.

The farther we got from the motel, the easier it became to breathe, and my wolf explained to me that some of the distress we'd been feeling there was coming from Eli through our bond.

Knowing how upset you were was agony to him, she told me in a far more subdued tone of voice than usual. *He was in so much pain.*

Maybe he shouldn't have hurt me first then, I shot back.

Out loud, I asked Storm a different question: "If he really was drunk when he did it, how could he have been sober already when we found him?"

"It's part of our physiology as werewolves," she explained, keeping her voice down so no one else would hear. "We heal fast, especially in our sleep. Going to sleep would have helped to rid his body of anything that was impairing him, and it could explain why he was in such a deep sleep when we found him. His body was still fighting to repair itself."

We fell silent again as I thought that over. Though it felt like forever, in reality, probably no more than half an hour passed before the doctor called us in to say the tests were complete.

He returned the vials of blood to Storm, as she'd requested, and handed over pages of tables filled with numbers and letters. "Are you sure you don't need help to interpret those?" he asked warily.

"I've got it," Storm replied, rolling her eyes in my direction. "Thanks for your help."

She handed the man the cheque she'd promised and we headed back out to her car where she tossed me the keys. "You can drive. I'm going to take a look at these."

I made my way back to the hotel while Storm sat beside me in the passenger seat, flipping through the pages of test results and muttering to herself. At one point, she pulled out her phone to look something up, and she must have found something just as we pulled into the parking lot because she suddenly swore loudly, making me jump in my seat.

"Don't do that!" I gasped as I turned the car off. "What is it?"

"Something a lot stronger than alcohol," she told me ominously. "Come on, let's go show the others. Oliver might know more about this than I do."

I tried to fight against the hope that was rising in me as we walked briskly towards the front door of the hotel. Maybe Eli really didn't know what he was doing? Did that make it better? I didn't know, and more than anything, I was afraid of having my hopes dashed once again. I couldn't keep going through these ups and downs, and we still hadn't even started to sort out the whole mess about him exposing me to everyone against my wishes.

The door was almost within reach when, out of nowhere, a strong pair of hands grabbed me from behind and another hand was placed over my mouth, muffling my scream before I could make a sound. Twisting my head around, the first thing I saw was Storm also being manhandled by several men in black, their faces covered in black masks. Understandably, she didn't take it very well. With fury in her eyes, she fought back valiantly, but her efforts were in vain. There were too many of them, and one man managed to inject her with something, causing her to lose consciousness as my heart pounded wildly.

What the hell is going on?

I was off the ground and lifted into the back of a van before I had a chance to even begin to figure that out, and the door slammed behind us.

"Drive!" a deep voice from behind me ordered and the van took off with me and the unconscious Storm inside. A gag was quickly fixed in place over my mouth to replace the man's hand, and panic ran through me as I tried to make sense of any of this. Who were these men? Where were they taking us and why?

Liz? Where are you? Are you okay?

Eli's voice was in my head, faint but unmistakable, and belatedly, I remembered about our mind-link. I was still getting used to it.

Eli, help! They've got me and Storm.

As mad as I was at him, he definitely seemed like the lesser of two evils right now.

Who's got you? Where? His voice was growing quieter by the second as the van sped away. Our mind-link only worked over a certain distance, like a radio frequency, and I didn't know how much longer we would be in range.

I don't know who. We're in a van, I don't know where they're taking us.

I strained to listen for his reply, but nothing came, and my heart beat even faster.

Eli? Can you hear me?

There was no response once again, and I closed my eyes in frustration. I wasn't sure if he heard that last part and even if he had, I hadn't given him much to go on.

"Cuff her," the same voice from before said as we took another sharp corner, and my arms were quickly yanked behind my back and hand-cuffs attached. These were no ordinary cuffs, though. They seemed to burn into my skin and my wolf whimpered in my head.

Silver.

These men must know what we were, and as I sniffed the air, I quickly realized they were werewolves too. I hadn't been paying any attention to their scents when they showed up, I had been too thrown off by the whole thing.

"Should we inject her too?" a different voice asked.

"I don't know what it would do to a wolf as strong as hers," the first man replied. "I'd rather not. The silver will keep her under control for now, and she's got no fight in her anyway."

That wasn't true; I did want to fight, I just no longer felt like I knew who or what I was fighting for. If this was all part of being a werewolf, I was beginning to wish I'd never found out I was one at all.

~Oliver~

Though the distance between me and Abby was killing me, not being able to reach out and take her in my arms, I was so grateful she was here with me, talking things through and trying to figure it out. No one in the world would blame her for being furious with me right now, but there was more to her than that; she could see as well as I could that something wasn't entirely right here, and although I knew her emotions were all over the place since I could feel them through our link, she was doing her best to stay calm and rational.

That was the brilliant Luna-to-be that I knew.

"Whose name was the room rented in?" she asked me on the way back to the hotel. She was guessing that I looked it up when I went to the motel office with the police officers to sort out the damage we'd caused to the doors, and she was completely right. That was the first thing I'd done when I got there.

"Mine," I admitted. It hadn't made me happy to see that, but there was no point in lying about it. "But the room was paid for with cash, and there's no cash missing from my wallet. Other than the drinks I ordered at the bar, I've got exactly as much as I left the hotel with earlier. I know there's no way I can prove that, but..."

"I believe you."

Those words were quiet but they might have been one of the best things I ever heard. She had every reason *not* to believe me right now after walking in on me as she did, but she was taking me at my word anyway, and it honestly meant the fucking world to me.

"The room we found Elijah in was also under my name," I added, which, to my mind, was the more interesting fact. "Why would I have paid for Eli's room? I didn't even see him at the bar and he got to the motel before me. He left with Jerrod, so if Elijah was too drunk or sick or whatever to sign out the room himself, why would Jerrod have put it in my name?"

"It doesn't make a lot of sense," Abby agreed as she looked out the window at the darkened city streets. She was still subdued, not her normal, energetic self, but I would take it. She was here and she was talking to me, that was good enough for me right now. "Why did you have a drink with Marissa?"

That was a good question, and if I could go back and do the night over again, I would definitely change that part. Since I couldn't, I simply told my mate the truth, as always. "I felt sorry for her. She was telling me how unhappy she was with her mate, and I was trying to be supportive. That's all that happened. There was *no* attraction there, not even a little. I only went to the motel with her to find Elijah."

"She's not happy with her mate?"

I recognized that note of empathy in her voice and I immediately shook my head at her. "Don't do that, Heels. Don't go feeling bad for her. Whatever happened tonight, you're the victim here, not her."

"I'm the one who put them together in the first place..." she started, but I didn't let her finish.

"No, the Moon Goddess put them together in the first place. You just tried to put them back together, with the kindest heart and the best of the intentions, so if it's not working out, that's 100% on them and not you. Don't feel guilty about it for even a second."

We arrived back at the hotel and went inside along with Elijah and Daniel, the latter of whom quickly said goodnight to us once we were inside. "My mate will be wondering where I am," he told us, giving Abby a quick hug. "I imagine you want me to keep all this to myself, so I'll have to come up with some other reason why it took us hours to get out of the escape room."

"If you could keep it quiet, I'd appreciate that," I told him. "At least until we figure out exactly what happened."

"You got it," he promised.

"Thank you for your help tonight," Abby said. "I'm sorry you got dragged into all this."

"I've got a feeling that being friends with you is never going to be dull," he teased her. "Anyway, you know where I am if you need me. Goodnight."

He seemed like a good guy, and I was glad Abby had some support with her tonight. I would have to find out exactly how they got to know each other in the first place, but their meeting wasn't really top of my mind at the moment. For now, Abby, Elijah and I headed back to Elijah's room to continue our conversation and wait for Storm and Liz, and almost as soon as we stepped inside, Abby's phone buzzed.

"Maybe this is Liz now," she suggested as she pulled out her phone and opened the message. As she looked down at the screen, her face immediately went pale and I could almost feel the wave of nausea that hit her, the same horrible feeling washing over me through our link.

"What is it, Heels?" I quickly took the phone from her, and my stomach dropped as I got a look at what she was seeing.

On the screen was a video of me and Marissa, in bed, wearing very little, and me looking like a man who very much knew what he was doing and wanted to be there.

How the hell is this possible?

I stared at the screen in disbelief and horror, my mind shutting down for just a second in the wake of this new proof of my infidelity. My heart thudded painfully hard in my chest and there was a ringing in my ears. It reminded me very much of how I felt when I saw the video of what looked like Abby and Liam together.

And, just like they did then, gradually, little doubts began to creep in.

"Wait, the cameras were set up in the *other* room, the one Elijah was in. How could this be me?"

Elijah grabbed the phone from me to see what we were looking at and he immediately grimaced. "Well, it sure as fuck isn't me. I don't even know this woman."

"It's got to be one of you," Abby pointed out quietly, her arms wrapped around her stomach like she was about to be sick. "And you both at least kissed someone else tonight, whether you want to believe it or not. The bond doesn't lie."

Elijah opened his mouth to reply but before any words came out, he inhaled sharply, putting his hand to his chest.

"What's wrong?" Abby asked, her brow furrowing in concern.

"I think it's Liz," he muttered just before his eyes glazed over, letting us know he was speaking to her through his mind-link.

His face grew paler and the concern on his face grew deeper as he continued to communicate with her, until finally his eyes cleared and he looked up at us in confusion and fear.

"She says someone has taken her and Storm."

"Taken them?" I repeated in bewilderment. "Who's taken them? Where?"

"I don't know." The frustration on his face was clear, along with his growing panic. "I lost the link, she's not answering."

This night was just one fucking thing after another. "I better go get my dad if Storm's involved," I said, giving Abby an apologetic look. "I know we're not done here."

"Just go," she assured me. "This whole mess will still be here once Storm and Liz are safe."

That was what I was afraid of, but for now I had to push it out of my mind as I went to wake my father. How much worse could this night get?

Chapter Thirteen

~Jerrod~

The van with the two women inside didn't go far. After driving along the main streets of the city for about five minutes, it turned off into an industrial area and I switched off my car lights as I followed them. Since it was the middle of the night, there was no one else around and I didn't want it to be too clear that we were on their tail.

"Well, this looks like something out of every mafia movie ever," my mate muttered beside me as the van stopped in front of a low, long building and the men jumped out. They carried the red-haired woman, who appeared to be unconscious, and shoved Elizabeth, who was now restrained, out of the van and into the building, the door slamming closed behind them.

Making out many details in the dim moonlight was difficult, and I couldn't see their faces which were all covered in masks, but they were either well-built humans or werewolves, and instinct told me it was the latter. It seemed like far too much of a coincidence that anyone else should just happen to stumble upon a powerful she-wolf and decide to kidnap her, and I didn't believe in coincidences anyway.

They must have been waiting for her outside the hotel and whatever they wanted her for, I couldn't imagine their intentions were good news for her.

I glanced over at Marissa, trying to judge what she was thinking. This night was the most time we'd ever spent together in one stretch and, surprisingly, I was glad she was here. Her company was better than being alone. "We could just drive away," I told her now. "It doesn't technically involve us."

She chewed on her bottom lip as she thought it over. "Technically, it doesn't, but she's already had a pretty rotten night because of us. It doesn't need to get any worse."

That was surprisingly empathetic of her, and I actually felt the same way; making her think her mate was cheating on her was one thing, but if her safety was actually being threatened, that was something I couldn't just ignore.

Maybe I did have a conscience after all. That was a surprise to me too.

Pulling out my phone, I dialed Elijah's number. It rang a few times and went to voicemail, so I tried again, and again, but there was still no response.

"He's probably ignoring you because of what happened earlier," Marissa pointed out. "Send him a text."

As she suggested, I typed out a quick message: *Your mate is in danger. I know where she is.*

"That sounds like a ransom note!" Marissa exclaimed as she read over my shoulder, but rather than mocking me as she used to, she just sounded concerned. "Don't make it sound like you're the one who took her."

"What do you want me to say, then?"

She grabbed the phone from me and rewrote it: *Your mate was abducted. I followed them but there's too many for me to take on alone. Bring backup.*

"He might still think this is a setup," I pointed out. After what happened earlier, he'd have reason to.

"He'll call you, at least," she countered, pressing send on the message and returning my phone to me. Sure enough, the phone rang a matter of seconds later.

"If you have my mate, I am going to reach down your throat and pull your balls up through your stomach," the voice on the other end growled.

That painted quite a picture.

"I don't have her," I explained calmly. "I'm sitting with my mate outside a warehouse where a group of men have just taken her inside. We were in the parking lot at the hotel when they took her so we followed them. I don't know who they are or what they want, but I figured you'd want to know."

"Is Storm with her?" a different voice asked, and it took me a moment to place it as Alpha Patrick.

"There's a red-haired woman, if that's who you mean, but I think they knocked her out."

A deep growl sounded through the phone, the growl of an Alpha whose mate was under attack. "Where are you?"

I gave them my location and they promised to be here as soon as possible.

"So, now we wait?" Marissa asked as I hung up the phone.

I nodded. "There's no point in us going in alone. It would just alert the men inside that they've been followed. I'll see what I can find out about the van and the building in the meantime, and we just have to hope that nothing too bad happens before the others arrive."

~Elijah~

I had never been so scared in my whole life. When Oliver returned with Alpha Patrick, he tried calling Storm's phone but there was no reply. I was desperate to go out and start looking for them, but Oliver pointed out that we had no idea where they had gone so we didn't even know where to begin. Although he was right, it didn't help. I needed to *do* something.

My phone rang as the discussion carried on around me, and I recognized the number as the same one that had texted me earlier about the meeting, meaning that had to be Jerrod's phone. Whatever he wanted right now was nowhere near as important as finding Liz, so I didn't answer, even when he called back a couple of more times.

"Storm's car is in the parking lot," Alpha Patrick announced, holding up his own phone to show us. "I have a tracker on it, like I do on all our pack cars. That must mean they made it back to the hotel at least, and the hotel must have security cameras outside. We might be able to see what happened or get a license plate number..."

I missed the rest of what he said because my phone buzzed again, this time with a text, and I swore loudly when I read it, making everyone else look over at me curiously.

"What's going on?" Abby asked, and I quickly relayed the message I'd just received and who it came from.

"Why am I not surprised that little shit has his fingerprints all over this?" Alpha Patrick seethed. "Call him back and put it on speaker."

A few minutes later, we had a location, but I still had no idea what to make of Jerrod's involvement. Was this some kind of setup? Had he invited me out tonight so that I would be away from Liz, so someone else could get to her? And what about his mate, who apparently slept with Oliver? What was the relation?

There was definitely more going on here than I understood and I hated being in the dark, but right now, my priority was definitely Liz. Once she was back with me, safe and sound, I could figure everything else out then.

Thanks to Alpha Patrick's not-entirely-legal driving techniques, we arrived at the address Jerrod gave us in less than ten minutes, and Abby spotted Jerrod and his mate sitting in their own car at the side of the road. We pulled over next to them and we all jumped out.

"Where are they?" I demanded.

Jerrod looked around. "Is this all of you? I said to bring backup."

"If you don't fucking tell me where my mate is right now..."

"Okay, call down, Elijah," Oliver interrupted, which was easy for him to say when his mate was right beside him. "Jerrod, tell us what you know."

Taking a deep breath, I tried to follow my brother's example and stay calm. It couldn't have been easy for him or Abby to be here with Jerrod and Marissa after everything that had just gone down, but Oliver was focused on Liz and Storm, and I appreciated that.

Jerrod told us about seeing the masked men taking Liz and Storm outside the hotel, which lined up with what Alpha Patrick had already deduced, and he pointed out the building they'd gone into.

"I've found some basic blueprints and we'll go in with you," Jerrod offered in summary. "But we need a plan. We can't just storm in unprepared."

"What's in it for you?" I asked suspiciously. Everything I knew about this guy suggested he did nothing that wasn't for his personal benefit.

"Call it my good deed for the day," he told me wryly. "Or for the year, maybe. I don't want to see her killed, alright? That's all I'm worried about."

Just the thought of Liz in that kind of danger made my stomach twist. Fuck, I wished we'd never come to this conference at all. Helping her take her rightful place suddenly paled in comparison to making sure she was safe and happy.

Maybe that was what I should have been worried about all along?

Changing what I'd done was impossible, though; I had to look forward, and for the time being, that involved getting my mate out of there as soon as possible. For that, I was going to need all the help I could get.

Looking around our small group, I asked for assistance, straight out. "Okay, so who's got a plan? I'm willing to listen."

~Liz~

I probably should have been terrified as the men took me and Storm inside the building, but at the moment, I was simply feeling tired and defeated. As the man in the van had said, all the fight had gone out of me. My whole life had been turned upside down, caught in a tsunami that was not of my own making, and the man I was relying on to be my anchor through it had betrayed me.

Compared to that, being randomly kidnapped wasn't even the worst thing to happen to me today.

We were taken into a large storeroom where the men quickly sat me in a chair and tied me to it with thick, sturdy ropes. *I didn't realize people actually did that*, I thought, my musings curiously aloof and detached. I assumed this kind of restraint was simply a plot device that moviemakers used. Did they actually base it on real life, or did people do it now because they had seen it in so many movies?

Storm was tied to the chair next to me, her head hanging low since she hadn't regained consciousness yet. Obviously, they didn't want to kill us, at least not right away, or they would have done it already. So what were they after? I decided to ask them straight out, my weariness making me bolder than I would have been normally.

"What do you want with us?"

The man in front of me removed his mask, letting me finally see his face. He was older than me, probably in his 40s, with a trim beard, thick eyebrows and dark eyes that looked down at me with curiosity and excitement.

"We don't want her at all," he replied, gesturing towards Storm. "If you cooperate with us, we'll let her go, unharmed. No harm will come to you either, Your Majesty, so long as you do what we say."

Your Majesty? *Shit.*

I knew these men were werewolves because of their scent and the fact that they'd been talking about my wolf before, but I hadn't put it together that they had taken us because of what Eli had revealed about me earlier. It looked like there was nothing random about this at all. Had they been waiting for me outside the hotel all night?

"You still haven't answered my question," I pointed out, my irritation with this whole situation starting to grow. Were there *any* men out there who didn't think they had the right to tell me what to do? "What do you want?"

"We only want what you want," he assured me nonsensically. "We want to put you in the position of power where you belong. I'm sorry we had to go to these measures but the stunt your mate pulled today forced our hand. We were hoping to approach you under more favourable conditions and do this all a bit more gradually, but now that everyone else knows about you, we had to move up the timeline."

What the hell was he talking about? "You knew about me before today?"

"We knew the source had been found," the man explained. "We just didn't know where or by whom until your mate drew a great big arrow for us."

It seemed like Oliver was right: Eli really had put a target on my back, and the odds of ever going back to my normal life were looking smaller by the minute.

"How did you know the source was found?" There was still a lot of this that wasn't making sense to me.

"My Alpha was funding one of the men who was looking for it, a human by the name of Darryn Reeves. He never knew werewolf money was funding him, he simply thought he had an anonymous benefactor. He was getting very, very close, and then he disappeared. A short time later, a Beta at another pack started doing research into the relationship between the royal family and their relatives who acted as guardians for them. My Alpha's not stupid; he put two and two together and realized the source must have been claimed."

I knew exactly what he was talking about now; Eli had told me all about Darryn Reeves. Along with other things, he was the man who had kidnapped Oliver, thinking he was Eli, and injected him with something that knocked his wolf out temporarily. Was that what they'd given Storm?

And the Beta who'd been doing research must have been Abby's dad. She told me that she had spoken to him a little bit about what she was meant to be doing to protect me, based on the connection between us.

The man continued speaking: "The Beta was from a pack attending this conference, so we came here hoping to get some more clues, and we got a whole lot more than that."

"Well, you've got the wrong girl," I told him firmly. "I don't have any interest in being Queen. So whatever grand scheme you've got, you can do it without me because I'm not going with you."

My declaration seemed to make little impression on him. "It doesn't matter if you're 'interested' or not. You *are* the Queen. The power is already in you. We'll teach you how to use it and what you should use it for. We want to work with you, Your Majesty. With our guidance, you can have everything you ever dreamed of"

"You have no idea what my dreams are." His words reminded me of nothing so much as the things Liam used to say to me, how he was going to teach me to be a great writer so long as I did what he said, and suddenly, my apathy and weariness were gone. In their place, a new fire flowed through my veins like molten lava. "If I *am* the Queen, like you say, then my needs come first."

"Of course they do," he agreed in that condescending, mansplaining way that men almost always spoke to me. "We will provide everything you need, in return for your cooperation."

"That won't work since what I truly need is freedom. I'm not your puppet or anyone else's, so you're going to let me and my friend go. *Right. Now.*"

Power flowed through my body and suddenly, the ropes holding me began to strain and fray, and the man in front of me looked down at them in disbelief.

"How is she doing that?" he asked the others who were still wearing their masks. "The silver should dull her strength."

*This **is** our dulled strength,* my wolf snarled in my head. *Show him, Liz.*

With a roar of frustration, I broke the ropes entirely and all the men took a step back.

"Inject her, now!" the man ordered.

"I thought you said..." one of the others began, but he was quickly cut off.

"I know what I said, but we can't let her leave. We'll just have to take the risk."

The second man pulled out a syringe, eyeing me nervously as I simply raised my eyebrows at him, daring him to come closer.

"I wouldn't do that if I were you," a new voice growled, and I turned to see Eli and Abby standing at the door. I had no idea how they found us, but I was glad to see them anyway. "Let her go."

Instead of being upset with their arrival, the man's face lit up in relief before his eyes quickly clouded over in a mind-link. "We were going to pick you up later," he told Eli. "You've saved us the trouble by coming here yourself."

More men came out of the woodwork, others I hadn't even realized were there since I'd been so focused on the man speaking to me, and Eli and Abby were quickly surrounded.

Eli, however, didn't look concerned. "You think you're the only one with backup?" he taunted, his face hard and cold. "No one tells my mate what to do. If this is the game you want to play, let's play."

~Oliver~

I tried not to breathe as we waited for Elijah's signal, partly because I didn't want to give our position away, but more because I didn't want to smell Marissa's perfume. Though it wasn't easy, I was trying not to think about everything that had happened earlier and especially the video that had been sent to Abby. I didn't think the guy in the video was me and I sure as hell didn't want it to be, but Abby had felt *something*, so I couldn't deny the possibility. The thought made me sick, as did the scent of Marissa's perfume which reminded me of it with every breath. She was right beside me with Jerrod on her other side and my dad on mine, the four of us standing with our backs to the wall, hidden in shadow so we wouldn't be seen if anyone happened to come by.

Jerrod had shown us the layout of the building from some blueprints he'd found. "This is the main room and it's deep enough into the building that I would bet it's where they've taken them. There are alternate entrances here and here," he pointed out. "There's a chance they might have someone on all the doors, but I'm guessing not. This isn't an entrenched position; nobody knew about Elizabeth until earlier today so they haven't had time to dig in too deep. I think this is just a temporary hideout so we don't need to worry too much about security aside from the main route in and out of the building."

Despite myself, I was impressed with his reasoning. I wasn't sure I'd have thought of all that, but then, I wasn't someone who regularly thought about how I would defend myself if I kidnapped someone's mate. That seemed much more in Jerrod's wheelhouse.

As much as I hated being around both him and Marissa right now, I had to put those feelings aside to focus on getting Liz and Storm back and outwardly, at least, it seemed they were doing the same. Like Elijah,

I also wondered if there was some kind of catch to Jerrod and Marissa agreeing to help us, but I had to admit that we wouldn't have had a clue where to begin looking if they hadn't gotten in touch with us.

I really hoped this wasn't some kind of trap.

Once we were all clear on the plan, we split into two groups, each of which went through one of the two back entrances to the building. Abby went with Elijah so that she could keep me updated on what was happening since my brother had no pack link to any of us, and her voice burst into my head now.

They're here. We can see them. Storm's unconscious, but they both seem okay.

That was good news and I quickly shared it with my dad, whose eyes filled with relief even as his face remained stoic. Despite his outward control, he must be panicking at the idea of his mate being in danger. They had only just found each other after waiting so long, and I was not going to let him lose another mate, nor was I about to let any harm come to Liz. We needed to get them both out of here safely.

There are seven of them that I can see, Abby told me next and quickly gave me their relative positions in the room. In a whisper, I relayed all that to my companions and we quickly divided responsibility for all of them while we waited for the signal.

A few seconds later, that sound came: a loud, piercing whistle that filtered through the door in front of us, and with a quick nod to each other, we burst into the room.

As planned, Jerrod and Marissa shifted into their wolves while my dad and I went for Storm and Liz. In the distraction that our entrance caused, Abby shifted, and Elijah landed a solid punch on the man standing in front of him.

"Are you okay?" I was with Liz in a matter of seconds, taking in the broken ropes at her feet and the silver cuffs around her wrists as I helped her to her feet. Next to me, my dad was pulling apart the ropes that bound Storm.

"I'm fine," she told me, but despite her words, her body was trembling. "How did you find us?"

"I'll explain later. For now, we just need to get you out of here…"

I didn't get to finish that sentence before another loud whistle sounded, but this time, it didn't come from our side. A large man, not wearing a mask like the rest of them, was now standing beside Elijah, the barrel of a gun pressed to my brother's head as Elijah struggled against the two other men who were holding him.

"I really wanted to do this the easy way," the man with the gun growled, looking between us all before focusing back on Liz. "There are silver bullets in this gun. If you don't call the others off and come with us now, he dies."

"She doesn't answer to you, you son of a bitch," Elijah snarled before looking over at his mate apologetically. "She can make her own decisions and no one has the right to try to make them for her. Not even me."

"Shut up," the man yelled at him, but my brother wasn't done yet.

"You're the one threatening my life. If I'm about to die, there are some things I need to say first."

"Eli, maybe this can wait…" Liz began, but he shook his head.

"No, it can't. These might be my last words, and I need to say them to you. I've been an idiot, Liz. A complete, fucking moron. I truly thought this was best for you and that I was doing it for the right reasons, but I see now that it doesn't matter what my reasons were. You know what's best for you, and I can help you work through it, but I don't have the right to make the decision for you. I'm sorry I didn't see that before, and I'm especially sorry that it led to this."

He raised his chin to indicate the whole situation we were in, and Liz grimaced.

"They were already looking for me before you said anything," she told him. "This isn't entirely your fault. Partly, but not entirely."

Elijah's lips twisted into a pained smile. "That's not all I have to apologize for. I don't know what the fuck happened earlier tonight, but

I'm so sorry I hurt you. I didn't mean to and I don't remember doing it, but if you say it happened, then I believe you and I'm sorry. I don't want anyone else. I haven't wanted anyone else since the moment I laid eyes on you. If we get out of this, I will spend the rest of my life making it up to you, I promise..."

He was cut off this time by a punch to the side of the face from the man next to him and Liz went rigid beside me.

"I already asked you nicely to shut up," the man reminded my brother, pressing the gun tighter to his head as he looked back at Liz. "Stop stalling. What's it going to be? Are you going to come quietly?"

The anger coming off of her at this point was so visceral that I was forced to take a step back. She held up her hands, the ones bound in the silver cuffs, and to the complete astonishment of everyone in the room, they cracked and broke apart, falling to the floor. "I'm tired of doing things quietly," she said, her voice hard as steel as the power emanating from her grew even stronger. "If you know how powerful I am, what makes you think I have to do anything you say?"

To prove her point, the man's head bowed, completely out of his control, and the gun began to lower.

Next to us, Storm stirred, as if Liz's power restored her own strength too, and my dad quickly embraced her.

The man with the gun stared at Liz in awe as his arm which was holding the gun began to shake. "Don't you see? This is incredible, but you need help to control it. You need..."

"I don't need anything from you!" A wave of energy left her, pushing across the room towards the man and knocking down everything in its path. Abby's wolf fell to the ground as did the others around her, and when it hit Elijah and the man with the gun, they staggered over too.

But as he fell, the man's finger must have slipped against the trigger, and the loud discharge echoed around the room making us all wince. The gun was no longer pointing at Elijah when it fired, at least, but when I turned in the direction the bullet went, my stomach sank anyway.

Chapter Fourteen

~**Marissa**~

Nobody moved while the man with the gun threatened Oliver's brother. If there really were silver bullets in that gun, we weren't about to mess around with it, and we didn't have any reason to think he was lying. He'd already abducted two women and knocked one of them out, so it didn't seem like he'd be bluffing about this.

When Elijah started telling his mate how sorry he was for the things he'd done, including being unfaithful to her, guilt shot through me again. Obviously, he loved this woman, and I knew he only made out with me because he was convinced I was her. That was exactly the reason why I put an end to it, and I didn't want him to die thinking he really cheated; I mean, I didn't want him to die at all, but if he was going to, I didn't want it to be with that on his conscience.

So I took a step forward, still in my wolf form, and Jerrod's voice immediately rang out in my head.

Stay out of it, Marissa. We don't know how far he'll go.

The words could have been insulting if they were said in his usual tone, but they weren't. They were tinged with concern instead, as if he really cared about my safety.

I have to tell him the truth, I replied simply.

To my very great surprise, he didn't disagree with that; he simply argued about the timing. *Not right now. Let them sort this out between themselves. If she really is as strong as everyone seems to think she is, I don't think he's in danger.*

His words proved prescient as the power Elizabeth was exhibiting grew stronger, to the point that everyone in the room could feel it, and when she sent it towards the man with the gun, I was truly in awe. They hadn't been kidding. She was the real deal.

No sooner had that thought crossed my mind than I saw the man with the gun stagger back, out of control, and his finger pulled the trigger accidentally.

With the gun aimed directly at me.

Time seemed to slow down as the crack of the discharge sounded and the bullet came towards me, but there was still nothing I could do. The bullet was moving too fast and my wolf's body was too big to move entirely out of the way. The fact that the bullet was silver meant that no matter where it hit me, the outcome was going to be bad.

Is this really where my life is going to end?

If so, my last night on earth was hardly something to be proud of. I had made mistakes, a lot of them, but I also felt I was on the verge of something important, something that might change my whole life for the better, and now, I might never have a chance to find out what could have been.

All of these thoughts flew through my head as the bullet hurtled across the room until, at the last moment, something else blocked my view.

Some*one* else.

Jerrod.

My mate reacted faster than I did and, at the very last second, stepped in front of me, so the bullet hit him instead of me. Blown back by the force of the impact, he fell to the floor at my feet.

Oh, Goddess, no.

Sounds of a scuffle echoed through the room around us as Elijah wrested the gun from the other wolf's hands and Oliver, Storm and

Alpha Patrick subdued the rest of the man's henchmen, but I didn't hear any of it. All I could see was the wolf in front of me, his brown eyes looking up at me almost in apology as he writhed in pain, the silver already seeping into his bloodstream. It must burn like hell.

Quickly, I shifted into my human form and reached out to cradle his head in my hands. "What did you do that for?" I asked him in disbelief, still trying to make sense of what was happening. Did he really just take a bullet for me? *On purpose?*

It was just instinct, his voice said in my head, sounding much more like the Jerrod I knew, and I swallowed down my disappointment even as I nodded. Of course that was why he did it. Why would I even think otherwise?

A moment later, however, his eyes closed and he spoke to me again through our link.

Shit, that's a lie. I guess if I'm going to die now, I might as well come clean, just like that idiot did.

His wolf's eyes reopened and he rolled them over in Elijah's direction, almost making me smile. Even at a time like this, he had no patience for sappiness. I actually kind of liked that about him.

"You're not going to die," I tried to tell him, but that was a lie too. Blood was already pooling beneath him, which was bad enough, but the silver was the real problem and we both knew it.

Don't bullshit me, Marissa. I like how you never sugarcoat things. It's one of my favourite things about you.

"I didn't know you had any favourite things about me." Tears were starting to fill the corners of my eyes now and I thought Jerrod might mock me for them, but he didn't. Instead, the look in his eyes softened even further as he took notice of them.

I didn't either. I thought I had it all figured out, who I was supposed to be and who I was supposed to be with, but maybe... maybe I was mistaken. Maybe you and I could have been good together. I guess we'll never know. I'm sorry.

Those were all words I never expected to hear out of his mouth, or from his mind in this case, and I wasn't sure what surprised me more: him saying them and actually meaning them, or the fact that I agreed with him. This whole crazy, ridiculous night had shown me a few things I never knew before, a few things about what love actually looked like.

It looked like Oliver fighting against the drugs in his body, his heart overruling his mind. It looked like Elijah apologizing to his mate and taking responsibility for the mistakes he'd made.

And it looked like Jerrod, stepping in front of that damn bullet for me and confessing that there might have been something between us all along, if only we hadn't been so lost in the narratives we'd already created for ourselves.

My tears slipped down my cheeks as his final 'I'm sorry' replayed in my head and his eyes closed in front of me, and I wished more than ever I could take back every single thing about this day, everything except for the things I'd learned.

If I could just start it all over, I would do so many things differently.

Maybe we didn't deserve another chance, but damn it, I wanted one anyway.

Just as my grief and regret threatened to overwhelm me, Elizabeth knelt down next to me, not seeming to notice or care about the blood on the floor beneath her.

"I might be able to save him," she told me, giving me a look of sympathy that was completely unexpected and completely undeserved. "I can't make any promises, but I'll try."

~Liz~

My hands were trembling as I knelt down next to Jerrod's wolf's body, but their fluttering wasn't caused by fear. My body shook from the power that was still flowing through me, the power that had been unlocked by seeing my mate threatened.

This power frightened me, even if it made me stronger. How easy it would be to give into it, to make people bend to my will whenever I wanted them to, just as the man who'd kidnapped me envisioned, but that wasn't who I was. My abilities seemed to get even more potent the more often I used them, and I was afraid that eventually they would swallow up everything else about me, everything that made me *me* long before I knew a thing about werewolves or mates or any of the rest of it.

But for now, at least, I could use this power for good to save the life of the man, or wolf, in front of me. Seeing the other wolf take on Marissa's form was a real surprise, and I figured it meant the wolf she was kneeling in front of must be her mate. What they were doing here, I couldn't begin to guess, but it seemed they were trying to help rescue me and I couldn't let Jerrod die because of it, even if he still seemed like a total creep otherwise.

Placing my hands next to where the bullet had gone in, where his fur was matted and stained with blood, I closed my eyes and let the energy flow through me just as it had when I saved Eli a few weeks ago, back on the day he asked me to be his.

His apology a few minutes ago had moved me, of course, but I wasn't sure I could trust it. The part about him cheating was one thing; I believed when he said he hadn't meant to, especially since I knew from Storm's reaction to the blood test results that there was more going on than we had initially realized. I still didn't know exactly what that something was, but I was willing to listen and find out. Eli's impassioned plea that he wouldn't hurt me that way rang true, so that wasn't where the true problem lay.

No, what concerned me more was him claiming he had seen the light about trying to make decisions for me and forcing me into a role I wasn't comfortable with. Though I wanted to believe that was true, he'd made me promises like that before. When he gave up his pack, he claimed he did it to support me, when what he really meant to do was mould me into who he thought I should be.

Now he was saying he could see that was a mistake, but was that the truth? Was it enough? Could I really trust him to change completely, especially when I hardly even trusted the power that existed inside me?

These swirling thoughts in my head distracted me so much that I almost jumped when I heard the bullet hit the concrete floor, propelled out of Jerrod's body by whatever force was at work inside me. From the hole where it had just exited, silver started to leak out, being drawn out of his blood by the energy inside me, and Abby quickly appeared on the other side of the wolf.

"Here," she said to Marissa, pulling off the cardigan she was wearing and offering it to her since Marissa had no clothes of her own at the moment. "Use this to wipe the silver away."

"Thanks." Marissa sounded almost confused as she took the piece of clothing, but she did as Abby said and dabbed at the silver with it, removing it from Jerrod's body so it couldn't do any further harm.

The hole began to close up, letting me know that the poison had been removed from his blood, but there was still the small matter of him already being dead.

Mostly dead, my wolf corrected me. *He's still within reach.*

With that encouragement, I focused even harder on my task, imagining the blood pumping through his body again, his heart beating, the synapses of his brain firing, and my hands began to glow as they had when I brought Eli back.

A moment later, the wolf shifted into its human form, making it a lot easier to see what was happening without all that fur in the way.

And only a few seconds after that, Jerrod opened his eyes and I let go, slumping back in exhaustion after the amount of energy that had taken.

His head was turned towards Abby when his eyes opened and a smile flashed across his face. Next to me, Marissa tensed, but Jerrod's smile was quickly replaced by a look of confusion. "Abby? Wait, where's..."

His head turned to our side, to me and to his mate, and when his eyes landed on her, the smile returned, even stronger than before.

"Marissa."

I leaned back even further, expecting her to throw herself on him as most mates would have done in that situation, but instead, Marissa looked down at him in what could only be called fury.

"Don't you dare scare me like that again! Look what you've done, my mascara is ruined."

Abby and I exchanged uncertain looks, but Jerrod's grin only grew. "It looks the same as usual to me."

They said they had a complicated relationship, and it seemed that was the case. I didn't need to be involved though, so I got shakily to my feet, my knees wet with blood from where I'd knelt, and Eli was instantly beside me, reaching out as if to put his arm around me, but at the last minute, he pulled it back.

"Do you need some help?"

He was obviously making an effort by asking rather than assuming, and in this case, I kind of did need help. The energy transfer had really drained me. "I'd like to sit down."

His strong arm circled me, taking most of my weight as he led me over to the same chair I'd been tied to earlier. The men who had been holding me had all been tied up instead now, thanks to Eli, Oliver, Storm and Alpha Patrick, and the Alpha was hanging up his phone as I sank into my seat.

"I've informed the Council about what's happened here. They're sending a security team to deal with these idiots, and then we can all go back to the hotel and get some sleep."

That sounded pretty damn good right now. It had been one hell of a night.

Storm, however, still had something to add. "Before you all relax too much, there's something you need to see. These are the test results from the blood I took from you two earlier."

She pulled out the papers from her pocket and handed them to Oliver as Abby came to stand beside him. We all watched as his eyes flicked across the sheets before landing on something that made his jaw clench and his neck turn red.

"What is it?" Abby asked, easily picking up on his agitation.

He said a word I'd never heard before and couldn't spell if my life depended on it, jabbing his finger at the paper. Abby looked as confused as I was, so he quickly explained. "It's a hallucinogen, and it makes the person very impressionable and easily manipulated. It's been used in psychology experiments to try to help people overcome past trauma, but the results are inconclusive. For now, it's illegal, and for good reason."

"That was in our blood?" Eli asked, still standing beside me even though I could tell he wanted to see the paper too. "Both of us?"

Oliver nodded. "There's no way in hell it got there accidentally. It would have had to have been ingested, through food or, more likely, drink."

Oliver and Eli looked at each before their heads turned in unison to where Jerrod and Marissa were, Jerrod sitting up now but still recovering. We all followed their gaze to where the couple sat speaking to each other, not paying any attention to the rest of us, until they seemed to feel everyone's eyes on them and turned our way.

"What?" Jerrod asked.

~Abby~

Normally, I liked to give people the benefit of the doubt. It was in my nature to at least *try* to be a tolerant, understanding person, but sometimes, people just went too far.

Liam went too far when he used me, and other girls like me, to satisfy his fantasies while flat-out lying to us about his intentions.

Oliver's biological father Adrian went too far when he killed Oliver's mother and manipulated his own sons into doing his dirty work for him, ready to sacrifice them too if it proved necessary.

And now, if I was putting the pieces together correctly, Jerrod and Marissa went too far when they drugged my mate to get him to cheat on me. If this was really what it looked like, they had just crossed over the line that marked the limit of my forgiveness. I had already forgiven Jerrod for the way he treated me in high school *and* for trying to kill Oliver when we first got together, nearly killing me in the process. Doing my best to see it from his point of view, I put it down to an undiagnosed mental health issue that led to an unhealthy obsession with me.

But now, he was supposed to have been receiving treatment and building his new life with his mate, and instead, it seemed he was still focused on destroying *my* life and causing me as much pain as possible. It even seemed he had a new accomplice in the form of the bleached blonde woman at his side, the one whom he must know played on every single one of my insecurities.

What did I ever do to deserve quite so much of his attention?

Oliver's usually warm grey eyes were stormy and cold as he looked over at the couple on the floor. "I'm guessing you know exactly how this drug got in our blood, so start talking. *Now.*"

"Maybe this can wait until we're back at the hotel..." Alpha Patrick suggested, but Oliver shook his head firmly.

"I'm not letting even a sliver of doubt linger in my mate's mind any longer than it already has. I want the truth and I want it right fucking now."

Jerrod and Marissa looked at each other, their eyes clouding as they communicated through their mind-link, and my anger got even stronger. If they were going to try to find a way to weasel out of this, if they told even one more lie...

"It's our fault."

Marissa's quiet admission was like a red flag to a bull as Oliver took a menacing step forward, Eli close behind him.

"What. Did. You. Do?" Each word out of Oliver's mouth was its own sentence, making it more than clear that he wouldn't tolerate anything less than the full story.

Marissa swallowed hard beneath the weight of Oliver's glare, but she didn't avoid the question. "We put the drug in your drinks, both of you. Only Oliver was supposed to get it, but then he didn't show up, so we gave it to Elijah, but then Oliver did show up and... well, long story short, you both got it."

That was too short. There was still an awful lot she was leaving out.

"*Why* did you give it to them?" was the question out of my own mouth.

Her eyes moved over to me even as her hands tightened around my cardigan that she was still holding. "I wanted Oliver to sleep with me."

"You have got to be fucking kidding me!" Oliver's words were growled as he moved towards them again. Jerrod quickly placed himself in front of his mate, while Eli and Alpha Patrick did their best to hold Oliver back.

"Let them finish," Eli instructed his brother before turning back to Marissa and Jerrod, his voice just as hard as Oliver's was. "Was there a point to this other than being complete and utter assholes?"

Jerrod fielded that one. "I still thought there was a chance Abby might choose to be with me if Oliver let her down."

"Are you fucking kidding me?!" I echoed Oliver's words because there were no better ones I could think of. "How much clearer can I make this? *I do not want you.* Even if Oliver and I did break up, which I can't imagine ever happening, you would still be at the bottom of my list!"

Maybe that was harsh, but at this moment, I truly didn't care. They did this on purpose, they set Oliver up to try to hurt us both. What kind of despicable, manipulative people would do such a thing?

Oliver was livid on my behalf, as well as his own. "She just lost her father, you son of a bitch, and you wanted to put her through this too? After you already made her life hell for years in high school? You have a massive screw loose, both of you."

He turned his furious gaze back on Marissa.

"Did we actually have sex?"

Again, she flinched at his angry tone, but answered him honestly.

"No. I kissed you, but you wouldn't even really kiss me back. The drug should have convinced you I was her, but it didn't work. You pushed me away."

That was a relief for Oliver, I could tell, but at this point his compliance in the whole scheme wasn't even close to my biggest concern. Even if he had slept with her, I wouldn't have blamed him for it, given the circumstances.

Glancing over at Liz, I tried to figure out the rest of the story. "How is Eli involved?"

Filling in the blanks, Marissa and Jerrod explained how they used Eli instead to stand in for Oliver, and how he only went along with it because he thought Marissa was Liz.

"We didn't have sex either," Marissa told him. "What you saw on the video was as far as it went."

"So I stopped you too?" Eli asked hopefully, but Marissa shook her head.

"No, you were completely convinced I was her and you wanted to show her how much you love her... which is when I stopped it. It felt kind of wrong."

"*KIND OF?!*"

I wasn't sure I'd ever shouted so loud in my life, and everyone in the room looked over at me in surprise.

"This is the sickest, most twisted, most self-absorbed thing I've ever heard! You hurt four people..." I pointed to each of us in turn. "... on a ridiculous whim to try to win back people who never belonged to you in the first place."

Marissa blinked rapidly, almost as if she were trying not to cry. "I understand that now. I know it's not enough, but if I could take it back, I would. We've learned a lot tonight, about ourselves, about each other, and about love in general."

She looked over at her mate who put his arm around her protectively before turning to face us. "You're right, Abby. It was a shitty thing to do. If we could take it back, we would, but we can't. All we can do is apologize, which we do. We're sorry."

Before anyone could respond to that, the men that Alpha Patrick had called arrived to take Liz's kidnappers into custody, and Oliver quickly came to my side, wrapping his strong arms around me.

"I'm so sorry you had to go through any of this, Heels."

I embraced him back tightly. "It's not your fault. Literally, it's not, as we just found out."

The extra squeeze he gave me let me know he appreciated those words. "What do you want to do about them?"

I glanced over to where Marissa and Jerrod were now whispering to each other, just as Oliver and I were doing. "I don't know. Right now, I basically just never want to see them again."

"I know the feeling," he assured me. "But there's one more thing I think we need to ask them first."

Liz and Elijah were busy talking to each other and Alpha Patrick and Storm were consulting with the other Alphas while Oliver and I walked over to Jerrod and Marissa, who eyed us warily as we approached.

"There will be consequences for this," Oliver told them both, his voice cold once more. "But first, I want to know where you got the drug."

"What?" Jerrod obviously hadn't been anticipating that question, so Oliver repeated it for him.

"The drug you gave me isn't available anywhere commercially. Where did you get it from?"

"Someone in the pack gave it to me," Marissa explained, but that wasn't enough information for my mate.

"Who?" he pressed, and I began to understand why this was important to him. If the chemical was difficult to get hold of, maybe the person who got it had access to other drugs, like the one that killed my father, for example.

Marissa looked over at me again with that slightly guilty expression she'd been giving me ever since I handed her my cardigan earlier. "Your sister gave it to me, Abby. I got it from Maddie."

Chapter Fifteen

~Elijah~

Liz sat next to me on the drive back to the hotel, which was a good step even though her body language still made it clear that she didn't want to be touched. She didn't say anything either, keeping her eyes focused on the darkness outside the window. I had no idea what she was thinking, and seeing her looking so tense and unhappy and not being able to do anything to help her was killing me.

What was killing me even more was knowing that she looked that way *because* of me.

After the truth came out about exactly what happened at the motel tonight, Abby and Oliver embraced, putting it all behind them, but things weren't that simple for me and Liz. I hadn't cheated, at least not consciously, but that wasn't the root of our problems right now anyway. It frustrated me that I hadn't managed to see through the drug's illusions as Oliver had, but perhaps the reason I didn't was that I wanted it to be true so badly that I actually helped the drug along instead, convincing myself the woman with me was Liz despite any evidence to the contrary.

Maybe that was what I'd done with this whole situation in general.

I saw Liz's power and her goodness and the queen she could be, and I convinced myself that taking on that role was not only what was destined, but that she wanted it too; she just needed me to show it to her. Now, I could see that, although the situations weren't exactly the same, it also wasn't all that different from Jerrod and Marissa drugging me and playing into the things I wanted. In both cases, they were only illusions in the end.

Even though I could understand all of that, I still didn't know how to make it right. I'd apologized and meant it, but that didn't change the fact that everyone knew about Liz now. People had already come for her, and there would be others like them, fanatical people with their own visions of the future just as I had been when I dedicated myself to tracking down the source in the first place. Any chance of a 'normal' life for us seemed next to impossible. Before today, that was absolutely fine with me, but after everything that had just happened, I finally understood that normality was what Liz really wanted and now, I couldn't see how I was going to be able to give it to her.

How could I possibly fix this?

When we arrived at the hotel, I tried not to assume anything. I wasn't sure if Liz would go to Abby's room for the night like she had originally planned, and I wouldn't have argued with her if she did. But when Liz looked over at Abby and Oliver, completely caught up in each other as they headed towards their room, she gave me an uncertain smile. "I guess I better give them some space, which means I'm back with you tonight or we could get another room."

"Of course we don't need another room," I quickly assured her. "You can sleep in the other bed if you want to, and you can just sleep or we can talk; whatever we do, it'll be your choice. I'll follow your lead, Liz."

Just as I should have done all along.

To my relief, she accepted that offer and we went to the room together. She had taken her bag to Abby's room so I gave her an extra t-shirt to sleep in and when she came out of the bathroom after getting ready for bed, I was surprised when she sat down on the bed next to me rather than going to the other bed.

"I'm kind of exhausted," she started. "But I think we need to talk anyway."

I was more than up for that. No matter how hard I thought about it on my own, the only way I was going to know for sure how to make things better was by asking her. I could see that now. "Of course."

I turned so that I was sitting cross-legged on the bed, facing her and giving her my complete and undivided attention.

She was looking a little more sure of herself now than she had been earlier, at least. "I think I want to go home tomorrow. I've had enough of this conference."

"Done." I had no problem with that. All my plans were useless now since she didn't want any part in them.

My quick reply made her smile, only for a second. "And there's something else too, something I've just decided on which I don't think you're going to like."

"What I don't like is seeing you unhappy. If your decision is going to bring you some peace, then it's okay with me." As soon as the words were out of my mouth, a horrible thought crossed my mind and my heart leapt into my throat as I quickly added a disclaimer: "Unless you're talking about leaving me, in which case, there has to be another solution."

That made her smile again, just that brief glimpse of her beautiful smile, before it disappeared once more. "That's not what I'm talking about. Although, after you hear what it is, *you* might want to leave *me*."

There was literally nothing I could think of that would make me want that, and I told her so. "That's not going to happen, Liz. Ever."

"Hold that thought."

She flashed me another quick smile, trying to be brave, but I could see the fear and uncertainty in her eyes. She really thought that whatever she was about to say might change the way I felt about her and I cursed myself once again for ever putting the thought in her head that she wasn't exactly what I wanted, all on her own.

"I've been talking to my wolf and she believes, like you do, that we deserve to rule. She's not going to be happy with a quiet life, never using her power."

Though I had a dozen questions already, I did my best not to interrupt. Maybe, somehow, I felt Liz's wolf's ambitions, which convinced me Liz wanted it too. Had I somehow felt that aspiration through our bond and mistaken its meaning?

"The problem is a life of power is not the kind of life I want, not at all. If I'm being honest, Eli, it scares me. I don't want to be able to decide who lives and who dies. I'm glad that I could use the power to save you and Jerrod, even if he is a jerk, and also that I could punish your father in the way he deserved, but what gives *me* the right to be able to make those decisions? I'm no better than anyone else."

"I have to disagree about that." I gave her a warm smile to let her know I was teasing, kind of. "But that's how royalty has always been, Liz. The kings and queens of the past, both werewolf and human, were no different from anyone else at a fundamental level. They just adapted to the position they were born into."

"And some were good at it and some were truly awful," she added, building on my example. "Some of them absolutely hated it."

I simply nodded, not wanting to interrupt again, especially since she was right. Some people were never suited to it, and if she was sure she was one of those people, who was I to disagree?

"So, my wolf has offered a solution," she told me. "You know how she was dormant inside me until we found the source?"

I nodded again.

"Well, she's explained to me how she has passed from generation to generation of my family, waiting for the time she could awaken. That is part of her power too. She is almost immortal."

I wasn't quite sure I understood. "So she's reborn in every new generation?"

"In a way," Liz agreed. "She was the king's wolf, the last king, the one who lost the source in the first place. When he lost it, she went into a state of hibernation. When his son turned eighteen, she passed to him instead, staying with him in that dormant state until his son came of age. In that way, she's moved through the generations, waiting for the one who would claim the source and restore her power."

This was all news to me, but I supposed it did make some sense as to why the royal bloodline was important in the first place. I still wasn't sure what it meant for Liz though. What was the solution her wolf had suggested?

She explained it before I had to ask. "Since we obviously want different things, she has offered to return to her hibernation and pass to my child instead, when the time is right. It would then be up to him or her to decide if this power was something they wanted to embrace or not, but at least I could prepare them for it. There would be time to make a real decision, not like the kind of ultimatum that's been thrust on me."

This was all entirely unexpected, but I could see as Liz spoke about it that she liked the idea and I had to respect that. There were still more things I wanted to understand, though.

"What does it mean for you? If your wolf is dormant, then you're..."

"Not really a werewolf anymore," she filled in for me, understanding the question precisely. "I wouldn't be able to shift and I would lose all the extra abilities I've gained. I'd have to go back to wearing my glasses again."

She gave me a sheepish shrug as she said it, but that was hardly what I cared about. There was really only one thing I wanted to know.

"What about our mate bond?"

"Well, you felt it even before my wolf woke up," Liz reminded me. "So I think you should still feel it afterwards too, but that's what I meant about you wanting to leave me. If I go through with this, and I really think I want to, I'm going to be human again, Eli, for all intents and purposes. You'd be mated to a human, and I know how you feel about them."

That certainly had been true in the past, but Liz had changed my opinion on that, just as she had on so many other things. "If you make this choice, Liz, you'll be stronger than any werewolf I know. Giving up your wolf is huge. You saw how my father begged and pleaded for you not to take his. It's the ultimate sacrifice, it's…"

As soon as those words came out of my mouth, I suddenly understood exactly what I had to do. There was one way I could prove to her beyond a doubt that I accepted her fully in whatever state she chose for herself, and that no ambition in the world was more important to me than she was.

"You still have the power to remove someone else's wolf, right?" I asked.

Confusion flashed across her face at my sudden change of subject, but she nodded anyway. "Yes, until my wolf goes dormant, I still have all her powers."

I nodded, my heart racing as I reviewed everything in my mind. I had never considered this before, or ever dreamed of doing it voluntarily, but right now, here with my mate who honestly thought I might leave her if she turned her back on the life I had pushed her towards, I knew this might be the best chance I ever had of proving to her just how sincere I was.

"In that case, before she goes back to sleep, I want you to remove my wolf too. You want a normal life, as humans? Then let's do it. Make me a human too, Liz."

Her mouth fell open in total shock, her eyes wide with disbelief as she stared at me. "You don't mean that."

"I do," I argued back simply. "There is nothing more important to me than you. I'm sorry it took all the madness of this night for me to finally realize it, but I mean it, and I will prove it to you, no matter what it takes."

"But… you love being a werewolf."

I couldn't argue with that. "Of course I do, but I love you more. If this is really what you want, then I'm willing to take that leap with you. As long as we're together, as long as you trust that you are what I need most in this world, then the rest of it truly doesn't matter."

~Jerrod~

Even though I knew we were in a lot of trouble, as I lay in bed back at the hotel with my mate in my arms, I was almost glad for the way this whole night had played out.

Sure, I'd taken the roundabout way of reaching a conclusion that I probably should have reached a long time ago, but finally, things were clear to me: Abby was never meant to be mine.

I thought she was because of the way she treated me when we were young, not like the future Alpha but as a trusted friend instead, and the way she made me feel, like there was something special and secret about her that I knew about and no one else did.

But now I could see that Marissa was the same, in a very different way. She didn't treat me as the future Alpha either: she had no trouble mocking me to my face or calling me on my bullshit. And there was part of her no one else got to see either: the part that, despite feeling alone and overlooked, had no problem taking risks and going after what she wanted.

In some ways, she was a lot like me, and those qualities, in the long run, were actually a far better match for me than Abby's were. It looked like there was some logic behind the Moon Goddess' match-making, I had just been too stubborn to see it and too convinced that I knew what everything meant all on my own.

If I had died tonight, not being able to do anything about that belated realization would have been my biggest regret.

I wouldn't say my life flashed before my eyes on the cold, concrete floor of that warehouse, but the parts of it that had to do with Marissa did, and now, I could see it all much more clearly.

"What do you say we start this over again?" I asked her once the others had left us and we were able to speak privately. "I'm not going to suddenly turn all sappy and I don't expect you to either. Hell, I'd be disappointed if you did. But how about we try more of this working together rather than against each other?"

"I'd like that," she replied, giving me an almost tentative smile. "You're actually kind of sexy when you're figuring out how to manipulate people."

To a lot of people, that might not have been a compliment, but I wasn't most people. "And it's kind of hot how you always say exactly what you mean."

I was tempted to kiss her right there and then but that was when Oliver confronted us about the drug and we quickly agreed by mind-link to come clean. Obviously, they were putting the pieces together anyway, and honestly, I just wanted to put it all behind us. He was pissed, and not without reason, but when he asked about where the drug came from, things took another interesting turn.

"I got it from Maddie," Marissa told them, and Abby's face went pale as Oliver looked at her in concern.

"Why is that important?" I asked. Maddie didn't know what Marissa intended to do with it; my mate was smart enough not to go into detail with someone so inconsequential.

Oliver glared at me like I was an idiot, which I didn't appreciate, but given the overall situation, I could hardly take offense. "Someone who could get their hands on this drug could probably have also procured the one that poisoned the Beta."

That *was* a good point, I had to admit, and Marissa looked at Oliver in surprise. "You think Maddie killed her own dad?"

Abby put her hand over her mouth in horror and Oliver's arm immediately went around her. For once, it didn't really bother me. "I think we need to find out," he said grimly. "First thing in the morning, we're going to Forest Ridge to talk to her. Let your team know we're coming."

His words were an order rather than a request which, again, would usually make me bristle, but under the circumstances, I couldn't complain. "We'll go with you," I offered instead. "If this is true, I want to deal with it personally."

There was no need for us to stay at the conference any longer. I'd already gotten far more out of it than I ever expected, and getting away from Elizabeth, who was powerful enough to bring me back from the dead *and* likely to be pissed off at us once she'd had time to digest everything that happened, was a good idea too.

First thing in the morning, I sent my dad a message saying something had come up back at the pack and Marissa and I were heading home. We met Oliver and Abby in the parking lot and they followed behind us in their car while we made the drive back to Forest Ridge. Our truce was an uneasy one; Oliver had said there would still be consequences for what we'd done and I had no doubt he meant it, but for now, getting to the bottom of the mystery surrounding the Beta's death was everyone's priority.

As soon as we were back at the pack house, I told Marissa to summon Maddie to speak with us in one of the meeting rooms. I could have used my dad's office since he wasn't there, but I didn't want her to think she was in any trouble until we had more information.

Anticipation was written across Maddie's face as she walked in, making it clear she thought she was about to be rewarded for providing Marissa with the drug in the first place, but her expression immediately turned guarded as she saw Abby and Oliver there.

"What's going on?" she asked warily.

"Come take a seat," I told her, keeping my voice calm and non-confrontational. "We just have a few questions for you."

"Questions about what?" She was looking paler by the second but she sat down anyway, as far from Abby as possible.

"About where you're sourcing illegal, experimental drugs from, and why," Oliver interjected, and his cool tone sent a chill through Maddie who literally shivered beneath his hard gaze.

"I don't... I'm not..." she tried to protest, glancing over at Marissa as if she thought there might be help coming from that side, but my mate simply raised her eyebrows, making it clear that Maddie was on her own. Not taking the hint, Maddie tried to appeal to her anyway. "You asked me to get it for you."

"I'm not concerned about the one you gave her," Oliver said, leaning forward as his voice turned even sharper. "I want to know where you got the one you gave your dad."

If I'd ever needed a picture of someone about to faint, Maddie provided the perfect image. There was no colour left in her face as she looked around the room from person to person, looking for any kind of lifeline, until she realized there was none.

Finally, she gave in. "How... how do you know about that? They said the tests didn't find anything."

Abby's eyes closed as her sister admitted her guilt and Oliver squeezed her hand even as his attention remained focused on Maddie.

"They lied." Oliver's reply was blunt. "We determined the real cause of death, and now, it seems like we know who killed him."

Maddie's face crumbled as she looked down at her hands. "The drug wasn't supposed to kill him."

"What was it supposed to do?"

"Just weaken him a little." Her voice was still whisper-soft but she was no longer resisting. "Just so he would feel like he needed a rest and decide to take his retirement a little early."

His retirement? A sudden clarity hit me as I realized what this was all about: the Beta position. It was no secret that Maddie and her mate, Grant, thought that he should get it, but I would have never expected them to go to these lengths for it.

And it drove home once again just how reckless and selfish Marissa and I had been too. What if the drug we'd given Oliver and Elijah had some horrible side-effect we hadn't considered? What if it had killed them? Could we have lived with that?

That was the danger of getting so fixated on our own story that we failed to take anything else into consideration. And apparently, that was what Maddie had done too, neglecting to remember that her father was a real person and not just his position, and that by hurting him, she also hurt everyone who loved him, including her own family.

That was the kind of person I'd been, but I didn't want to be that way anymore. At last, that was clear to me.

"Did Grant know about this?" I asked, and Maddie nodded her head, not even trying to protect her mate.

"He had the idea but I'm the one who found the chemical. That was how I knew about the one I got for Marissa."

"Why would you offer to help me when it could implicate you like this?" my mate asked, which was a good question. Flaunting her connections was the complete opposite of covering her tracks.

"The tests didn't show it killed him," Maddie repeated weakly. "And you still hadn't chosen Grant as your Beta, so I thought this might help to convince you."

"Why couldn't you just wait for him to retire on his own?" When Abby spoke for the first time, her voice was laced with pain. "He was going to step down in a matter of months anyway. I don't understand."

Maddie couldn't bring herself to look at her sister. She kept her head down instead. "If the decision was up to the Alpha, he wouldn't choose Grant. We needed Jerrod to make the choice, and after everything that happened with you, there were rumours in the pack that Jerrod would screw up again and lose the Alpha position. We wanted the new Beta chosen before that happened."

My pack really thought that about me? I knew that wasn't the most important thing right now, but as I thought it over, I realized that in a way, this was my fault too. The way I'd played who wanted to be my Beta off each other, dangling the prospect in front of them, was part of what drove Grant and Maddie to such desperate measures in the first place. It didn't excuse what they'd done, not by a long shot, but I could see how my own behaviour played into it too.

I didn't like the picture of me that she was painting, not any more than I liked the things I had done last night.

"Are you going to tell Mom?" Maddie asked in a small, pathetic voice, finally looking up at her sister.

Abby's eyes were full of sadness and disbelief. "It's a little too late to be worried about her now."

Maddie's head dropped again and I quickly mind-linked pack security, ordering them to lock up both Grant and Maddie until my father returned and decided what was to be done with them.

When Maddie was gone, I turned to Abby. "I'm sorry you had to go through this. All of it."

By 'all of it', I meant everything: her father's death, obviously, but also what Marissa and I had done to Oliver, and what I'd done to Abby too back in high school. *All of it.*

She nodded in acknowledgement before putting a question to me: "What do you plan to do to make it right?"

I knew she was talking about all of it too, not just Maddie and Grant.

"I'm not sure," I admitted, looking over at my mate who gave me an encouraging nod. "I need to speak to my dad but I think maybe I need to take a step back and focus on what's really important. I think it might be best for us to have a fresh start."

"We'll be in touch," Oliver assured me, in what sounded a lot more like a threat than an offer of support. "But for now, I'm taking my mate home."

I gave my agreement and they both exited the room, leaving Marissa and I alone.

After a few moments' silence, I offered her a shrug. "That wasn't exactly the way I expected this conference to go."

She snorted at the understatement. "I'm a little surprised he didn't just rip our heads off. Any of them, actually."

I had been surprised at first too, but after everything that had just happened, I thought maybe I could understand it a bit more. "Maybe forcing us to come up with our own punishment is the real punishment. What do you think we deserve?"

She winced at the question, understandably. "I guess it's not really how an Alpha and Luna are supposed to behave."

She glanced back towards the door, making the comparison to Oliver and Abby clear, and once again, I couldn't argue. "The thought has crossed my mind too. I guess we'll talk to my dad when he gets back and see what he says. Right now, though, we didn't get a lot of sleep last night. What do you think about just going to bed?"

That spark of desire in her golden-brown eyes was all I needed. The future might be uncertain, but at least I had a true partner now and somehow, that made everything seem a whole lot easier.

~Oliver~

Once again, I was in awe of my mate. Throughout this whole crazy mess, everything that happened last night and today, she kept her head, not jumping to conclusions, searching for the truth. But now that we had it, now that we knew that her own sister was responsible for their father's death, she looked far more fragile than usual, so brittle she might shatter with the lightest push, and I wanted to give her the space to do that.

Sometimes, we needed to keep it together, and sometimes we needed to just let it go. I wanted her to know that she could always do both with me, that I would be there for her either way, and that we would always, always get through it together.

We were almost at the door of the Forest Ridge pack house when someone called out her name. "Abby?"

We both stopped and turned to see Abby's oldest brother, Keaton, the current acting Beta, coming up behind us. He gave me a friendly nod before turning back to his sister.

"What are you doing here?"

"Jerrod can explain it to you," I quickly interjected. Abby had no responsibility to have to share what we'd just learned. The news was going to come as a blow to her whole family, and if she didn't want to be the one to deliver it, she shouldn't have to.

Her brother seemed to accept that, but he had more to say. "I actually have something for you. I was going to mail it over to you at the Jade Moon pack but you can take it now if you want to."

"What is it?" Abby's voice was quiet and small, not at all like herself, and I knew she was just barely holding it together.

"It's an envelope from Dad with your name on it. I found it in his office when I was cleaning up after... well, you know."

We certainly did know, and though I wasn't sure what the contents might be, I was sure Abby would want to see it eventually if not right this moment, so I stepped in. "Go and get it, we'll wait here."

When he walked away, Abby looked up at me sadly. "It's probably just the information he looked up for me about Liz's family and our family."

"Could be. Let's wait and see." I couldn't say for sure, but it would be better to have it than to wonder about it later.

Her brother returned in a couple of minutes, handed the letter-sized manilla envelope over and wished us a safe trip home. Abby held the envelope tightly in her lap as I drove us off Forest Ridge land and out onto the highway, heading for home.

For at least ten minutes, she kept silent, her breathing uneven as she looked out the window. Though keeping silent was hard for me, I kept my mouth shut, not wanting to interrupt whatever she was thinking about. She knew I was here for her, and I knew she liked to process things on her own. I would wait until she was ready to share whatever she was thinking about with me.

"Maybe there's something in the water there," she finally said. "First Jerrod and now Maddie. What makes people do things like that? How can they be so selfish? It doesn't make any sense."

Affection ran through me as I glanced over at her. "It doesn't make sense to you because it's not the kind of person you are, Heels. I know that when you saw me and Marissa in bed together, you had a moment of doubt, and I totally get that. I know what it looked like. But I would never, ever choose someone like her over you because the difference between the two of you is far more than skin deep. It doesn't shock me that she would do what she did; it's still surprising and ridiculous, but with everything I know about her, it's plausible. Whereas you would never cause someone else pain on purpose. You simply don't have it in you, Abby, and that's an amazing thing. It's one of my very favourite things about you, and so I don't ever want it to make sense to you how anyone could do those kinds of things. I don't want you to ever understand it because I love your pure heart just as it is."

Her hand slid over onto my thigh, giving it a squeeze as I kept my hands on the steering wheel. "I love your heart too," she whispered.

We fell into silence again as she continued to think things over, and after a few more minutes, I gestured down to the envelope in her lap. "Why don't you open it and see what it is?"

The envelope crinkled as she opened it up, sliding out a few sheets of white paper. From the corner of my eye, I could see there were a few printed pages of typewritten text accompanied by a handwritten note, almost a page long.

"It's the information I asked for, like I thought," Abby said, flipping through the printed pages. "Everything he could find on the royal bloodline and our family history."

That could be interesting, but I knew her mind wasn't focused on that right now. "What does the note say?"

Her fingers trembled a little as she held up the handwritten page and began to read it out loud.

Dear Abby,

I was going to call you to share this information, but I thought you would want to read through everything yourself. I could send it by email, but I know you always get excited to get some real mail too, so I thought I'd do it this way instead. I hope it brings a smile to your face.

The information about the royal bloodline and our family is all news to me and it's fascinating, I'm sure you'll agree. But what struck me the most was how it talks about the way the guardian is chosen.

Not everyone in our family is automatically a guardian. It's not the oldest either, as is the case with the royal wolf themselves. Instead, the wolf chosen for the task is the one that the royal wolf believes is best suited to the responsibility. You might think that's the strongest or the bravest or the smartest, but it's not purely because of any of those things either.

The legends suggest that the wolf chosen is the one who best embodies the spirit of guardianship. It is the one who can recognize the needs of the royal wolf without needing to be told, someone full of empathy and compassion, strength and wisdom, with a strong moral compass and a strong backbone too. Someone who sees the value in others but can also stand up for themselves and those they are protecting.

In short, Abby, it's you. You said the royal wolf spoke to your wolf and chose you, and based on this, I am not at all surprised.

I know you have had your doubts since meeting Oliver about whether you were suited to be the Luna of his pack, but I can honestly tell you I have no such qualms. The Jade Moon pack is very lucky to have you. Your mate sees your true worth and I'm sure his pack will as well. You deserve all the love and happiness that your future holds, and I couldn't be prouder of the woman you've become.

This has gotten a little too sentimental, even for me, but these are things I've wanted to say for a while. Sometimes we wait for the perfect time but it's better just to say them when we have the chance. I love you, Abby, and I'll see you again soon.

Love, Dad

There were tears streaming down Abby's face by the time she finished and tears in my eyes too. I agreed with every single word, and I could only imagine how much it meant for Abby to have those words from her father, in writing, to keep and cherish forever.

"He's right, you know," I said when I thought I could speak again without my voice wobbling. "The pack is lucky to have you, almost as lucky as I am."

I expected her to blush or look away or change the subject as she usually did whenever we talked about her being Luna, but looking down at the paper in her hands, she nodded instead. "I think I have to stop being afraid of it and stop comparing myself to anyone else. We've been through so much together already, Oliver, and we're still here, still as strong as ever. We can handle the rest of it too, I'm sure."

The certainty in her voice filled me with warmth from head to toe. "You bet your sexy ass we can."

That made her smile, as I'd hoped, and we talked the rest of the way home, sometimes laughing, sometimes serious, but never holding back from each other.

As long as we always did just that, I knew whatever our future held, we would handle it together.

Chapter Sixteen

~Liz~

Everything had changed in the last 24 hours. When I woke up the day before, I was in the arms of my mate, nervous and excited about the conference and learning more about this new supernatural world that I'd found myself unexpectedly thrust into.

Since then, Eli and I had been through trial after trial, some of our own making and some that definitely weren't, and as the new day dawned, we were both facing a choice that could change our lives forever.

My conversation with my wolf began on the drive back to the hotel last night while I was staring out the car window. *Is using my powers supposed to drain me this much?* I asked her as I did my best to keep my eyes open. It would have been so easy to simply drift off to sleep if I let myself.

Not really, she admitted. *Many thrive off it, but you seem to have the opposite reaction.*

That was when she entrusted me with everything I told Eli, from how she had lived with so many of my ancestors, helping them to wield the special power she carried, to how some people took to it better than others.

So you could share this power with someone else? I asked curiously. *Without hurting yourself, you could leave me and choose someone else to live with?*

It must be someone from your bloodline, the next person in the succession, but yes. We could separate.

We discussed it more when I went to the bathroom to get ready for bed, and by the time I emerged, I was clear about what I wanted. She could simply go back to sleep and the source would rest with her. Other wolves would no longer feel it in me; in fact, they wouldn't sense that I was a werewolf at all. In every way that mattered, I wouldn't be; it would simply be carried in my blood as before, waiting to pass to my child when the time was right.

Once everyone knew that I was no one important, hopefully they would all just leave me alone.

But would Eli want to leave me alone too? That was the piece of the puzzle I still wasn't sure about. If I was nothing special, would I still be special to him? Despite everything that had taken place between us, I still loved him. The thought of losing him forever, of him leaving me because I wasn't the mate he thought he was getting, terrified me. After all this time, I thought I had finally found a love that would last, and if that love was only an illusion, I was going to be devastated.

However, when I told him exactly what I was feeling and what I was thinking, he didn't want to leave me. Instead, he offered to give up his own wolf and embrace life with me in whatever form I wanted it.

Although he insisted he meant it, it had been a hell of a long day for both of us and the middle of the night was never a good time for making life-changing decisions. I told him we should sleep on it and we could discuss it in the morning, so when I woke up in the bed beside him, that conversation was still hanging over our heads.

Eli was already awake, sitting up in bed and looking at something on his phone, but he put it down immediately when he saw me move, his gray eyes softening as they came to rest on me. "Good morning."

"Good morning," I replied, blinking in the bright sunshine. "What time is it?"

"Almost eleven," he said, and when my eyes widened in surprise, he chuckled. "You needed the sleep, obviously. There's no rush for us to check out, we can leave whenever you're ready."

Right. I told him last night that I wanted to go back home and he didn't argue with me at all. He seemed sincere about wanting to make things right between us, even after I told him what I intended to do.

"What were you looking at?" I asked next, pointing to the phone he'd just placed down, and without hesitation, he picked it back up and showed it to me.

"College courses. If you're going to school then I'm going with you, so I'll need something to do with myself. What do you see me as? I was thinking either a lawyer or a stripper."

I nearly choked on my laughter as his eyes sparkled in amusement. "I don't think they have any classes for the second option."

"Not at the college," he conceded. "But I'm sure there are classes somewhere."

"I'm not sure I want other women staring at your body," I admitted, letting my eyes wander over it now. He always slept shirtless and the view was incredible.

A low growl sounded from the depths of his chest. "I like this possessive side of you."

When he leaned over to kiss me, I met him eagerly. Even though we still had a lot to talk about, being back in a place where we felt comfortable to tease and laugh with each other was a relief. There were several points yesterday where I didn't think that was going to happen, and certainly not so soon.

However, we did still need to talk, so I pulled back from him reluctantly. "So, does the fact that you're looking at college classes mean you still want to give up your wolf?"

He nodded firmly. "I've thought it through, Liz. If living as a human is really what you want to do, then I'll do it with you. We're in this together from now on. No more hidden agendas, just you and me, working together."

That was just what I needed to hear, but there was still a tiny part of me that was afraid he was just saying it. Was he trying to manipulate me into changing my mind? I didn't want to think so, but then I hadn't expected him to do what he did yesterday either. Where he was concerned, I felt I could no longer completely trust my instincts.

There was one way to find out for sure if he was sincere, and so I put him to the test one more time. "Let's do it, then."

Surprise and perhaps a touch of fear flashed in his eyes, but only for a moment before he nodded resolutely. "Right now? I mean, it's fast, but sure, if you're certain, then we can do it. It's fine. I'm ready if you are."

Closing his eyes, he leaned forward, obviously remembering how I had placed my hands on his father's temple when I removed his wolf.

And as I looked at the man in front of me, willing to change his entire life for me, willing to give up the part of himself that had been his primary identity his whole life, I knew for sure that he truly meant what he said.

He *would* give it all up for me, but that didn't mean he should *have* to.

I did place my hands on either side of his head, but not in power. My touch was filled with love instead as I pulled him towards me and kissed him again, soft and gentle.

"Liz?" he murmured in confusion against my lips. "What are you doing?"

"Accepting your apology. You don't need to give up your wolf for us to live the life we want. I just need you to accept me for who I am, and now that you've done that, we can move on."

"I don't understand." He looked truly bewildered as he pulled back to see me properly, his eyes searching mine. "I thought you wanted to live as a human."

"I do," I confirmed. "But it doesn't mean *you* have to. I don't want you to give up who you are for me, just like you shouldn't have expected me to change who I was to fit your plans. We don't have to be the same for this to work, we just have to be ourselves and love each other for who we are. And I *love* that you are a strong, sexy Alpha werewolf."

A smile played on his lips, but there was still hesitancy mingled with it.

"I'm not an Alpha anymore," he reminded me. "I don't know what I am. First, I thought the source was my destiny, then I thought my purpose was to support you, and last night, I was convinced I was meant to become human. If it's not any of those things, then I really don't know what the fuck I'm supposed to be doing."

"That sounds a lot like being human already," I teased him. "Most of us don't have a clue what we're doing. Our lives aren't laid out for us like yours are; there are no preassigned roles and no predestined mates. It's scary and confusing at times, but it's exciting too. You can do whatever you want to do... except for being a stripper."

That made him laugh, and I placed my hand on his cheek again.

"And until you figure it out, you still have me. Someday, maybe you'll have our kids too. That's a good place to start."

A look of wonder passed over his face as I mentioned kids. "So our firstborn would be the new royal wolf, wouldn't they? Maybe that's what I'm meant to do, to prepare him or her to take on that role..."

"Eli!" That wasn't at all what I meant, but when he grinned, I realized he was only teasing me.

"Don't worry, Liz, I'm done trying to plan out anyone's life for them. *If* our son or daughter wants to use your wolf's power, then I'll be there to help. If not, I'll be there for them anyway."

"Thank you." This time, I truly did believe that he meant it. Against the odds, he managed to erase my doubts and somehow, our bond felt even stronger than it had before.

"So when are you going to turn your wolf off?" he asked me curiously. The phrasing made me smile, but he was right: that was pretty much what I was going to do.

And I had already decided that too. "Now. This morning. I want to go stand in front of the council again before we leave so that everyone can see and feel that my wolf is gone."

To my relief, he agreed immediately. "That's a great idea. They'll spread the word that you're human and that should make it safe for you to go back to your old life."

That was exactly what I hoped, but as I imagined standing up in front of everyone, insecurity ran through me again. "You'll come with me, right?"

This time, he placed his hands on my head, looking deep into my eyes. "Always. And speaking of coming together…"

He didn't finish that sentence, his kiss making it more than clear what he meant, and as we shed our clothes, the sparks of our mate bond lit up once again. With each touch, the pain of our brief separation was healed, each caress was a new promise for the future, and when he filled me, our bodies joined as one, we had never been so connected.

At last, we were truly together, hearts, bodies and minds all wanting the same thing, and now, it felt like there was nothing that could stand in our way.

~Abby~

One week later

Life never stopped for either the good times or the bad, so all we could do was make the most of each moment we had.

That was the key lesson I took from the whole crazy summer, starting with our trip to San Francisco and meeting Elijah, and ending with my father's death and the insanity of the Alpha conference. Things could turn on a dime, and sometimes the best you could do was hold on and try to ride it out until everything slowed down and you could catch your breath.

And other times, you had the chance to take things by the reins and make your own moments, which was what I decided to do when I told Oliver I wanted to have our own mating ceremony before the summer was over.

"Really?" His warm gray eyes lit up in excitement. "In front of the whole pack?"

"In front of *our* whole pack."

He kissed me hard before pulling me by the hand to his dad's office, where we interrupted Alpha Patrick and Storm in the middle of a rather heated embrace against the Alpha's desk. At least they were still fully clothed.

"I know I said the fact you had kids wasn't a deal-breaker, but I might be changing my mind," Storm grumbled as she stood up and straightened out her shirt.

"Sorry," Oliver apologized, though he really didn't sound very sorry at all. "I should have knocked but I wanted to share the good news."

Any annoyance on the faces of Oliver's dad and stepmother quickly disappeared when he told them the reason for our visit, and Storm came over to give me a fist bump before her smile faded into a look of trepidation. "This doesn't mean another trip to the dress store, does it?"

"I'm afraid so," Oliver teased her. "Being a Luna isn't all leather and knives."

"Well, hopefully I won't have to deal with it too much longer," Storm replied. "Now that you two are making it official, taking over as Alpha can't be too far behind?"

Oliver deferred to me on that one, not wanting to put any words in my mouth, though I could see the hope in his eyes. As I thought back to the letter my dad had left for me and everything else that had happened, I was more certain than ever that here, at the Jade Moon pack with my mate, was where I was meant to be.

"As soon as Oliver's ready. Maybe I can start helping you out with some Luna duties in the meantime?"

Once more, my mate's eyes lit up in appreciation and happiness, and I could have lived on the love in that look forever.

Since we had just finished having Alpha Patrick and Storm's ceremony, there wasn't a lot of work to be done to plan ours. We could recycle a lot of their preparations, and other than picking out my dress, which I got Whitney and Liz's help with, letting Storm off the hook, I didn't have much to do other than send out a few invitations to people outside our pack.

I invited Whitney and Jack, of course. Having humans at a mating ceremony wasn't typical, but they already knew about what we truly were so we wouldn't have to hide anything from them. And besides, they were such an important part of my and Oliver's story, I couldn't imagine not having them there.

My whole family was invited too, minus Maddie and Grant. Maddie had always been my mother's favourite, so my mom was having a hard time accepting that her daughter had caused the death of her husband, even if the end result was unintentional as Maddie claimed. Her maternal instincts were so strong that my mother argued against a lengthy imprisonment for them, which left Alpha Easton with little choice but to exile them from the pack. For someone like Maddie who had always been fixated on seniority and rank, it was a bitter pill to swallow. She might have preferred imprisonment to life as a rogue; I was told she cried more at their sentencing than she did at our father's funeral.

I sent an invitation to Luna Daniel whom I met at the Alpha conference, hoping we could get to know him and his mate, Malcolm, better. I could use all the Luna allies I could get, and I could really see us becoming good friends.

And finally, I invited Jerrod and Marissa, which certainly took Oliver by surprise when I told him my intention.

"Why the fuck would you want them there? No offense, Heels."

"None taken." I knew him better than that. "But this ceremony is looking forward to our future, right? What better way to do that than to put the past to rest? Besides, Marissa probably misses her old pack and would like to see everyone anyway."

"You're too damn nice for your own good." His words were so full of affection that I knew he meant it as a compliment.

Whitney and Liz helped me get ready before the ceremony, arguing good-naturedly with each other about how to do my hair and whether I should have my glasses on or off.

"Oliver likes them on," I told them, which settled the topic in my mind. "And I think I should have my hair down since I usually wear it up."

The dress I'd chosen was a shimmering pearl-and-pink colour that reminded me of the frozen bubbles Oliver made for me when we were first getting to know each other. My jewelry was a gift from him for Valentine's Day, but the lingerie I wore beneath the dress was something entirely new. That was my gift to him later.

As we headed downstairs, the chattering of hundreds of voices reached my ears and Liz squeezed my hand supportively. "Are you ready for this?"

"Completely."

The hall was full of people, all of whom turned to look at me when I walked in, and I gave them all my most serene, Luna-like smile. It could have been intimidating, but it actually wasn't too bad; everyone here was happy for me and Oliver and they were ready to accept me into the pack as their future Luna. I still didn't know all their names but I was getting there, and with Oliver to help me, I trusted it would all work out.

As long as I had the amazing man standing at the front of the room, staring at me like I was the greatest treasure he could ever find, every-thing would be just fine.

Oliver asked if I wanted to write any special words for us to say, but I was happy to use the traditional words of his pack. There were times I thought a traditional werewolf mating ceremony was the last thing in the world I would want, but now, with him, I was ready to embrace it.

As the officiant made the incisions in our palms that would bind me not only to Oliver but also to his pack, he spoke those words to us: "Bound by blood, by the connection between your souls granted to you by the Moon Goddess, and deepened by your own love and devotion to each other, may you enjoy a long and happy mating full of far more of life's joys than its sorrows."

That was all anyone could really ask for, wasn't it? More good times than bad, and someone to help us through the hard times.

The party that followed the ceremony carried on for hours, but Oliver and I didn't see most of it. After we had accepted congratulations from most of the pack, he leaned over and whispered in my ear. "I am dying to see what surprise you've got for me under that dress, Heels."

"How do you know it's anything different?" I tried to demur. "It could be the same thing I put on this morning."

"I know you better than that." His eyes were full of love and lust in almost equal measure. "I know *everything* about you, my perfect mate."

If that was ever true of anyone, it was true of Oliver. "Let's go, then."

With a grin, he quickly pulled me up to the front of the room and said goodnight to everyone, leaving a trail of cheers and whistles in our wake as everyone knew exactly where we were going and why. My cheeks flushed in embarrassment but also in anticipation as we made our way up the stairs to our room, our hands already all over each other.

By the time we finally got through the door, I was already breathless with desire for him. He pulled my glasses off first, growling in approval. "You look amazing tonight, Abby. Absolutely perfect."

"Not anywhere near as good as you look," I protested, hooking my fingers over the top of the waistband of his pants and pulling him to me. He had bought a new suit for the occasion, one that did *not* match his brother's, and it looked incredible on him.

It would look even better off of him though.

I started to undo his pants, working towards that aim, but Oliver shook his head at me. "Not yet, Heels. Not until you show me what you've got."

I pouted at him for just a second but I couldn't hold it, breaking into a grin instead. "You'll need to unzip me then."

My mate growled again as I turned around and he pulled the zipper down, getting his first glimpse of the white satin teddy I was wearing underneath. "Fuck, Abby."

He slid the dress down over my shoulders, letting it fall to the floor, and when I turned around to let him see the whole thing, his mouth was hanging open, his eyes dark with need.

"I know I say this a lot, but that might be the sexiest thing I have ever seen." His eyes drank me in, inch by inch, and I could see his cock twitching beneath his pants, letting me know those weren't empty words. "I don't even want to take it off, but I need to be inside you too, so I guess I'm going to have to."

"Not necessarily." I reached down between my legs, feeling the heat that was already coming off me. I was aching for him already, just as he was for me. "There are snaps."

I undid them now to give him complete access, the pop they made echoing through the room, and Oliver gave me a wolfish grin. "That is the most brilliant fucking thing I have ever seen."

My laugh was swallowed up in his kiss as his strong arms surrounded me, pressing me tightly against his straining erection, and this time when I went to set him free, he made no attempt to stop me. My hand wrapped around his hard cock, warm and eager for me as he pulled off the rest of his clothes, tossing them furiously to the floor. Soon he was fully naked and we tumbled onto the bed together, as eager as we had been on our very first night together, if not more. Because now we knew each other even better, and we knew exactly how good this was going to be.

Being with him was the closest thing to perfection I had ever found.

Oliver seemed to agree as he sank into me, his solid body covering mine and his gray eyes looking down on me in adoration. "There will never be a time when I don't want this."

"I love you, Oliver."

My words and the perfect feel of our bodies joined together drew out one more growl from him. "I love you too, Abby. Today and forever."

Taking advantage of his werewolf stamina, we tried out multiple positions before the night was done. He wanted to see the teddy from every angle, and I was happy to oblige so long as he kept filling me and using those magic fingers against my clit. I lost track of the number of orgasms I had but he definitely set a new record, and I was pretty sure Oliver was keeping score anyway.

Even once we finally lay down in bed together, having taken the lingerie off at last and cuddled up with him behind me, he slid into me one more time. "I think we should just sleep like this, Heels."

"If you're expecting me to argue, you're in for a disappointment."

We laughed, as we did so often together, and then we made love one last time, soft and sensuous and slow.

There had never been a more perfect night.

Chapter Seventeen

The invitation to Oliver and Abby's mating ceremony came completely out of the blue. Jerrod and I were in his office together when it arrived, which was where we seemed to spend a lot of time since returning from the conference, and when he pulled the elegant notecard out of the envelope, we both stared at it in confusion.

"Do you think they meant to send it to us?" I wondered.

It made more sense that the invitation was meant for one of Abby's brothers and got delivered to us by mistake, but when I checked the envelope, it read 'Jerrod and Marissa' in a neat, even script.

"Maybe they want to rub our noses in it?" Jerrod suggested, obviously trying to imagine what he would do in their shoes. "To show us that despite all our efforts, they're still together?"

A week ago, I might have agreed, but now I really didn't think that was it. "Honestly, I don't think they spend that much time thinking about us."

Though I could have taken offense at that, after everything that had happened, realizing that they were just living their lives without bothering about us was actually kind of freeing.

All the anger and resentment I'd been harbouring towards Abby hadn't done me any good; if anything, it ate away at my own self-worth while shutting me off from making any kind of effort to try to build anything with my mate. I'd been jealous of her and I'd projected a lot of my own feelings onto her. I truly believed that she went out of her way to hurt and humiliate me because I was Oliver's ex, but now I could see that it simply wasn't the case. She didn't think about me enough to plot any kind of revenge. While I'd been fixating on her for months, I had probably never crossed her mind.

In her life, I was nothing more than a guest star, showing up for a scene or two, and quickly forgotten.

And in the end, that was a good thing, because it meant I could stop waiting around for my starring role in Oliver's story, which was never going to come, and focus on my own life instead, one that was looking more interesting every day.

"I think we should go," Jerrod said, his mind calculating the probabilities and possibilities like it always did. "It'll prove to them that we've moved on, and it'll give us a chance to speak to Elijah too."

I quickly agreed, first because he was right, and second because I was excited at the idea of spending time with my old pack and all my friends there. I cut myself off from them too, bitter that no one had stood up for me after what happened with my dad, but maybe I had been too harsh. Maybe the time had come for all of us to mend fences and move on.

On the drive over to Jade Moon, I told Jerrod stories about my friends and what growing up there was like, things I'd never told him before, and he listened with real interest, asking questions and making mental notes about who was who. He was actually really smart; not like Oliver was, not with science and formulas and chemicals, but he was smart about people, understanding the relationships between them and what drove people to act the way they did.

We just needed to find the proper outlet for those skills, and I was sure he could accomplish great things.

The Jade Moon pack house was decorated in an understated, graceful way, kind of like Abby herself. She wasn't showy or ostentatious, but it seemed to work for her anyway, and it definitely worked for Oliver.

The look on his face when she walked through the door of the hall in her dress was a look he had never given me, not in all the time we were together.

I had, however, started to see it in Jerrod's eyes from time to time.

We waited in line afterwards to offer our congratulations to the happy couple. Oliver's smile was tight, but he thanked us for coming, and I thanked them both for the invitation.

"It's a little strange to be back here," I admitted, looking around the once-familiar hall and all the members of my former pack. I had spent the last few months wishing more than anything that I was still here, but now that I was, it didn't feel the same. People had moved on, and so had I.

"I hope you get a chance to catch up with everyone," Abby said, and whereas before I would have been searching for some insult in the words, now I took them at face value. She honestly did hope we had a good time.

I wasn't sure I would ever fully understand her, but I could respect the effort she was making to put everything behind us.

And speaking of moving on, Oliver brought it up now. "Have you decided on your next steps?"

We all knew what that meant; had we decided how we were going to atone for what we'd done to them at the conference?

"We're almost there," Jerrod explained. "Hopefully, we can finalize it tonight and then we'll let you know."

Oliver nodded in acknowledgement, and then we stepped aside to let the next people in the line give the happy couple their best wishes. I lingered just a moment longer, watching Abby and Oliver as they smiled and made conversation, and I knew that we had already left their thoughts, fading to the background of their lives where we belonged.

That was fine with me. We had our own lives to be living, and taking my hand, Jerrod led me towards the next stage of ours now.

"Can we have a few minutes of your time?"

Elijah and Elizabeth were standing on their own, talking to each other when we approached. They both eyed us warily once Jerrod spoke, and I could hardly blame them. They barely knew us when we threw a grenade into their relationship, and they would be completely justified in telling us to fuck right off if that's what they decided to do.

But they didn't. After exchanging glances with each other, Elijah gave us a nod. "Here, or somewhere private?"

He seemed to recognize that we weren't there for idle chat, which was completely accurate. "Private would be better," Jerrod confirmed, and we followed them out of the hall and into one of the small sitting rooms down the hall.

Once we were all settled, I kicked things off, addressing Elizabeth. "First of all, we wanted to say thank you for saving Jerrod's life. With everything else that was going on that night, we didn't get a chance to thank you properly."

She nodded, looking a little uncomfortable with the praise. "Anyone would have done the same, if they could."

I wasn't so sure about that, especially given the other part of what happened that night, which I brought up now.

"And we're sorry for everything else that happened that night. I know it sounds stupid now, but we never set out to hurt either of you."

"Only Oliver and Abby," Elijah pointed out, sounding unimpressed.

I couldn't argue with that. "Yeah. That was a stupid thing to do too. I know it doesn't mean much, but we really have learned from it."

It didn't mean much to him, I could tell, and he started to get to his feet. "Well, if that's all..."

"It's not." Jerrod's firm tone caught him by surprise and he lowered himself slowly back into his seat, not out of submission, but with curiosity. "We actually have a proposition for the two of you, if you'll hear us out."

Once again, they exchanged looks, reading things in each other's eyes that I couldn't guess at, before Elijah leaned back and spread his hands in invitation. "Let's hear it."

~Elijah~

The last time Jerrod approached me with a proposition, it ended up with me drugged and making out with his mate who I believed was my own mate. No one could blame me for being a little leery when he said he had another one for me now.

Still, I was curious. There was nothing obvious they had to offer us. Once Liz made the decision to allow her wolf to go dormant, we went back to the conference as she suggested. Bursting into the middle of the meeting of the council and all the highest-ranked Alphas, I led Liz to the front of the room.

"What's the meaning of this?" the chairman demanded as every pair of eyes in the room followed our progress.

"It won't take long," I assured him. "I just need to make an amendment to what I told you yesterday. I need everyone here to take a look and a sniff of the woman beside me."

Immediately, all attention in the room went to Liz, and though her hand trembled in mine, she did her best to hold steady. I had never been prouder of her.

"She's human." The chairman was the first to speak, his brow lined in confusion as all the men around the room inhaled deeply. "How can she be human?"

Whispers quickly circulated, a few questions standing out to my ears.

"Wasn't that the queen?"

"She looks different with those glasses on."

"Did she lose her power?"

"What's happening?"

That was exactly what we'd come here to explain. "Yesterday, I stood before you and told you that the royal bloodline had returned. You felt the power that my mate had. Since then, a few new things have come to light, including the fact that she was abducted late last night by a group of wolves who wanted to use her power for their own benefit and force her to promote their own agenda."

As I expected, that set off another round of furious whispers, but I kept speaking over them.

"But more importantly than that, I found out that the role I'd envisioned for my mate wasn't one that she wanted for herself. I thought I knew what was best without checking in with her first, and that was a mistake."

I offered Liz a small smile of apology and she squeezed my hand in reply.

"Since one of the powers she possessed was the ability to separate a werewolf from its wolf, she has decided to use that power on herself. Her wolf is gone, as you can all see and smell for yourselves. She is human now and the royal bloodline has ended once more. For the record, I still think she would have been an amazing queen. She is compassionate and intelligent and fair and brave and everything a queen should be. It is our loss that she won't be able to use that power to help guide us, but this is her choice and it's one I support fully. She may not be a queen anymore among wolves, but she will always be the queen of my heart."

The words were cheesy, of course, but there wasn't a single mated werewolf in the room who didn't know exactly how I felt. And even if I was made fun of later on, the look in Liz's eyes when I said them made it all worthwhile.

News spread quickly, and by the time we got back to the Jade Moon pack later that afternoon, Oliver and Abby had already heard about it.

"Did you really remove your own wolf?" Abby asked Liz in disbelief.

"Not exactly." Liz explained to them both how her wolf was just resting, undetectable, but how we both felt that letting people believe the wolf was gone entirely was the safer choice. For her to be completely safe, we needed people to believe there was no chance of her wolf resurfacing, and it wasn't a hard sell since no one had ever heard of a wolf hibernating in this way before.

We told Oliver and Abby the truth, and Patrick and Storm too once they returned from the conference the next day, but they were the only ones who knew. As far as the rest of the world was concerned, Liz was 100% human again and there was no chance of our children being anything other than half-wolf, half-human hybrids. For now, that was exactly how we wanted things to be.

Given all of that, I couldn't really guess what Jerrod wanted to speak to me about now. There was nothing left for him here, no powers that he could try to exploit. So when he explained exactly what he had in mind, I couldn't have been more surprised.

"I want you to take over as Alpha of the Forest Ridge pack."

"What?" The question was on the tip of my tongue but Liz was the one who spoke it out loud. "Why would Eli be Alpha of your pack?"

"My father is ready to retire," Jerrod explained. "He's been ready for a while, but he's been holding back until I could prove I was ready to take his place. It goes without saying that what happened at the conference hasn't exactly helped my case."

I could imagine. Respecting the mate bond was one of the most important unspoken rules between Alphas, and he and Marissa had pissed all over it with the stunt they pulled.

"I know that I don't deserve to take over after everything that's happened," he continued, and honestly, I hadn't expected that level of self-awareness from him. Maybe he really had learned his lesson. "But I've seen the dangers that power struggles can cause within a pack. It led to Abby's father losing his life, and I'm afraid that if someone else from within the pack is appointed Alpha in my stead, there will be some who won't accept it. It could lead to scheming and backstabbing, and it could tear the pack apart."

He had a point. I had seen similar things happen in other packs when there was no clear heir; that was part of the reason Alphas were usually so desperate to have their own heirs, going to lengths like the ones Alpha Patrick had gone to in order to secure a child he could call his own.

"Bringing in someone from the outside seems like a smarter move," Jerrod said. "And someone who has already been an Alpha but is currently without a pack makes even more sense."

I could see his point, but I had a lot of questions. "What about you? You're going to be okay with living in your own pack with a different Alpha?"

Jerrod reached over and took Marissa's hand. "Actually, we're going to leave for a while. We think it would be better to have some time away. I've put in an application to act as a diplomatic apprentice with the Council and they've accepted me. We'll be leaving the pack at the end of the week."

An apprentice? That was a far cry from the position he'd been envisioning for himself when I spoke to him at the bar at the conference. Back then, he had pictured himself as chairman, the person running the show, not the one doing the grunt work.

"I'm going to be working there too," Marissa explained. "I've put in a proposal to start up a new support system for she-wolves who are rejected by their mates, to help them deal with it in a healthy way. I wish there had been someone I could talk to when it happened to me."

I could see the guilt in her mate's eyes, and so could she, apparently, since she squeezed his hand in acknowledgement.

I turned to my own mate. "What do you think about this, Liz?"

We had spoken about the future over the last week, of course, but so far we hadn't made any firm decisions. She wanted to continue with college, but despite my best efforts, I hadn't found any courses that really appealed to me. My whole life, I'd been raised to be an Alpha; leading a pack was what I knew and what I loved, and though I didn't regret giving it up to be with her, I had to admit that Jerrod's suggestion held some appeal. The Forest Ridge pack wasn't very far from the town where Liz's college was; she could live with me and commute in for classes, or stay in town during the week if she wanted to and come home on the weekends. It really could work.

But that was only if she wanted it to. I wasn't going to make any decisions that she wasn't completely on board with; that was one thing I had definitely learned the hard way.

"Would it be permanent?" she asked Jerrod, which was a good question. Was he actually handing over the pack to me fully, as I'd done in giving my old pack to my dad's rejected mate, Jenny, or was he asking me to be his regent?

"I thought we could do a trial run to start off with," he told us. "Maybe three years? After that, we could reevaluate. You never know, you might be sick of the pack by then."

I could tell he didn't mean that; he loved his pack just like any Alpha did. But three years was actually perfect for us: that was how long Liz had left in her degree, so by then we should have a much better idea of exactly what kind of life we wanted in the long term, and it would give me something useful and productive to do in the meantime.

"I think this could be great for you," Liz told me, her eyes full of affection. "And you want to do it, don't you?"

I did, if I was being honest. None of the courses or jobs I'd looked at in the last week excited me nearly as much as this did within mere minutes of it being suggested.

"I think it could work for me, but only if it works for you too."

Her smile told me just how much it meant to her that I was seeking her input. "I think it's a great idea."

We shook hands with Jerrod and Marissa on principle and made plans to visit them in two days' time to meet with the current Alpha and some of the pack's leadership team. Jerrod was convinced they would all agree once they met me and he laid out his reasoning, and I believed it too.

This was definitely not the path I'd expected to find myself on when the summer began, but as Liz and I went up to bed at the end of the party, it felt right. I'd misread a few signs along the way, but with my mate at my side and a new challenge ahead of me, it felt like I'd finally found where I was meant to be, at least for now.

Things would probably change again later, but that was the nature of life. And as long as Liz was by my side through it all, I would never be completely lost again.

Epilogue

~Oliver~

Two years later

"Come to bed, Heels." I stood in the doorway of the Luna's office, giving my mate a look that was part affection and part disapproval. "Your characters aren't going to do anything without you. They'll be right there where you left them in the morning."

"You don't know that," Abby muttered back to me, her eyes still on the computer screen. "They have a mind of their own sometimes. I just need to finish this chapter and then..."

"You just need to sleep," I contradicted her, stepping inside the office and walking around behind her desk to place my hands on her shoulders. My thumbs rubbed the tense muscles of her neck and she groaned in pleasure, her fingers coming to a standstill over the keyboard. "And the pups need you to rest too, so let's go to bed."

At the mention of our pups, her hand went to her stomach, her *very* swollen stomach that was currently playing host to the babies that would be joining us any day now. Perhaps unsurprisingly, given my family history, we were having twins, but we didn't know yet if they were boys or girls. Abby had decided she wanted to wait and be surprised, and I was helpless to resist that beautiful smile of hers when she asked me to agree, especially when she was giving me everything I ever wanted.

I had my pack, which I took over as Alpha from my dad a year ago, I had my Luna, and now, in a matter of days, I would have a family too.

Life had been very good to me ever since the day that I ran into Abby in the woods.

Every day wasn't smooth sailing, of course; we had our challenges just like anyone else, but when I looked at the balance sheet, adding up the good things and the bad, the good side outweighed the bad by so much, I think we might have broken the scale. The day she told me she was expecting was one of the happiest days of my life, though I had a feeling the babies' actual arrival might surpass it.

The gentle kneading motion of my fingers was probably more effective at luring Abby away than my words were, but she gave in either way, closing the laptop lid and pushing herself awkwardly to her feet. My arm was immediately around her to offer support and together we walked to the base of the stairs that led up to our bedroom.

Abby looked up at the stairs and sighed. "I think we need to install an elevator."

She was struggling with stairs these days, telling me that the pups put pressure on her bladder that got even worse when she went up the stairs. Our bedroom was up on the second floor, and we usually had to stop on the first floor for a pee break.

"It's only for a few more days," I reminded her. "Your body will be your own again soon, and in the meantime, I can carry you if you want."

I always offered, but she always declined, determined to do it on her own. With one hand on the handrail and the other holding onto me, she took the first step and immediately let out a surprised yelp.

"Abby? What's wrong?" That was a sound she'd never made before.

"I think... I think that was a contraction," she told me, her hand going to her stomach again. "It's stopped now though."

"Okay, change of plan, then. We're going to the hospital."

She gave me a look that was very similar to the one I'd given her earlier, amused but with a touch of disagreement. "You've read as much as I have about all of this, Oliver, or maybe even more. You know labour can take a long time and we don't need to worry until the contractions are consistent."

"I also know that it makes more sense to go to the hospital now rather than going to sleep and waking up in the middle of the night in a panic because you wet the bed."

Her mock indignation was adorable, and I kissed her before she could protest again.

"Do it for me, okay? I'll be right there with you the whole time."

As soon as she nodded, I was mind-linking the hospital to tell them we were coming, and my Beta to ask him to grab the bag we'd already prepared and bring it over to us. With that taken care of, I let myself concentrate entirely on my mate for the short walk to the pack hospital.

"How're you feeling, Heels? Are you scared?"

I really couldn't imagine what this was going to be like for her. I'd read everything I could get my hands on, watched the videos and attended the prenatal classes, but I could never truly understand.

"Of course I'm scared," she told me honestly, giving my hand a squeeze. "I was scared the first time we slept together too, and what you were putting in there was a heck of a lot smaller than what's going to come out now!"

As always, she made me laugh, though I couldn't help defending myself. "I don't know if I would say 'a heck of a lot' smaller."

She gave me a playful nudge, rolling her eyes at me.

"And I don't remember you being scared that night, Abby. I remember you taking charge and having me practically on my knees for you. I remember you being sexy and confident and a dream come true."

"I was still scared," she told me. "But I knew it would be worth it, and I know this will too."

Everything was ready for us when we arrived and while Abby got changed and settled, I called my dad and my brother to let them know what was happening. My dad and Storm were on holiday but were due back tomorrow anyway, not wanting to miss the arrival of their grandkids, although Storm had threatened to maim anyone who tried to call her 'grandma'.

Elijah was with Liz when I called and I could hear her excited squeal in the background.

"Do you want us to come now?" he asked me.

Having Elijah and Liz so close to us was one of the best things about the last couple of years. He and I often bounced ideas off each other, Abby and Liz worked together on their college courses, and the four of us got together whenever we could. My brother and I were still very different people, but we understood each other a lot better now, and deep down, he was one of the best guys I knew.

I had always wanted a brother, and now, I couldn't really imagine my life without him.

"There's no rush," I told him. "It could be hours yet and Abby will feel bad if you guys stay up all night waiting. Get some sleep and come over first thing in the morning. Can you also let Abby's mom know what's happening?"

He agreed to that and I returned to Abby after hanging up. As we expected, there was a bit of a wait, but around five in the morning, things began to pick up, and suddenly it seemed like everything was happening all at once.

"This is it, Heels," I said, even though she really didn't need me to tell her that. I just wanted to feel like I was being helpful, though there was nothing I could do.

She smiled up at me despite the pain and the fear, my beautiful, brave Luna. "Let's meet our pups."

The next half hour was probably the most useless I had ever felt in my whole life, but finally, the first baby was out. "It's a girl!" the doctor announced, handing the baby to me while Abby got ready to push the next one.

A girl. A daughter, who wailed unhappily at being wrenched from her cozy, warm home.

"Don't worry," I whispered to her. "Things'll get better, I promise."

The second baby followed quickly, and this time we were fully expecting another girl, so when the doctor told us this one was a boy, Abby and I looked at each other in surprise.

"I guess they're not identical then," I pointed out.

"I always knew you were smart," Abby teased me, looking exhausted but happy as our son was placed in her arms. As we looked down at the two beautiful, perfect pups, *our* pups, Abby's eyes filled with happy tears, and mine weren't far behind. "We're a family, Oliver."

"We've always been a family, Heels," I corrected her gently. "Now, there are just a few more of us."

~Abby~

After spending a bit of time with our son and daughter, the nurses put them both to bed and Oliver told me to get some rest too. "We're going to have a steady stream of visitors in the morning," he warned me. "Better sleep while you can."

I knew he was right, and once I closed my eyes, it really didn't take me long to fall asleep after the excitement of the last few hours. When I woke up, Oliver was still there, looking freshly showered and changed, and he helped me to get ready too.

Each step I took was painful and my whole body felt like it had gone through the wringer. I could see why women swore they were never going to do this again after giving birth for the first time, but when I looked at the excitement and happiness in my mate's eyes, and the two beautiful bundles that were ours, I had a feeling we'd be back here again, sooner or later, though hopefully *not* with twins again the next time.

Once I was ready and I had taken a go at breastfeeding both babies, Oliver began to call in some of the people who were waiting to see us.

Patrick and Storm were first. Their clothes were crumpled, looking like they hadn't got much sleep themselves, and Storm quickly confirmed it. "We bumped up our flight after Oliver's call. We didn't want to miss any of this."

"You're the first ones to meet them," Oliver promised them. "Our new son and daughter."

He placed one of the babies in each of his parents' hands and stepped back to come and sit next to me as we enjoyed their very different reactions.

Storm stared at the baby boy in what seemed to be confusion. "He's so small and defenseless. Whoever thought making kids so frail was a good idea?"

Meanwhile, tears gathered in the corners of Patrick's eyes as he gazed down at his granddaughter. "She's perfect. Congratulations."

I could only imagine how he was feeling, having never been able to have children of his own, but as far as we were concerned, he *was* Oliver's dad, and these babies were his grandchildren, just as surely as if they were related by blood.

There was a knock at the door a moment later. "There's got to be room for us in there too," Eli's voice filtered through the door and, with a chuckle, Oliver went over to let his brother and Liz in.

"You were next," he promised them, but they didn't seem to hear him, making a beeline for the pups instead.

"Boys or girls?" Eli asked as he looked over Patrick's shoulders.

Liz took a quick peek too before coming to sit next to me. "How are you feeling?"

"One boy and one girl," I answered Eli before turning to Liz. "And I'm doing okay. Labour wasn't fun, but it's over now and they're both healthy. That's what matters."

"What are their names?" Eli asked next, and everyone in the room turned to look at Oliver and me, who had just come back to sit on my other side.

"Go ahead, Heels," he offered with a smile. "You can tell them."

We already had two names for each gender picked out, assuming we were having identical twins, but now that we had one of each, narrowing down the choices was easy.

"Our son is Jonathan, after my father."

Everyone smiled and nodded in acknowledgement, and I wondered if they guessed the second one even before I said it.

"And our daughter is Nicole, for Oliver's mother."

Patrick's lips pressed tightly together as he looked down at the little girl in his arms and Storm leaned into him supportively. "I think it's beautiful," she murmured, and everyone else quickly agreed.

"I guess that one's off our list then," Eli said to Liz, who blushed, and I gasped as I quickly connected the dots.

"Wait, are you pregnant?"

"I didn't want to say anything just yet," she explained, giving Eli a disapproving look. "And especially not today. This day is about you guys."

"Are you kidding? That's amazing news, I'm so happy for you!" I gave her a big hug and Oliver went to congratulate his brother too. "Our kids will get to grow up together. This is perfect!"

My mom and my brothers and their mates were waiting to see us too and the room was filled with joy and laughter the whole day as people came and went.

We still didn't know for sure if Eli and Liz would be staying at Forest Ridge permanently, but so far, everything had been going well with their leadership of the pack there. Oliver and Eli had forged a lot of connections between the two packs, undertaking joint projects together, and both packs were thriving.

Jerrod and Marissa had also taken to their new roles; I heard nothing but good things about them both whenever they were mentioned. A woman my own age in our pack had recently been rejected by her mate and I had referred her to Marissa's program. She told me afterwards how helpful the support was, and I could see the difference it made to her too. With all their success, I wasn't sure if returning to Forest Ridge was in their future or not, but either way, I was sure that Eli and Liz would always be a close part of our lives.

We actually received a message of congratulations from Jerrod and Marissa later that day, as well as from Daniel and Malcolm, and of course well-wishes from the entire pack. Just as Oliver had always promised me they would, they had embraced me as their Luna and I knew they wished nothing but the best for us both, and now for our children too.

Whitney and Jack sent their best wishes too. They were living in Buffalo where Jack played for the NFL team there. They already had a son of their own, having been married last summer, and Whitney promised me they would come for a visit as soon as the season was over so the kids could all meet each other. Though Oliver tried to hide it, I knew he was a little bit jealous that Jack got to play pro football when he never could, but when I mentioned it to him, he brushed it off.

"We can't get everything we want in life, Heels, and trust me, I'd take our life here with you over playing football every single day of the week."

As for me, I already had the first draft of my first novel accepted by an agent and I was working on some revisions before we started looking for a publisher. I had hoped to have it finished before the babies arrived, but obviously, that wasn't going to happen. I would just have to fit it in around feedings and diaper changes and all the rest of it, but knowing Oliver would have my back the whole way made it seem a lot less daunting.

Everything I'd ever dreamed of was right there at my fingertips, and so much more besides. I never could have imagined anything quite this good because I never knew how good my life could truly be, not until I met my perfect match.

~~THE END~~

Thank you
for reading

If you enjoyed the book, please take a moment to leave a review.
Thank you!

This is the end of Abby and Oliver's story, but many more adventures await in my other series. Turn the page for a full book listing, or other ways you can keep in touch.

More From the Author

Contemporary Romance – New Adult/Clean

It Figures duet
It Figures
Figuring It Out

Historical Romance – 18+

Lady in Waiting Series
Lady in Waiting
King in Training
Princess in Hiding

Paranormal Romance – 18+

Cold Lake Pack Series
The Curse and the Prophecy
The Spell and the Legacy
The Dream and the Destiny

Mismatched Mates Series
Mismatched Mates
Misguided Motives
Mistaken Meanings

Serena's Story
The Alpha's Second Chance
The Returned Mate
The Vampire's Consort

Sacrifice Series
Blood Donor
Life Giver

Paranormal Romance – New Adult/Clean

The Alpha's Prey

Keep in Touch

My Patreon account has daily updates from my works-in-progress, bonus chapters and more – join me there to comment and read along as my next books are being written:
www.patreon.com/melodytyden

You can find and follow me on Facebook at:
facebook.com/melodytyden

Join the Facebook group Melody's Romance Corner for fun games, interaction with the author and exclusive news and excerpts.

You can also sign up to my newsletter at www.melodytyden.com for all the latest news.

www.ingramcontent.com/pod-product-compliance
Lightning Source LLC
Chambersburg PA
CBHW061152210726
48294CB00006B/1654